KATE CONSTABLE was born in Melbourne and spent part of her childhood in Papua New Guinea, where her father was a pilot in the Highlands. When she returned to Australia, she knew nothing about TV, football, pop music, fashion or swapcards, but quite a lot about King Arthur, Greek myths and *The Phoenix and the Carpet*. During her childhood she lived in nine different houses and changed schools nine times.

While studying for an Arts/Law degree she worked as a poet's assistant, a doughnut girl at Cowes Bakery, a drinks waitress at the Swagman Restaurant, and for a record, company. After a backpacker's tour of Europe, Kate returned to the record company, married her boss, then retired to bring up her two daughters, and write fantasy novels for teenagers.

Her enthralling fantasy trilogy, The Chanters of Tremaris, published in Australia and the US and translated into several languages, has delighted young readers all over the world.

ALSO BY KATE CONSTABLE

The Chanters of Tremaris

The Singer of All Songs
The Waterless Sea
The Tenth Power

Kate Constable

The Taste of Lightning

ALLEN&UNWIN

First published in 2007

Copyright © Kate Constable 2007

Allen & Unwin
83 Alexander Street
Crows Nest NSW 2065
Australia
Phone: (61 2) 8425 0100
Fax: (61 2) 9906 2218
Email: info@allenandunwin.com
Web: www.allenandunwin.com

National Library of Australia
Cataloguing-in-Publication entry:

Constable, Kate, 1966– .
The taste of lightning.
For children.
ISBN 978 174114 863 3 (pbk).
1. Fantasy fiction – Juvenile literature. I. Title.
A823.4

Designed by Ruth Grüner
Cover photographs: Anja Peternelj, Dawn Hudson, Bo Insogna
and Vladimir Ivanov; cover digital image by Ruth Grüner
Text photographs: Dainis Derics, Eric Foltz, Geoffrey Hammond,
sierrarat and Vladimir Ivanov
Set in 11½ on 14½ pt Granjon by Ruth Grüner
Printed by McPherson's Printing Group

1 3 5 7 9 10 8 6 4 2

www.kateconstable.com

FOR EVIE

PART ONE

Arvestel

CHAPTER 1

What Happens in Darkness

THE Palace clocks were striking midnight and distant thunder growled from an early summer storm. Tansy hurried to the laundries. She had come this way hundreds of times since she'd first arrived at Arvestel a year ago, but everything looked different at night. There were no lamps to light her path, and the three moons were covered by cloud; if she hadn't known the way so well, she might have lost herself in the warren of stairs and corridors and store-cupboards that made up the servants' territory beneath the Palace.

She was afraid she'd be late. It was bad enough being empty-handed. She didn't have what Lorison had asked for, and she knew that this request was more important than the others. This time Lorison hadn't asked for a mere cake of scented soap, or a tin of boot-blacking. Everyone helped themselves to that kind of thing. But this – this was different, and the fact that Lorison had told Tansy to meet her at night, in the deserted laundries, was proof.

Tansy picked her way across the washing room, feeling for the damp stone of the troughs on either side. During the day, the laundries rang with noise: the grumbling of the women, the heavy slap of wet cloth, the bangs and rattles of paddles and washboards, the gush of emptied buckets. But now Tansy could hear smaller sounds: the steady drip ... drip of the troughs, the gurgle of pipes.

The ironing room was beyond, with its circle of hearths in their metal cages, and the felt-covered ironing boards. By day it was stiflingly hot in both rooms; often Tansy would leave her work dripping with sweat and steam, her face red, her shirt and pinafore damp from top to toe. But now the great fire in the centre of the ironing room was out, and the night air rushed down the chimney.

'Good girl. No candle, just like I told you.' Lorison's nasal whine came from the doorway. 'I've always said you were a good girl, always stuck up for you. The others say you think you're better than the rest of us, but I say no. She's clever, is all. Doesn't belong in service, I say. Deserves more from life than washing other people's underpants, don't you, Tansy?'

Tansy didn't answer. She wasn't sure if Lorison was making fun of her. She knew she was no cleverer than most people. She didn't want to be in service, that was true. Even in well-paid service – and there was none better paid than service at the Palace of Arvestel, the seat of the Royal House, the heart of the Kingdom of Baltimar – you still had to take orders. You didn't own yourself; you weren't free.

'You got yourself one step nearer to that horse farm of yours tonight, my girl.' Lorison chuckled. 'Well, let's see it.'

Tansy swallowed. 'I – I ain't –'

Lorison's voice sharpened. 'You telling me you ain't got it?'

'I looked out every day –'

Lorison seized her arm and shook it. 'You didn't look hard enough. There must've been something come through the

4

laundries. Ten days I gave you, there must've been *something*!'

There was an edge of panic in the older woman's voice. Tansy tried to shake herself free. 'Let go! It ain't my fault.'

'You think *she'll* care whose fault it is?' Lorison's grip tightened as thunder rumbled around them. 'She won't. It'll be my fault, and your fault, and we'll pay –'

'Who? Who's *she*?' Tansy tried to prise Lorison's fingers from her arm.

'Don't tell me you don't know. Bright girl like you, and you ain't guessed? You think I wanted all that stuff for myself? Who do you think we're working for, girl?' Lorison squeezed Tansy's arm. 'This is all for Madam, for the Witch-Woman.' She lowered her voice and glanced around at the looming shadows. 'For Lady Wanion.'

Tansy tried to back away. 'I don't believe you.'

'You better believe me, girl.' Suddenly Lorison was brisk and ruthless. She dragged Tansy toward the doorway. 'Come on. You can tell her yourself. I got no interest in your excuses. You can give your excuses to her.'

'What, *now*?'

'Madam does her business in the dark. She sleeps in the day, like a spider. She's busy now, doing what she does. Ready for visitors.'

'Let me go!'

'You going to scream?' sneered Lorison. 'No guard's going to come running for you, girl, not this time of night. Respectable girls oughta be in bed.'

'What about you, then?' Tansy had to half-run to keep up with Lorison.

'I got no need to worry. Madam protects me.'

Lorison tugged her round corners, up stairs and into

a tangle of dim corridors crammed with objects. Tallboys leaned drunkenly against the walls; giant vases nestled beside mirrored sideboards laden with porcelain. From high brackets, carved lamps threw eerie shadows. Tapestries and curtains whispered in the draught, and behind the faint grumble of the thunderstorm came the chime of ancient clocks as they marked off the quarters of the night.

'You're hurting me!' said Tansy.

'Run faster then.'

There was no one about. At this time of night, feasts and concerts had ended; only rust parties gathered here and there in secret corners of the Palace. A group of addicts with their telltale twitches and red-stained nostrils would be seated around the paraphernalia of their drug: the tray, the knife, the sniff-pipe and the lamp. But the rust parties were quiet affairs. If they made any noise, Tansy didn't hear it.

Without warning, Lorison stopped in the shadow of a carved cabinet. 'Here's something not many in this place has ever seen,' she said, and she reached behind the cabinet to press on one of the wall panels. It swung open to reveal a set of stone steps that led down into the darkness.

'This is one of Madam's secret ways,' said Lorison with a hint of pride. 'They run all over the Palace, and out of it, if you know where to look.' She grabbed Tansy's hand and pressed it to the panel, and Tansy recoiled as her fingers traced the shape of a slender-legged spider carved into the wood.

'I'll get it tomorrow, I swear I will!' she whispered to Lorison. 'Don't take me to *her*.'

'Too late now.' Lorison pushed Tansy down the steps, and pulled the panel closed. Darkness engulfed them, and Tansy clutched at Lorison's arm.

'Are we going to the Pit? Lorison? We ain't going to the Pit?'

Lorison laughed, and tugged her forward. With relief Tansy realised that there were torches in these passages, but small, and far apart, with long stretches of suffocating dark between. Tansy was frightened of Lady Wanion, but she was even more frightened of being shut up alone in the dark, and she clung to Lorison's arm as they stumbled from one murky splash of light to the next, round corners, up and down stairs. Sometimes Lorison whispered, 'That way goes to the kitchens – that way leads right out to the picnic pavilion in the woods. Those steps go to the picture gallery. Madam's got her secret ways to everywhere in Arvestel.'

At last they halted before a low door studded with iron bolts. 'We're here,' whispered Lorison, and Tansy smelled the sour whiff of her fear. Lorison raised her knuckles and knocked, two quick raps and two slow.

'Enter,' came a voice from inside, and Lorison lifted the latch and shoved Tansy into the room.

Tansy had to stifle a cough in her sleeve. The enormous, dimly lit room was full of sweet, sickly smoke, and crowded with objects: cabinets with glass doors, boxes and crates of all sizes, tables piled with jars and vials. Just in front of Tansy and Lorison stood an immense bowl, waist-high. Its contents shimmered in the candlelight: water, or oil, or some kind of liquid. Surely it couldn't be – could it be *blood*?

Tansy recoiled, but Lorison pushed her forward. Now she could make out the figure of a woman, seated on a high, throne-like chair. There were candles behind the woman's head, so it was difficult to see her face. Tansy had an impression of a massive, squatting presence, like a toad. The woman's face was broad and flat, and her wide, thin-lipped mouth turned down. Her head was wound around with a silk turban, her eyes half-closed. The hands clutching at the arms of the chair were no more than withered claws, incongruously attached to the bulky body. The woman wore an embroidered robe of rich brocade, and huge jewelled earrings dragged the lobes of her ears almost to her shoulders.

'This is the girl I told you about, Madam. Tansy, the laundry-maid.' Lorison's voice squeaked with fear. She gave Tansy a vicious nudge, and whispered, 'Bow down to Madam!'

Tansy bowed so low she almost lost her balance. Everyone in Baltimar had heard tales about Lady Wanion. Tansy knew she was a witch; that she wove powerful, secret magic and prisoners were sent to her if they refused to co-operate: not just Renganis and Cragonlanders captured in the war, Baltimaran criminals too. Lady Wanion, they said, was very persuasive. One old soldier had told Tansy that Wanion *persuaded this one Gani's eyeballs clean out of his skull*. Tansy's stomach had lurched.

'I see it is the laundry-maid. Why have you brought her here?' To Tansy's surprise, the voice that issued from the toad-like mouth was deep and rich and full of music.

'She didn't do what she was told, Madam.'

'I see.' There was a pause; Tansy was too frightened to look up. She stared at the ground. Shadows slithered and scuttled at the edges of her vision.

'This is the girl who likes to ride horses, yes?'

'That's right, Madam,' said Lorison promptly. 'Every morning, since the start of spring, down to the stables she goes, rain or shine. She loves it, don't you, Tansy? Speak up, girl. Answer Madam when she talks to you.'

Tansy whispered, 'Yes, Madam.'

Wanion's taloned nail tapped softly on the arm of her chair.

'Perhaps Tansy does not understand that her mornings with the horses are my gift to her. Does she not wish to show her thankfulness?'

Tansy swallowed, unsure if she was supposed to reply, until Lorison dug her sharply in the ribs. 'Yes, Madam. Yes, I'm very grateful.' A lump rose in her throat. When Lorison had told her she could go to the stables before dawn and help with the horses, her miserable life at Arvestel had become worth living at last. Those precious times were the only happiness she'd known since she'd come here.

The low, musical voice filled Tansy's ears. 'I have given you a great gift, yes? A great gift. And in return, I asked this little thing only. One small task. Remind me what it was we asked of you. Perhaps you did not understand.'

Tansy's mouth was dry. 'You – Lorison asked me to, to steal something. A piece of clothes, from the laundries. Something grey.'

'Yes.' Wanion let out a long sigh. 'Yes. That is all. A small thing only. A stocking, a glove. Something worn next to the skin. Only this I asked of you, and the mornings with the horses would be yours for as long as you wished so long as you lived at Arvestel.' Wanion laughed, a warm, embracing laugh. Lorison gave a nervous snigger. 'And more than this I promised, yes? Gold, to buy whatever you wished, to buy horses of your own one day, and a farm to raise them?'

'Yes, Madam.' Tansy stared at the floor. She didn't care about the gold Lorison had promised as much as she cared about being near the horses.

Wanion gave another sigh, heavy with disappointment. 'You work in the laundries, yes? Washing and ironing, soaping and rinsing, starching and folding.'

'Yes, Madam.'

'Washing the dirty clothes of everyone in Arvestel, yes? The servants, the noble lords and ladies. Even the King's stockings are washed there, yes?'

'Not – not by me,' said Tansy, with a stab of confusion. Must she steal the King's clothes now?

'No, no, I do not ask you to interfere with the undergarments of the King.' Once again that rich, warm laugh filled the room. 'The token I asked for belongs to a boy. Not a Baltimaran noble boy, a foreigner. What is his name? Steer, Sneer? No – Skir, that is it. You have not heard of him, no?'

Tansy shook her head.

'No. You see how unimportant he is. But his clothes pass through the laundries, like everyone's, yes? You have seen them? All grey he wears, like a little mouse.'

Tansy opened her mouth, and closed it again. She *had* seen him, just once, last autumn, before her own rides began: he was the red-haired, skinny boy, about her own age. He'd been taking his first riding lesson, on a grey pony. He was hopeless – hands everywhere, no seat at all. Strange to think that she'd envied him then, envied him the fat docile pony. *Skir*. The name meant nothing to her. But yes, she had seen his clothes in the wash-troughs and on the drying-lines. No one else in Arvestel wore grey, grey, nothing but grey.

Wanion said, 'I see in your face that you do know him, that you know his clothes, yes? You must be careful, my dear. Your face is easy to read. So. You have seen this boy's clothes. Why is it you could not find even one grey sock or a glove or a vest?'

'I did look, Madam, truly I did. But there was nothing grey at all.'

'Was it fear of the Pit that prevented you? Because you must know that the Pit belongs to me.' Wanion laughed, and this time the laugh was not pleasant. 'Those who do my bidding must have no fear of *that*, even for thieving.'

'I – I'll try again, Madam,' said Tansy. 'But you know how boys are. Likely he didn't send nothing to the wash these last days. I got five brothers and they never –'

Lorison was pulling furious faces at her and she fell silent.

Wanion said heavily, 'It is too late for that now.'

The room grew very still. Tansy heard the hiss of a lamp, and a faint whisper as the thick curtain behind Wanion shifted slightly in the draught. She wondered what lay behind that curtain. She felt sick from the perfumed smoke; she longed to run out of this too-hot, too-sweet room into the fresh night air.

'I gave you a chance, yes, and you did not take it. Now I must ask another thing. Still a small thing, but not so easy. You must fetch for me something else. A lock of hair, a fingernail. You understand? Something that belongs to his *body*.'

Tansy gasped. 'But Madam, how can I do that?'

'You must find a way. You will find the token, and bring it to me. You have two days, no more. After that, I go back to the Fastness of Rarr, to my home. I must have the token before I leave. And, of course, no one must know about this, especially the boy himself. Do you understand? If you do this simple thing, then there are horses for you. To ride now; later, to own. But if you fail –' Wanion sucked in her breath. 'Do not fail,' she said.

Tansy whispered, 'Yes, Madam.'

'That is good. We understand each other, yes? I have another gift for you. Lorison!'

'Yes, Madam.' Lorison darted across the room and returned with something clutched tightly in her hand. 'Here, girl, take it.'

Dazed, Tansy opened her hand, and Lorison dropped something into her palm: a luckpiece. Almost everyone in Baltimar had at least one luckbit, a little doll strung around their neck or tucked into a pocket. But even in the wavering light, Tansy could see that this was no ordinary luckpiece. It was made of mother-of-pearl, ivory and white satin, stitched with white silk. Without meaning to, Tansy closed her hand around it, and Wanion let out a pleased, hissing sigh.

'It is good. This little one is my friend, you understand? It listens to you, watches with my eyes. It is part of me. Even when I am far away, I am with you. Do not try to destroy it, or you will be destroyed also. Now you are bound to me, yes?'

Wanion's beady, almost invisible eyes were fixed on her. The little doll seemed glued to Tansy's hand; she was sure that if she tried to drop it, it would tear the flesh from her bones. Tansy's mouth opened, and she heard herself say, 'How can I get what you're asking for? I'm a laundry-maid. I ain't even allowed upstairs. How can I get near this boy?'

Lorison giggled in pure terror. Tansy's head swam. Wanion leaned forward in her massive chair, tipped slowly toward Tansy like a boulder about to crush her. She hissed, 'You will help me, Tansy. Or it will not be a piece of this boy's hair I take from you. It will be a piece of *yourself*.'

Lorison seized Tansy by the arm and tugged her to the door, gabbling. 'She'll do it, Madam, I'll see to that, don't you worry, we'll have it for you, night after next, I promise. She don't understand, see, she's a country girl, off a farm, she don't mean no disrespect, just a bit simple in the head is all. Don't you fret, Madam, I'll see she does what she's told this time.'

With a flurry of curtsies, Lorison hustled them out into the secret corridor and slammed the iron-studded door. Then she shook Tansy so fiercely her teeth rattled. 'You lost your senses? I picked you cos I thought you was a bright one! Would've done better to ask Pipkin the halfwit!' She thrust Tansy away so hard her head banged on the stone wall and she saw stars. Lorison was crying. 'See that? See that, you lackwit?' She waved her left hand in Tansy's face. All that remained of her little finger was a neat stump. 'I tell people I got my hand caught in a hinge. But *she* did it. Oh, you stupid girl. You don't know what she does. You got no idea. You know where my finger is now? *Do you?*'

'No,' said Tansy faintly. The sickly smoke had followed them into the corridor, or perhaps it clung to their clothes. Lorison's face rippled.

'*She's* got it. So I ain't never out of her power, and I never will be, so long as she's got a piece of me. Why do you think she wants a bit of that boy? The part rules the whole, that's why. She wants to make him her puppet –'

'Why? Why him?'

Lorison flipped her hand impatiently. 'I don't know. I don't care, neither. All I know is, better him than me. That's what you gotta think, too, better him than you. Oh you fool. You want her magic on you? You want to be like me? Want her finger and thumb pinching on your shoulder day and night like I got?' Tears coursed down Lorison's face as she pulled Tansy through the darkness. 'Just you do what she says. Find a way. Don't ask questions, don't *answer back*. Who do you think you are? You're a servant, same as me. Only I serve *her* now. She owns me. You, you might be lucky. Just this one thing she wants from you, a bit of this boy's hair.'

Tansy stumbled along, feeling stupid. 'But how can I?'

Lorison snorted. 'You'd be pretty enough if you didn't chop

your hair so short. He's a foreigner, they got strange tastes, maybe he'll like you. What is he, halfway to a man? That age, they'll touch anything with bosoms, even little ones like yours, if you let em. Oh, you'll see. Get close enough and he'll let you take more than a bit of hair. She'll like that better, that'd please her.'

'But I ain't never even kissed a boy.'

'Well you better learn, girl, and learn fast. You get what Madam wants, you give it to her, and that's it, all over, and you can ride your precious horses till they drop dead under you. Me, I got no choice. She got a piece of me, see? *Don't let her get a piece of you.*'

The white luckpiece grinned up at Tansy from the palm of her hand; it burned her like a coal from the fire, and when she thrust it into her shirt pocket, it burned through the cloth like a brand above her heart.

They emerged from the secret passages into a broom cupboard near the women-servants' quarters. Lorison vanished, and Tansy was left, dizzy and sick, to grope her way to bed, with the thunder of the Witch-Woman's laughter rolling in her ears.

CHAPTER 2

The Priest-King of Cragonlands

SKIR watched the storm crawl across the horizon. Thunder rumbled like distant drums, and sheet lightning flickered in purple and silver fireworks over the northern sky.

Skir's heart raced. The hair prickled at the back of his neck, and he tasted a metallic tang on his tongue. He gripped the windowsill, forcing himself not to turn away, not to sweep the heavy curtains closed. It would be so easy to shut out the storm, and enclose himself instead in this safe, luxurious room.

Beeman came in quietly. 'All right, Skir?' He knew how his pupil hated and feared thunderstorms. He came to stand beside Skir at the window. 'A long way off,' he said after a few moments. 'You can count twenty between the lightning and the thunder. And it's moving east. It won't come any closer to Arvestel.'

'I know,' said Skir crossly, annoyed that his tutor felt the need to reassure him, as if he were a little boy hiding under the quilts. Yet he was grateful. After a moment he said, 'It's not near, Skir, as you can hear. No need to fear, or shed a tear.'

Beeman gave a snort of laughter. 'You still remember that?'

'I remember.'

Together they watched the convulsions of the storm as it drifted across the shallow hills. The mountains of Cragonlands were invisible from this far south, but Skir's rooms faced north, holding the promise of a view that he would never be able to see. Actually, if anyone had asked, he would have preferred south-facing rooms. Then he might have glimpsed the sea, or at least the river-mouth. But a view of the water was not prized among the Baltimarans, and his northern rooms were considered a privilege: the windows framed the famous gardens of the Palace of Arvestel. Skir couldn't understand why the Baltimarans took such pride in them: they were all hedges and fountains and geometric patterns; not a single wild thing growing anywhere. Even the flowers were grown in hothouses, all lined up in neat rows waiting to be drowned with fertiliser.

Now the gardens, and the hills and woodlands that rolled away beyond them, were lit up by the erratic dazzle of lightning.

As a tiny child, Skir had been struck by lightning. He had no memory of it, though his body seemed to remember: his hair crackling, the taste of metal in his mouth. He did have a vague memory of his mother singing, to comfort him. It was all he could recall of his mother.

Someone had told him about the lightning, one of the priests in the Temple at Gleve, long before he came to Arvestel. The priest – who was it? Not Bettenwey – had been reprimanded for telling him; he was still quite small then, maybe six years old. Beeman knew that he knew, but they never talked about it. There were many things they never talked about.

Beeman said, 'It's awfully hot in here. Do you really need that fire?'

Skir glanced indifferently at the hearth. 'I told the maid to build it up while I was in the bath. I hate drying myself in a cold room.'

'Haven't you noticed it's summer? I'll open the window.'

'No!' said Skir. 'No. Maybe later.' He shivered, and glanced involuntarily outside, where the storm still flickered about the horizon.

Beeman followed his look. 'If you're not going to bed yet, I'll light the lamps.'

Skir leaned on the windowsill as his tutor moved around the room. 'Do you always have to be so damn *tactful*?'

'I do my best,' said Beeman in his mild, dry way. 'I won't light too many. Let's be cosy.' He set the taper to one lamp, then another, and made a puddle of golden light around the fireplace that softly lit the rest of the room.

The floor was thickly carpeted, and long velvet curtains framed the windows. There were carved chairs and sofas piled with embroidered cushions, paintings in gilt frames, and fine porcelain vases filled with flowers. Scattered about the room were a harp, a flute, several paintboxes, an abandoned clay sculpture of a girl's head, and an empty birdcage woven from silver wire. There were throw rugs of woven silk, and lamps in golden brackets.

Through a doorway stood a curtained bed, heaped with sumptuous quilts in subtle shades of crimson and purple. Dirty shirts and crumpled socks were strewn across the floor around it. Skir's clothes were all beautifully made and delicately embroidered, but without a single splash of colour. High-ranking priests of the Faith should wear dark blue, but the Baltimarans had declared that too, too dreary; they'd compromised on soft dove-grey. Skir's shoulder-length red hair, damp after his bath, was tied at the nape of his neck with a grey ribbon, and he wore a grey silk dressing-gown.

He was pale-skinned, slightly built, and looked younger than his sixteen years. He had a thin, clever face, dusted with freckles. His eyes were wide-set, the grey-green of the ocean on a miserable day. The last time he'd seen the ocean was on his journey from Cragonlands, five years before.

Beeman drew the velvet curtains across the windows and blotted out the storm. 'I forgot to ask, how was your riding lesson?'

'Cancelled. Old Ingle said we should give the pony a rest.' Skir looked up. 'What?'

'Give the pony a rest, indeed! How these people won a war, I do not understand . . . I'll speak to Ingle.'

'I don't care, Beeman. I can't be bothered with it, really.'

'I'll speak to Ingle,' said Beeman, pretending he hadn't heard, which was his usual way of defying Skir's orders. 'Your riding lessons are important. It's good exercise, and it teaches you other things, too. You need to be firm, but gentle. You must make the horse trust you, and you must learn to trust the horse. Just like the relationship between the ruler and the ruled.'

'In that case, it would be more useful for me to learn it from the point of view of the horse,' said Skir caustically.

Beeman laughed. 'You'll see I'm right one day.'

'Oh, you're always right. It's very annoying of you.' Skir sighed. 'It hasn't been as bad as I expected, actually. I've only fallen off three or four times, and I've hardly hurt myself at all. And at least I don't *wobble* like the Baltimarans. No wonder the horses need a rest.'

The Baltimarans were nervous about Skir's riding lessons. He took them under the strict supervision of armed guards, and he was not permitted to ride anything but the smallest, tamest ponies, supposedly for his own safety. But really they were afraid that he might suddenly gallop off over the hills and head north for the border. Although everyone maintained the polite fiction that Skir was an honoured guest of the Baltimaran King, in reality he was a prisoner, a hostage.

A nearer rumble of thunder rattled the ornaments on the mantel, and Skir jumped. Beeman said hastily, 'Why don't you finish your drawing?'

Skir wandered to the table and peered at the half-finished hunting scene on its square of canvas. 'Is it worth finishing?'

'Certainly. The shadows are excellent. And the trees in the snow.'

Skir held the picture at arm's length. 'But dogs aren't my strong point.'

'Oh, they're dogs, are they? I thought they were goats. Perhaps, if you smudged them out, it could become a picnic.'

'In the snow? They'd freeze their backsides. Maybe a Rengani picnic. Renganis wouldn't let a bit of snow spoil their fun.'

'Renganis don't believe in fun, or picnics. Better make it a military training exercise. Well, if you don't feel like drawing, shall we do some exercises of our own?'

Skir rolled his eyes. 'You mean the ceremonies? Again?'

'Yes, review the rituals,' said Beeman. 'We've been neglectful the last few days.'

'So?'

'Skir, please don't take that moody tone with me. You know as well as I do that you must keep up your practice. When this is all over –'

'When I've expired from a mysterious illness, you mean?

Or fallen from the window in a tragic accident?'

'I mean, when you're restored to the throne. When you go home to Cragonlands. These are rituals the Priest-King performs every day. Every word and gesture must be perfect.'

Skir slouched over the table. 'But I'm never going home, am I? I'm stuck in this – this *room*.' He flicked a contemptuous hand at the satin and velvet. 'His Highness, King of the Northern Territories of Baltimar! I wish they'd put me in the dungeons! At least that would be honest.'

'If you had ever seen a dungeon, you wouldn't make such a fatuous remark,' Beeman said quietly.

Skir pushed the charcoals around the table. 'Why pretend?' he said. 'Even if I *do* go back to Cragonlands one day, it won't be as ruler. I might have the Circle of Attar on my head and the Staff of the Temple in my hand, but the Baltimarans will be pulling the strings and everyone will know it.' Skir let his hands rise and fall limply, in imitation of a puppet.

Beeman didn't flinch. 'Don't try to out-guess fate, Skir. None of us knows what the future may bring.'

Skir kicked at the table leg. 'I know those ceremonies inside out. I'd rather practise writing the Signs.'

'Not here. Let's keep the Signs for when we're safely outside the Palace, with no one watching.'

'Don't *fuss*. No one's watching now.'

Beeman was unmoved. 'Spies are everywhere. We can't be too careful. The Baltimarans may be rich, but they know nothing of the Signs.'

'The way you carry on, you'd think the whole court was teeming with spies, instead of fat young men who've got out of fighting and lounge around pretending that they don't sniff rust, and fat young women who spend all their time flirting with the fat young men, and fat *old* men who moan on and on about the war, and fat old women who moan on and on about the young people –' Skir stopped; Beeman was laughing. Skir laughed too, a little ashamed of his own vitriol.

'Nevertheless, there are spies,' said Beeman, rubbing his eye. 'That's why I didn't teach you to write for so long. It's secret knowledge, priestly knowledge.'

'But you're not a priest, Beeman. How did you learn about writing?'

'Oh, I picked it up along the way,' said Beeman vaguely.

Skir sat down near the fire and rested his chin on his hands. 'Why you?'

'Sir?'

'Don't call me sir. You sound like the Balts.'

'Don't call them the Balts,' said his tutor automatically. 'Try to speak respectfully, even if you can't think of them with respect.'

Skir was not to be diverted. Tonight felt special, different from ordinary nights. He and Beeman usually went to bed early, unless there was a banquet or a concert or some revelry that Skir had to attend. They never sat up talking like this. Perhaps tonight Beeman might tell him things. There was one topic in particular that Skir both longed and dreaded to talk about; but he wouldn't ask about that, not yet.

'Why you, Beeman? Why did the Baltimarans choose you to be my tutor?'

'They didn't.' Beeman drew up a chair on the other side of the fire to face his pupil. His melancholy face relaxed a little, and he stroked his drooping brown moustache. 'The priests sent me, with the King's consent. They had to send someone. You were only a child.'

'I was eleven. Boys of eleven fight, in Rengan. They fight in the war, beside the men.'

Beeman frowned. 'That's Baltimaran propaganda. The conscription age for the Rengani Army is sixteen, for five years' minimum service. It's true, quite young children help to make the weapons in the manufactories. But they don't fight. And anyway, as you know, a Priest of the Faith is not permitted to take the life of another.'

'Have you noticed how the Balts – sorry – the Baltimarans always skim over the "Priest" part of my title? They don't mind calling me "King", even here, with their own King spitting-distance away. But not "Priest".'

'It makes them uncomfortable,' said Beeman. 'It's not like Cragonlands. Baltimar has no Faith, no chantment, nothing to believe in.'

'They believe in wealth. And winning wars. And they have their own magic.'

'Superstitious rubbish. The magic of shreds and scraps.' Beeman frowned. 'They don't understand what a chanter is, let alone a priest.'

'I'm not sure that I know what a priest is, either,' said Skir. He darted a glance at Beeman. But Beeman wore his usual absent-minded look, as if he were only half-listening. Skir leaned forward. He would make Beeman pay attention. He said loudly, 'At least I know what I'm not.'

Beeman unfolded himself and reached down to poke the fire. He said mildly, 'What do you mean by that, Skir?'

'You know. I'm not really the Priest-King, am I? I'm a fraud.'

Beeman looked puzzled.

'No,' he said carefully. 'You are the boy the priests recognised as the new embodiment of the Priest-King, when you were four years old.'

'But they made a mistake, didn't they.' Skir's heart was thumping. This was the subject he had never dared to discuss with Beeman, though they'd skirted around it often enough. 'The Priest-King is always a chanter. Every Priest-King that's ever been has had the power of ironcraft: they can sing to the earth and make it move. But not me. Never.'

The storm had moved away, and the Palace was hushed. The ticking of the clock on the mantel sounded very loud in the silent room.

At last Beeman said, 'There's plenty of time, Skir. Be patient.'

'I *have* been patient. I've waited and waited. But the gift won't come! I've been practising the damn chantments for years, and *nothing*.'

Beeman sighed. He plunged his hand into his pocket and drew out one of the little machines of wire and wheels that he liked to build: his own equivalent, Skir often thought, of a Baltimaran luckpiece. He began to fiddle with it, frowning.

'Well?' said Skir.

'Don't be bitter.'

'I'm not – I just don't – how could they make a mistake?' Suddenly exhausted, Skir slumped in his chair. 'Didn't they ask for proof? Bettenwey was there, wasn't he? He's no fool.'

'Bettenwey was not High Priest then. It was Devenwey who recognised you.'

'Well, anyway – why didn't they ask for a demonstration? And what about my parents? Why didn't they tell the priests I wasn't a chanter? Were they so keen to see the back of me?'

'It is a great honour to be chosen by the priests,' said Beeman quietly.

'I suppose the priests gave them money,' said Skir.

'Now you're talking like a Baltimaran. Your parents...' Beeman paused.

'Was it because of the lightning?'

Beeman looked at him sharply. 'What do you mean?'

'When I was struck. Did they think it was an omen?'

'No, no, nothing like that.'

'Did they think it was a curse then? Is that why they wanted to get rid of me?'

'No one wanted to get rid of you. Your parents thought you would have a better life in Gleve. They didn't know what would happen.'

'That the Baltimarans would invade, and kidnap me? Why didn't anyone see *that* coming? I would have thought it was absolutely predictable. The Baltimarans and the Renganis have been fighting over Cragonlands for generations. Fighting over *rust*. Whoever controls Cragonlands controls the supply of rust, because Cragonlands is where the chaka-weeds grow, and since half of Baltimar is addicted to rust and pays the other half to get hold of it, there's a lot of money tied up in the rust harvest...' Skir's voice trailed away; he'd forgotten the point he was trying to make.

Beeman said dryly, 'I'm glad to see you've been listening to my lessons after all. I was rather afraid I'd been wasting my breath.'

'Like I wasted my breath when the soldiers came,' said Skir. 'They saw me, trying to sing. Trying to shake the pillars down. Hands in the air, shrieking away, making a fool of myself. What a joke. They must have had a fine laugh over *that* sight.'

'Sometimes the gift lies dormant through childhood. When you become a man –'

'But my voice has dropped. There are hairs on my chest.' There was an edge of desperation in Skir's voice. 'Do you think I should grow a beard? Or lie with a woman?'

'I'd wait a while for the beard, if I were you. As for the woman – well, that would be easy enough to arrange, if that's what you want.'

'Well, of course I *want* it. But would it do any good?'

Beeman put the tips of his fingers together. He said carefully, 'I don't believe that is the answer. There have been Priest-Kings who married, and those who fathered children without marrying. And there have been some who lay with men, like Devenwey. But there were also many who never lay with women or men, and their magic was supposed to be all the stronger for it.'

'Maybe I should do it anyway. It might cheer me up.'

'You would regret it. It is not an action to be taken lightly. Not by you.'

Skir stared at the fire. In some ways that was a relief. The Baltimarans expected him to hop from bed to bed the way they did; the painted bosomy girls at Court giggled about nothing else all day long. In fact it would have been easier to do it than to keep *not* doing it. But he was nervous about it, and it was good to be able to tell himself that he shouldn't – for the sake of his sacred office, for his magic . . . Just in case.

There was one girl he'd seen. She'd been standing on the fence when he had his first riding lesson. Skir had taken her for a stable-hand at first, her hair was so short. She had no bosoms to speak of, and no paint either. She'd looked *clean*. She was watching, very steadily. Critically, as if they were equals. But then something went wrong with Skir's stirrups, and when he looked back, she was gone. He'd never seen her again.

Skir shifted restlessly in his chair. 'Have you ever been in love, Beeman?'

'Yes,' said Beeman shortly. 'She died.'

'Oh.'

Beeman gazed into the fire. In the soft glow of the firelight he seemed oddly young and vulnerable, hardly older than Skir himself. 'Don't worry about your chantment, Skir. It will come.'

'Beeman?'

'Yes?'

'What if – what if there's no such thing as chantment? You say the Baltimaran magic is a sham, why not chantment too? What if the priests have been tricking everybody all these years?'

Beeman smiled. 'When I was your age, I didn't believe in chantment either. But it is real. Just because we rarely see it here in the Threelands, doesn't mean it doesn't exist.'

'I suppose if we were across the seas in the Westlands, in the middle of the Chanters' Rising, we'd be *surrounded* by magic,' said Skir. 'Magic battles in the streets, the Witch-Singer shrieking out her songs of ice to freeze the enemy in their tracks –'

'I *don't* think so,' said Beeman. 'You shouldn't listen to banquet gossip. And the leader of the Rising is the Singer of All Songs, not the Witch-Singer. Name the Ten Powers,' he rapped out, suddenly becoming a tutor again.

'Oh . . . um. The Power of Signs, of course. The Power of Tongue, which is speech and singing. Power of Winds. Power of Beasts. Power of . . . um, Ice. Power of Fire, Power of Iron, of course. Power of Healing.'

'You mean the Power of Becoming.'

'Becoming – yes – that's what I meant. Power of Seeming, which is illusions. And the Great Power, which is served by the Faith.'

'Very good, though you put them in the wrong order. Revision tomorrow.' Beeman unfolded himself from his chair. 'Time for bed. Goodnight, Skir.'

'Night.'

Skir watched his tutor withdraw to his own room, which opened off the large one. Beeman never allowed Skir into his room. Perhaps he kept a woman in there. Or a horse. More likely it was lined with all the little contraptions Beeman had put together over the years. Good old Beeman . . .

It had never before occurred to Skir that Beeman's life was not particularly happy either.

He sat hunched beside the fire, thinking. Whatever Beeman said, and whatever luxuries surrounded him, he was a prisoner. Until the last rust-maker pulled up the last chaka-weed, or the last Baltimaran addict sniffed the last pinch of rust, until the last shreds of resistance in Cragonlands were wiped out, the Baltimarans would keep him. Skir was their insurance for the future. He was the luckbit in their pocket.

If I was an ironcrafter, Skir thought, *I could escape from here*. He knew the chantment that would punch a hole in the wall. He crossed over to the window, and gathered his breath the way Beeman had taught him. Deep inside, hope flickered like a candle flame. Maybe this time, maybe at last, the gift would surge up inside him. He would deserve to be the Priest-King after all.

He held out his hands and sang.

The chantments of iron were guttural and growling, sung in the throat and the nose. Skir sang with all his might, grinding out the noises that were supposed to summon magic, supposed to shift stones, supposed to hurl rocks through the air. He screwed up his face as he sang, forcing breath from deeper and deeper in his lungs. The room closed in around him –

Suddenly he was lying on the carpet, and Beeman was bent over him.

'Skir! Skir, are you all right? Here, drink this.'

Skir's hands shook as he took the tumbler; water spilled down his chin and onto his dressing-gown.

'I heard an almighty crash – look, you knocked over the side table. What *were* you doing?'

'Practising chantment,' mumbled Skir.

'I told you it was too hot in here.' Beeman tugged at the window and a fresh breeze flowed into the room. 'There, that's better. Are you sure you're all right?'

'*Yes*. Go away.'

'Should I ring for some warmed wine?'

'*No*. I said go away. Leave me alone.' Skir sat up. 'Why are you always so calm? Why don't you ever get angry with me?'

'Why should I be angry? You fainted.'

'Typical, isn't it? I wanted to make something *happen*, and instead I pass out! What's the *point*?'

'Keep your voice down, Skir.'

'Why should I? Who cares? *They* wouldn't care if I went stark raving mad in here; in fact, they'd probably prefer it –' The possibility struck him for the first time. 'Perhaps I'm mad already, and you're my keeper! Am I, Beeman? Am I mad?'

'Don't be absurd.' Beeman's face went red, then white. 'You spend altogether too much time thinking about yourself, Skir.'

Skir hurled the tumbler across the room as hard as he could. But instead of the satisfying smash of broken glass, it landed with a soft thud on the thick carpet. There was a brief silence.

'I'm sorry,' said Beeman at last.

'*You're* sorry? What are *you* sorry for?'

'I should be more patient. I know how difficult it is.'

Skir lowered his head and mumbled into his chest. 'You know the worst of it? I – I actually quite like it here, sometimes.'

Beeman hung his head, and laughed. He gave Skir's shoulder a brief, rough shake. 'Change will come, you know.'

'I know,' said Skir; but he didn't believe it.

CHAPTER 3

Perrin's Orders

'PERRIN! Anyone seen Perrin? Frug it, where is the little –'

The expletive was lost in a mutter of derision as half the mess tent turned to stare at the wild-eyed, filthy soldier.

'Shut yer frugging trap, mate, he's here somewhere. What do you want him for?'

Several obscene suggestions followed, and a ripple of bitter laughter.

'Frug you! This is serious. I need Perrin, the one who tames snakes. Is he here or not?'

The jokes died away into wary muttering. Someone jerked a thumb to the trestle, crusted with stale food, where Perrin sat wiping his tin plate with a hunk of grey bread.

'Out the way, you frugging idiots.' The ranker shoved through the men milling about the greasy, bubbling cauldrons of stew. 'Perrin. Hey. Perrin?'

Swordsman Perrin, Second Class, gave his plate a final swipe and looked up coolly. With his long eyelashes, fine features and curling dark hair, he was known as a pretty boy. Since being drafted into the Rengani Army two years before, he'd learned how to handle soldiers who were interested in pretty boys.

'I'm Perrin.'

'You the frugger that tames snakes?'

Perrin grinned lazily. 'Got a snake, have you?'

A few of the men guffawed.

'Ah, frug off. Come on, quick!'

Perrin gazed around at his audience, gave a theatrical shrug and rose from his seat with the lazy grace of a surroan cat. But once they were outside the mess tent Perrin seized the other man's arm and broke into a run past the long, straggling rows of muddy tents.

'So what about this snake?' panted Perrin as they ran.

The wild-eyed soldier gasped, 'Digging latrines on the west side of camp – near them woods there – Bayley screams –'

'What kind of snake?'

'One of them big black ones, with red on the tail.'

Perrin slowed his pace when he saw the ring of men gathered; by the time he reached them, he was sauntering, hands in pockets, cool and unhurried.

'Let him through!' shouted the wild-eyed soldier. 'It's the one that tames snakes. I got him, let him through.'

The small crowd parted. Perrin saw a terrified ranker huddled on the ground beside the half-dug pits. He was holding out his muddied spade with two hands to fend off the serpent. The red-tailed snake rose high and swaying, poised to strike, only three paces away.

'Everyone quiet,' said Perrin, and the buzz of the onlookers subsided. Calmly Perrin stretched himself flat on the ground, with his cheek pillowed on his left arm, not far from the snake, and much closer to it than the ranker, Bayley.

Someone hawked, and spat a juicy gobbet near Perrin's head. 'What, going to take a nap now, is he? Little snooze?'

'Quiet,' said Perrin. The snake swayed, and turned its shining head toward the vibration. Softly, Perrin began to sing a song in a foreign tongue none of the men present could understand. The words rose and fell, a crooning lullaby, and the snake swayed to the song's rhythm, forward and back.

Perrin lay still, eyes half-closed, as he sang. He looked drowsy, but he was as alert as the deadly snake itself. The soldiers began to sway slightly too, without realising it, and Perrin allowed himself a private grin. He sang louder, and his right hand crept across the grass, out of the snake's view. The snake's head swayed in wide, sleepy arcs.

Perrin's right hand crept nearer; it touched the snake. His gentle song rose and fell, and the snake swayed as his hand slid along its glossy body. He was just about to grasp it behind the jaws –

Whack! The snake exploded into spatters of blood and writhing muscle. Two more blows from the spade and the snake was dead. Bayley sneered in triumph.

Perrin sprang up. 'You frugging idiot! I nearly had it.'

'It's dead now, you frugger! What were you going to do, let it loose in the forest so it could slink back at night and fang us all in our tents?'

Perrin said nothing, but his blue eyes burned with cold fire.

'Settle down, mate. It's just a frugging snake.'

'You could have taken my hand off.'

Someone jeered, 'Pretty Boy's upset you spoilt his show.'

Perrin swung around, and again there was an air of a wild cat about him, tensed to spring and tear its prey apart. But then his face fell into an easy, charming smile, and he laughed. 'You got it. I was having frugging fun playing with that deadly red-tail. I wanted to sing to that damn snake all night long.'

Laughter bubbled and lapped around Perrin like warm water. The men were on his side again. Perrin made an elaborate bow. 'Any more wildlife you'd like me to deal with – spiders, roaches, bears? No? Then I'll go back and see if those bastards have left me any dinner.'

One of the men slapped his back as he departed. That was all the thanks he'd get; but Perrin knew the whole camp would be humming with the story before morning. A square-headed sergeant with a scarred cheek and a missing ear began shouting. 'All right, lads, show's over! Still got three pits to dig by nightfall. Frug off back to your stations. Unless you fancy digging pits and filling em in all day tomorrow . . .'

The Fifth were back in Rengan at last, after a long stint in Cragonlands. Officially, they'd come home for extra training, to learn more about the new exploders that High Command had brought across from Mithates, in the Westlands. Unofficially, as everyone knew, they'd been driven back across the border by the Balts. With the exception of a handful of special agents who remained behind to help the local insurgents plan their resistance, the war was as good as over – for now. There'd be a fresh offensive next spring. There always was.

Perrin, like most of the men, was just glad to get away from the fighting. Especially if they could pretend it was a strategic withdrawal rather than a defeat. But the absence of fighting meant other work had to be invented, and no one liked digging pits.

Grumbling and swearing, the men melted away into the dusk.

Someone cleared his throat quietly, and the sergeant swung round to see an officer with a tanned brown face. Hastily the sergeant touched his shoulder in salute.

'Sorry Major, didn't see you there.'

The major shrugged aside the apology. 'I saw the trick with the snake. You know him?'

'Swordsman Perrin? Don't think it's a trick, sir. Seen him do it once before, down on Wilker's Plain. Only a grass adder that time, not a big fr – big one like this.'

'Just snakes?'

The sergeant pulled a face. 'Lads say he can charm a fish out the water. Let's say, he don't mind showing off what he can do.'

'And?' the major prompted quietly.

The sergeant sniffed, and wiped his nose. 'Stories spread. You know, sir, when there's not much fighting.'

'War's not over, Sergeant.'

'No, sir. Course not, sir.' The sergeant spoke smartly; but his spit on the ground showed his true feelings.

The major ignored it. 'So, what about Perrin?'

'Well, only rumour, but they say it's not just beasts he can tame.'

The major waited in silence, and the sergeant continued uneasily.

'There were rumours of an incident, sir, the winter before you joined us, before the Battle of the Falls. We were stationed not far from the border. They say some of the lads were giving Perrin a hard time. Kid with looks like that, well . . . He was just a drafty then, and apparently didn't take it too well. Next thing you know, there's two men in the river. Lads fished em out just before they went over the falls. The story that went round was, Perrin *forced* em to jump in the river somehow – they had to do it. But I don't know, sir. Lads see what he can do with snakes and . . .'

The major was silent for a moment, watching the diggers

34

spray clots of mud across the trampled grass. The thick smell of human sweat was sticky in the air. 'I'd like to speak to those two men.'

'Thing is, sir. Both were killed in the Battle of the Falls. We lost so many. Never was able to confirm it really happened.'

'I see.'

'Sir – he's not a bad kid.'

'No,' said the major thoughtfully. 'No, I'm sure you're right.'

He turned to go; a moment later he'd disappeared into the bedraggled wilderness of the camp.

A few evenings later, an officer tapped Perrin on the shoulder. 'The Commander wants you in his tent. Now.'

Though the man spoke softly, the usual heckling started up. 'The Donn fancies a tune, does he?'

Perrin played the finger-harp as well as any man in the Rengani Army, and better than most. In the evenings, when the men gathered round the fires to trade rumours and swap crude stories and polish their weapons, they'd call for Perrin to play and sing a ballad or two; it was the only time that Perrin didn't loathe being a soldier.

Sometimes the men wanted dancing, and then Perrin would play with a piper and a drummer; he didn't like that so well. What he enjoyed was feeling all eyes on him as he sang, and the knowledge that he could bring tears to those eyes with a tremor of his voice or the strumming of the harp. He liked to make people laugh, too, but that was easy. Any idiot could make a fool of himself. But to make the battle-hardened troops of the Fifth weep – that took a true master.

'Old bastard must want a pretty face to look at over his roast duck.'

'Or after his roast duck –'

With one look from the lieutenant, the jokes died away. They'd been half-hearted anyway, directed more at Perrin than at Commander Donn. The Commander of the Fifth wasn't one of those generals who'd wander round the camp pretending to be mates with his men. He was a cunning old bastard, but he was straight with you. He knew he was better than the soldiers, smarter and tougher; that was why he was a general, and they weren't.

Perrin shrugged, for the benefit of the others, and turned toward his tent.

'Where are you going, Swordsman?'

'To get my harp, sir.'

'Won't need that. Now move, before my boot meets your frugging arse.'

Perrin moved. He hurried between the tents after the lieutenant, through the filth and stink of the military camp: sweat and rancid food, piss and excrement. He racked his brains for a reason he might be in trouble. He hadn't annoyed anyone recently, at least no more than usual. He was learning to watch his tongue; he hadn't argued with an order since – since the Battle of the Falls.

Still, he wasn't seriously worried. Perrin had never met a problem he couldn't talk his way out of.

The front part of the Commander's tent was well lit; Perrin blinked as he came into the light out of the shadows of the camp. Surprisingly, the Commander was alone, seated on a folding chair at a folding table, reading dispatch scrolls. Perrin eyed them with interest: he'd seen scrolls before, of course, but rarely close enough to make out the writing.

The Commander looked up, and Perrin remembered

to snap to attention just in time, hand to shoulder. 'At ease, soldier.' The Commander returned to his scrolls. Perrin stood waiting. One of the old man's legs was propped on a stool; he'd stepped on an exploder twenty years ago and blown away half his foot.

If not for the pips and stripes on his sleeves, Commander Donn might have been mistaken for a small-town administrator. He had shrewd eyes and a pinched, humourless mouth; his most distinguishing feature was his teased-up cloud of hair. Perrin took the opportunity to examine it up close. The overall effect was too fluffy for the rumoured special creams from Baltimar, he decided; it must be a wig after all.

The Commander thrust the last scroll into a carry-bag and knotted the ties. Perrin stared carefully into the middle distance, but he was aware of Donn's eyes on him, appraising, measuring. For the first time, Perrin felt a twinge of unease.

'Swordsman Perrin.'

'Sir.'

'I've been checking your records.'

'Sir.'

'Very useful, these new Signs, this *writing*. Means we can keep track of people more easily.'

'Sir?'

The Commander leaned back. 'I believe you're familiar with the Signs, Swordsman?'

Perrin's heart sank. So that's what this was about. It was his own fault, showing off again. None of the other men could read, and only a handful of the officers. And when Cronsie had borrowed that battle report, Perrin hadn't been able to resist reading it out to the rest of the squad. Some frugger must have reported it. Perrin said, 'I know some of the Signs, sir.

My mother learned them in – in the Westlands. I picked it up from her.'

'Born in the Westlands, Swordsman?'

'Yes, sir. A place called Nadalin. On the coast of Kalysons.' Perrin stopped, but the Commander gestured to him to continue. 'My parents took a ship to Rengan when I was six years old. My father was a baker. My mother taught children.'

Commander Donn frowned. 'Taught the Signs?'

'No, sir. Not once she knew it was classified. She never betrayed military secrets.' *Except to me.*

'A wise woman.'

'Yes, sir.' Perrin stared straight ahead. His mother had wanted to teach the Signs, to share her knowledge. The village council of Chaplet, which was directly answerable to High Command, had soon put a stop to that.

'Parents both dead now, I believe?'

'Yes, sir, both dead. There was a fire in the bakery, after I was drafted.'

'Sorry to hear that, Swordsman. Always a hazard, fire, in a bakery.'

'Yes.' Perrin's voice was bitter. He was certain that the fire was no accident. The village council couldn't tolerate foreigners, let alone foreigners with secret knowledge. Perrin's mother had been a risk, even after ten years as a Rengani citizen. But a dead woman couldn't teach the Signs to the Balts, so they'd had her killed. Of course he had no proof.

'No brothers or sisters?'

'No, just me.'

'Why did your parents leave the Westlands, Swordsman?'

Perrin lifted his chin. 'Isn't that in my records? Sir?'

'I'm asking the questions, soldier.' The Commander spoke

mildly enough, but his eyes narrowed. Perrin was reminded of what the men said: that a reprimand from Donn was as bad as a whipping from any other general.

Perrin took half a heartbeat to decide that it wasn't worth risking a lie: at any rate, not a complete one. 'They left because of me, sir. I was a handful as a kid, up to all sorts of mischief. They heard about life in Rengan – the, er, the moral standards, the simplicity of life here. Everyone pulling together for the larger purpose. Rengan's health is our common wealth, and all that. Sir.' Perrin grinned disarmingly. 'They thought it would be good for me. An Army life is a straight and narrow life, as they say.'

The Commander put the tips of his fingers together. 'A pretty story, Swordsman. But that's not the real reason your family left the Westlands.'

There was a pause, while Perrin calculated how much the Commander might know, and how much he could keep hidden. Probably not much, he decided. Not after the snake thing. He said, 'Well, I had a – a voice, sir.'

'You mean they left the Westlands because you were a sorcerer. *Are* a sorcerer, I should say.'

'A chanter,' Perrin corrected him automatically. The Commander frowned. Perrin said hastily, 'That's right, sir. I'm a sorcerer, sir.'

'And they hoped that in this country, away from the influence of other sorcerers, you might forget your magic. They hoped you might be *straightened out*.'

'It wasn't just that, sir. Life was risky for chanters, for sorcerers, in the Westlands, when the Witch-Singer appeared and the Chanters' Rising began. I suppose things might be different there now, I don't know, we don't hear much news of the Westlands.'

'No, we don't.' The Commander frowned again. 'Except through the weapon-makers of Mithates. But you can take it for granted that we're all better off, and safer, here in the Threelands, war or no war, than in that nest of sorcery in the west.'

'Sir.' Perrin was expressionless. 'As you say, sir, my parents hoped I'd forget about chantment.'

'But you haven't forgotten, have you, Perrin?'

'No, sir.'

Satisfied, the Commander leaned back in his chair. 'Swordsman Perrin, you're guilty of a serious offence. You've been hiding your gifts. We can make much better use of you.'

'Yes, sir,' said Perrin smartly. Oh, well. Now they'd send him somewhere where his skills could be used properly for the war effort, for the larger purpose, for the good of the nation. But doing what? The Balts fought with horses, but the Renganis didn't know much about them. Maybe High Command wanted him to tame horses. That would be a nice soft job. Better than endless sword drills on the practice paddock. Definitely better than being slashed to ribbons on the front line, when the fighting started again.

Perrin could have kicked himself. He should have thought of this before; he could have drawn his talents to the attention of High Command long ago. It was the old soldiers' attitude that had held him back: *Never volunteer. Keep your head down.* He'd started to believe that was the only way to survive. But this was a better way . . .

The Commander inclined his head toward the darkened rear of the tent, and a second figure emerged into the light.

'Swordsman Perrin, this is –' Commander Donn hesitated fractionally.

'He can call me Tugger,' the second man said easily, and instead of saluting, he held out his hand. 'He doesn't need to know anything else.'

Perrin darted a look at the Commander, whose lip had curled in the rare grimace that passed for one of his smiles.

'It's all right, Perrin. Shake the man's hand.'

Tugger's grip was tight, his hand brown and strong. Though he was dressed in nondescript dull greens and browns rather than a uniform, he was unmistakably a life-long soldier. He had the slight squint of someone who'd spent years staring into the sunlight, and he was weathered and tough as a strip of leather.

'You don't need to know my rank, son.' He released Perrin's hand. 'You only need to know it's higher than yours.'

'Yes, sir.'

'Don't call me sir. From now on, you call me Tugger, and I call you Snake. Where we're going, there are no names, no salutes, no uniforms. Clear? Of course,' Tugger grinned, 'you'll still obey me without frugging question.'

'Yes, sir. I mean, yes, Tugger.' Puzzled, Perrin looked from one man to the other. This didn't smell like the lead-up to a soft job behind the lines playing with captive Baltimaran horses. There seemed to be some kind of private joke going on. Perrin preferred to be the one who made the jokes.

Tugger pulled up a stool for himself and dragged another into range with his foot for Perrin. So here he was, sitting cosily around a table with the old bastard himself, and some other high-up frugger. The lads were never going to believe this story . . .

But even as Perrin formed the thought, he knew that he'd never tell the other soldiers about this meeting. With that

41

handshake, he'd crossed into another world; without setting foot out of the tent, he'd left the camp, and the Fifth, forever. Something was up. And like it or not, he was part of it.

Tugger said, 'You're a chanter. You sing songs that tame animals.'

It was a statement, not a question. Perrin nodded.

'Heard you sang a red-tail to sleep the other day. That right?'

'Yes, that's right.'

'Mind if we ask for a little demonstration?'

'No, Tugger.' Perrin's heart thumped.

Tugger called softly. A ranker dragged a large, canvas-draped box into the tent. He saluted, threw a curious glance at Perrin, and departed. Perrin shifted to the edge of his stool. It was a surroan cat; he knew it even before the low, eerie growls began to roll through the tent.

'Take off the cover,' said Tugger.

Perrin flicked the canvas aside. It was a cage, not a box, and a flimsy cage at that. Behind the bars the big cat crouched with its back arched, its green eyes wide and gleaming with fear; its spotted fur bristled. The sharp stink of urine filled the tent, and the growling intensified. One good run at the bars and the whole cage would fall apart.

'Should we open the cage?' The Commander wasn't looking at the surroan; he was watching Perrin.

'If you like,' said Perrin. He held the cat's gaze; he didn't think about whether he was being insolent, and he didn't notice the glance that the two senior officers exchanged. He held out his hand to the cage and crooned softly, deep in his throat. As he sang, he lowered himself to his haunches, to the same level as the cat. The surroan growled a warning, flexed her claws, and spat.

Perrin chuckled. 'Easy now, easy.' He resumed his song, creeping closer to the cage. Slowly the surroan's fur flattened, as if stroked by a friendly hand, then she lowered her tail, and sat. Perrin's chantment became a rhythmic purr, and the cat's growl softened into a purr too. 'Good girl, good girl,' murmured Perrin. He put his hand through the bars, just to show off, and the cat rubbed her cheek against his fist.

'Nice,' said Tugger.

'Thanks.' Perrin didn't look up; it was dangerous to take your eyes off them once the song was finished. He'd been caught like that early on, with a street dog in Nadalin. He still had the scar on the back of his leg. But even with his head turned away, he was aware of Tugger and Donn looking at each other.

'Can you do that with any animal?'

'Never met one yet that could resist me.'

'Women too?' said Tugger dryly.

'Never thought of trying it on a woman.'

'Hmmm. I'll bet.' There was the hint of a twinkle in Tugger's eye.

The cat stretched, yawned, and curled up to sleep.

'Tamed a surroan before, Snake?'

Perrin liked his new name; it was better than Pretty Boy, anyway. 'Only met one once before. In the woods by the border, a few turns of the moons ago, when the war was still – when the fighting was still –'

'Before the strategic withdrawal of our forces from Cragon-lands,' said Tugger. The twinkle in his eye was almost a wink.

'Yes. We were in retreat, Balts pursuing. One of my squad nearly stepped on a cat and her kittens. She would have torn us to shreds if I hadn't been able to – redirect her.'

'Onto the enemy?'

Perrin nodded. 'She took two of them. The squad dealt with the rest.'

'Never saw that in any report, Swordsman.'

Of course not; it never happened. Perrin said easily, 'My squad leader's a sceptical man. He didn't see anything. Or hear it.'

Tugger said, 'Cats. Snakes. What about birds? Fishes? Woodlice?'

'Woodlice can't hear too well, Tugger.'

'So how do you sing to snakes? Thought they were deaf too.'

'They are, almost. You have to get onto the ground, so they can feel the vibrations.' He added, 'It's more than the songs. Animals just seem to like me.'

'Yes,' said Tugger. 'Everyone seems to like you.'

Perrin risked a grin, a half-shrug. It was true. Even the bastards in the squad who gave him a hard time teased him without malice. Everyone liked him, everyone wanted to get near him. There was nothing he could do about it; it had always been like that, ever since he could remember.

'Could be an asset,' said the Commander to Tugger.

Tugger nodded. 'If the boy's suspicious. Yes. Help us win his trust.' He gazed at Perrin. It was a shrewd gaze. Perrin realised that, for the first time in his life, here was someone who could see past his charm, and his good looks, and his little tricks, and miraculously liked him anyway. Here was someone who liked him *despite* his charm, not because of it; someone who wouldn't let him frug about. Suddenly Perrin felt something he'd never felt for any member of the Rengani Army: respect. This Tugger was a man worth following.

Perrin was sure now that he wouldn't be playing games with Baltish horses. He didn't really want to know, but he half-raised his hand. 'Excuse me. What's this all about?'

'Thought you'd never ask,' said Tugger. 'You're a lucky man, Snake. You've won yourself a place in my squad. Going on a little mission, a raid on Baltimar. Not just over the border – deep into the heartland, deep into the south. Fair chance we won't come back. Clear?'

'Yes.'

'I mean we'll probably die, Snake. That all right with you?'

'Yes.' Perrin felt sick. But what else could he say? A rapid series of images flashed through his mind: fleeing into the night, crawling through fields until – the soldiers' shouts. The ropes, the cell. His body swinging in the town square at Chaplet. Traitor, coward, deserter.

Perrin stood up and looked Tugger full in the face. 'Whatever you say.'

Tugger's brown eyes crinkled. 'Plenty of time for details later, but here's the rough plan. You, me, four other men, a boat. You know boats, is that right?'

'Yes.' A skip of surprise. Renganis, like the Baltimarans, disliked and distrusted boats. But Perrin had grown up scrambling round the cliffs and coves of Nadalin, and had handled little boats as soon as he could walk. And then came the long ocean voyage to Rengan; by the end of that, though he was still only a child, Perrin regarded himself as a proper sailor. 'Yeah, I know my way round a boat. I can swim, too.'

'Swim? That's good. Six men. We take a boat round the coast. South, to Arvestel.'

'Arvestel!' exclaimed Perrin.

'That's right. Up the river-mouth. Take them by surprise.

Bit of luck, they won't even know we've been there till it's too late. Retrieve the boy. Sail back round the coast, rendezvous with the second team at the border and hand over the boy. Break into pairs, melt away. Make our own way home. Handle that, Snake?'

'Yes.'

'Any questions? Not that I'll guarantee to answer them.'

'Who's the boy?'

'The Priest-King of Cragonlands. The Balts abducted him five years ago. Now we're going to take him back.'

'Back to Cragonlands?'

There was a slight pause; the two officers avoided looking at each other. Tugger said, 'That's right. Eventually.'

Perrin could smell a lie; he'd told enough of his own. He didn't care. He wasn't particularly interested in the boy or his fate; he just wanted to sound intelligent in front of Tugger.

'Why me? Specifically?'

Tugger's eyes crinkled. 'You never heard of the Guardians of Arvestel? I thought every kid in Rengan heard those stories at his mother's knee.'

'I wasn't brought up in Rengan,' Perrin reminded him. He felt sick again.

Tugger lowered his voice. 'They do bad magic down there, Snake. Not nice. Stitch things together that don't belong. The Guardians of Arvestel are half-man, half-beast. Surroans that run on two legs, horses with men's heads. Dogs with hands that can hold a sword. We don't know what other filth, what abominations there might be.'

Perrin swallowed. 'And you want me to – to sing to them?'

The Commander barked, 'If you think you're not up to it, now's the time to speak.'

There was a long pause. At last Perrin said, 'No sir, I can handle it.'

Tugger smiled slowly. 'Lucky you said that. If you weren't up to it, well . . . Let's say we couldn't let you leave this tent with a tongue in your head after what you've heard tonight.'

The Commander said, 'You should know that if you return without the boy, there will be consequences. Fatal consequences.'

'You mean I'll hang, sir,' said Perrin bleakly.

'Yes, you'll hang,' said Donn brusquely. There was a short silence. 'But on the bright side, if – *when* you succeed, High Command will show their appreciation. Promotion, naturally. Land on the east coast, perhaps. Sort that out later. Any other questions?'

Perrin looked blankly into the darkness that hedged the tent. A question – could he think of a question? He dredged one up from the depths of his mind. 'Yes, sir. When do we leave?'

'Tonight.' Tugger nodded to the door of the tent. 'There's your kit.'

Perrin spun around. There was his bed-roll and his knap-sack. He could even see the distinctive outline of his finger-harp wedged under the canvas. Whoever had done his packing hadn't forgotten a thing.

CHAPTER 4

A Hair from His Head

IT was the dead of night when Skir woke. He knew it must be long after midnight, because the dancing on the terraces had ceased. The small uncurtained window by his bed let in faint light from a single moon. Dawn was still far away.

'Beeman?' he whispered. 'Is that you?'

There was no reply, only a sinister silence. Skir found himself thinking *assassins*.

Beeman had warned Skir a thousand times to be alert for danger, and every time Skir scoffed at him. 'Arvestel's stuffed so full of guards you can't walk down the corridor without poking your eye out on a spear. Not to mention the dogs. An assassin couldn't get in here unless they flew up to the balcony.'

'Stranger things have happened. Just be careful.'

There: a definite noise. A rustle in the outer room. Skir's heart skipped a beat. He opened his mouth to croak for Beeman, but no sound came out. Then, with a surge of relief, he remembered that he'd left a plate of pancakes from supper half-eaten on the table. Not assassins – mice. He almost laughed.

The scuffling came again. Stealthily Skir groped for a slipper and hurled it through the doorway.

There was a thud and a squeak. But not from a mouse.

Skir gasped, 'Beeman! *Beeman!*'

Silence.

'I'm calling the guards!' cried Skir.

'No!' came an urgent whisper out of the darkness. 'They'll kill me!'

'Assassins deserve to be killed,' declared Skir. Then, 'You're a *girl*.'

'I ain't an assassin,' hissed the unseen girl indignantly. Then, less certainly, 'Least, I don't think so. Not exactly.'

'Oh, good, I feel completely reassured.' Skir lit a candle. How many times had he wished *something* would happen? And this was certainly something. 'Come in here and let me see you.'

The flare of the flame showed a girl of about Skir's age, with fair hair cropped close to her head, and fine, straight features. She didn't look at all frightened; she stared at him fiercely. She was wearing a cloak with the hood pushed back, and, underneath it, a man's shirt and breeches, too large for her. The breeches were held up with a twist of rope. Her hands were empty; if she had a weapon, it was well hidden. Her eyes were large and grey, with long lashes. There was a dent above her lips; suddenly feeling faint, Skir imagined laying his finger gently on that dent.

He cleared his throat. 'What's your name?'

'Tansy.'

'Do you know who I am?'

'You're called Skir.'

This unexpected familiarity took Skir by surprise. 'Well, yes. But my formal title is the Priest-King of Cragonlands.'

The girl looked at him blankly, clearly unimpressed. Skir felt a flicker of annoyance. 'What are you doing here?'

The girl looked down, and a pink flush spread over her cheeks and up to her hairline. She muttered something.

'Sorry? I couldn't hear you.'

'I *said*, do you want to touch my bosoms?'

'What? *No*.'

There was an awkward silence. 'I'm sure they're very nice,' said Skir. He wished he'd said yes, now.

The girl bowed her head lower.

'Did you come to – to see me?'

'No. I thought you were asleep.'

'Oh. But then why –'

'Listen,' said the girl in a desperate rush. 'I don't mean you no harm, I swear it. I didn't know what she wanted, what she'd do. I didn't know it were for *her*.'

'Wait, slow down. Who's *her*?'

'Her. The Witch-Woman. Lady Wanion.'

He'd heard of Wanion, of course; she was one of the King's most powerful advisers. But he'd never met her. Wanion didn't attend feasts and concerts; she had other work to do. He hadn't heard she was supposed to be a witch. Interesting.

Skir thought for a moment. 'Wanion has magical powers, does she? Well, I'm a magician too, a very strong, very powerful magician.'

Tansy looked up, and such a fierce hope blazed in her eyes that Skir was almost frightened. He managed to keep his voice steady. 'Yes, as long as you're with me, within these walls, no harm can come to you. These rooms are part of Cragonlands. No Baltimaran magic can reach you here. But you must swear to tell me the whole truth.'

Tansy's chin went up. 'I don't tell lies.'

'All right,' said Skir. 'Sit down. Go on, there's plenty of room. Now, who are you? Where did you come from?'

'I'm a laundry-maid,' said Tansy dully.

'How did you get in?'

'Followed your supper tray up from the kitchens. Then I hid in a cupboard outside till it was quiet. I'm good at keeping quiet.'

'Not that good. I heard you, didn't I?'

Tansy covered her face with her hands.

'Don't cry!' said Skir in alarm.

'I ain't crying,' said Tansy in a muffled voice. 'It's just – her magic'll get me, or yours will. Either way I'm good as dead.'

'I won't hurt you, I promise. As long as you tell me the whole story.'

Tansy took her hands from her face. 'It were – someone. Not from the laundries. I don't want to say her name. She knew what I wanted more than anything; she knew I wanted to be with the horses. She told me she were courting a groom in the stables, and she could arrange for me to go down there in the mornings early and help out. And I did. All through spring. I rode Bray, and Thimble, and Kite, the Queen's own mare, and once I held Penthesi's leading rein . . .'

'That's good, is it?' The names meant nothing to Skir. His own riding lessons were conducted on the ponies of the little princesses; he didn't know their names.

'Penthesi's the King's best hunter. You must have seen him. Black, with a white star. He's huge. The cleverest horse in the stables, old Ingle says.' Tansy's voice was reverent.

'They all look the same to me. Anyway, what happened? Did someone scold you? I assume you're forbidden to hang around the stables.'

'I weren't *hanging around*. I had a job to do, same as the stable-hands. Tern said I was handy as any of the lads, handier than some. There was one day I calmed Kite when none of them could get near her, not even Ingle. But then Lor – the person who arranged it all, she said she weren't courting with Tern no more, and if I didn't want to get into trouble, I better do as she said.'

'And?' Skir was fascinated by this glimpse of life on the other side of the servants' doors, the hidden world to which even Beeman had hardly any access. He'd never realised that the servants had lives as complicated, as riddled with secrets and intrigue and strict rules of behaviour, as their masters and mistresses in the golden and ivory rooms of the Palace. And he was fascinated by this girl who spoke to him as frankly and easily as if – well, as if they were equals.

Tansy jumped. 'What's that?'

A clink of armour and the muffled whine of dogs floated up from outside the window.

'Just a patrol. Don't they go past your quarters?'

'I guess I sleep through it,' said Tansy with a shiver. 'I sleep pretty hard, most nights.'

'Go on. Tell me what happened next.'

'Lori – the person, well, she only asked for little things at first. Boot wax, a cake of special soap. She said it weren't stealing, because it weren't taking off a person. She said, don't I ever help myself to a bit of leftover meat from the platter? Don't I ever have a nice warm wash in the hot laundry water? Don't I ever take a rag out of the basket?'

'And do you?'

'Course I do. Everyone does. Can't get by in this place unless you do. Still, it's different taking stuff for someone else. She said she'd give me gold, but I didn't do it for that. It were so I could work with the horses.'

'Never mind,' said Skir. 'No one'll miss a cake of soap here and there, surely. They give me a fresh soap in my own bathroom every day. No one'd throw you in the Pit for that.'

Tansy stared at him. 'Course they would,' she said flatly. 'If I got caught. And that's nothing. I ain't told you the worst yet.' She took a breath. 'She asked me to take something of yours.'

'Oh.'

'I waited for something to come by the laundries, but nothing did.'

Skir glanced down at his grey silk pyjamas, stained with hot chocolate and paint and jam. 'Well, it's true, I'm not very good at putting things in the wash-hamper. And Beeman's told the maids not to do it for me. It's supposed to teach me self-discipline.'

'I knew it. Just like my brothers.'

Skir jumped up and yanked open some drawers. 'If it'll save you getting into trouble – here, help yourself. Take a necktie or a scarf or something. I've got thousands I never wear, look.'

'You don't understand,' said Tansy. 'It's worse than that now. She don't want clothes no more. She wants a piece of you. Hair, or fingernail trimmings.' She lowered her voice. 'I reckon what she'd really like is blood or – something like that.'

Skir laughed. 'That's *mad*. What's she want that for?'

'You say you're a magician, and you don't know! It's for her, for the Witch-Woman to do magic with. Dark magic.' Her voice became lower still. 'She cuts off people's fingers for her magic, too. Peels the skin off them like carrots. Then she can do what she wants with you.'

Skir sank back onto the bed. His skin prickled. Tansy was

so distressed that for an instant he actually felt frightened too. But Beeman would say the only true magic was chantment; the Baltimaran superstitions of hair and bone and rhyme were powerless. Weren't they? Poor Tansy obviously believed it, though. The price of ignorance is fear, Beeman would say. Skir suddenly felt immensely old and wise.

He said, 'There's a hairbrush in my bathroom, it's *full* of hair. Disgusting. I'll get it.'

Tansy straightened herself up. 'No, don't! I don't want it no more. *Stop*. It's different now I met you. Call the guards if you want, I deserve it. But I'd rather die quick than rot in the Pit. And I'd rather rot in the Pit than go back to *her*.' Tansy shuddered.

Skir sat down again. 'Well, it makes no difference to me. Give Lady Wanion handfuls of my hair if you like, I don't care, but if that's how you feel . . . Why don't you just say no?'

Mutely, Tansy fished under her cloak and held out the tiny, exquisite luckpiece on her hand. She whispered, 'That come from the Witch-Woman. Now I'm bound to her. It's watching me all the time, see? And if I don't give her what she wants, she'll take a piece of *me*.'

The two of them stared at the little doll. Silent, malevolent, it stared back up at them from Tansy's palm.

Skir shook himself. 'Rubbish,' he said briskly, and before Tansy could stop him, he plucked up the luckpiece between finger and thumb and held it over the candle-flame.

'No! No!' Tansy shouted. The flame sizzled up the threads of white silk. Tansy made a frantic grab for the burning doll, but Skir held her off; in desperation she snatched up the crystal water jug by Skir's bed. Water fanned through the air, hissed onto the burning luckpiece, but it was too late; charred fragments of ivory and mother-of-pearl fell to the carpet.

'Hey!' Skir ducked away, knocking over the candle and snuffing it out.

Tansy scrabbled on the floor. 'Where is it?'

Skir caught up his other slipper and smashed the heel down as he'd seen other people squash spiders. As a priest, he was forbidden to kill any living thing, but grinding the burned, sodden fragments of the little doll into powder was extremely satisfying. He sat back on his heels, breathless and triumphant.

Tansy clapped her hands over her mouth; in the moonlight her eyes were like saucers. Then she took a deep, sobbing breath, and ran her hands up and down her arms. 'I ain't burned,' she whispered. 'I ain't hurt at all. You *are* a sorcerer.'

'Of course I am,' said Skir, and for the briefest moment he almost believed he was a chanter after all, a master of magical power, holding life and death between his finger and thumb.

The doorknob of the outer room rattled.

Skir forgot he was a master magician, and panicked. 'What do we do?'

'The bed.' For a heartbeat they both stared at the shadowy, curtained expanse of Skir's bed, heaped with quilts and cushions. Three or four girls could have hidden in it quite easily. Tansy dived under the covers.

Breathless and dishevelled, Skir scrambled back into bed, acutely aware of Tansy's warm, breathing body close to his own beneath the quilts. 'Come in!' he called, just as Beeman poked his head around the door.

'I am coming in,' said Beeman mildly. 'What's the matter? I heard shouting.'

'I had a bad dream. I must have screamed.'

'Odd. I could have sworn it was a woman's voice.'

'I dreamt, yes, you know, I dreamt I was a woman. Yes. It was a very strange dream.'

'Are you all right? Would you like some water?'

'If I want water I can pour it myself, I'm not a child. Go away, Beeman. Wait. Beeman? Where were you?'

'In my bed next door, of course.'

'Were you? I thought you must have gone out.'

'Gone *out*? Where?'

'That's what I wondered.'

'I didn't go anywhere. Are you delirious? Do you have a fever?'

'No. I'm perfectly all right.'

'Goodnight then.'

'Goodnight.'

The door clicked closed as Beeman withdrew. At once, Tansy shook herself violently free of the covers.

'I hate that, hate having stuff over my head,' she whispered. 'I couldn't breathe . . . He did go out, your servant. I was watching. He sneaked off without a light. He must have a woman.'

'Beeman's my tutor, not my servant. And he doesn't have women,' whispered Skir. 'At least, he never has before.'

'There's a first time for everything,' whispered Tansy, and for some reason this struck them both as supremely funny. They had to stifle their laughter with pillows.

Then Tansy sat up and gazed at him soberly in the moonlight. 'I can't leave here now. Madam'll know I destroyed her luckpiece. You'll have to protect me, like you said.'

'Well – yes, all right,' said Skir, taken aback. He felt cornered. 'Fair enough. But you can't stay in my bed forever.'

56

At once his face grew hot. He hoped Tansy couldn't see.

'No, not in your bed.' Tansy frowned, deep in thought. 'Only for a few days.'

'A few *days*! But Beeman is always here.' He paused. 'I could tell Beeman. I think I should tell Beeman.'

'No! You mustn't tell anyone! What about *under* the bed?'

'No – wait. There's my bathroom. The maids don't clean in there, I'm supposed to clean it myself, to teach me responsibility and humility. Beeman won't use it because it's too filthy; he goes to the gentlemen's baths in the east wing.'

Tansy considered, then nodded her head. 'The Witch-Woman's going away after tomorrow. While I'm with you, she can't hurt me. And in four days the wagon comes that goes up north. Once I get away from Arvestel, she won't find me, not now the luckbit's gone. You better give me some gold.'

'Gold? I don't have any jewellery.'

'Not jewels. I mean money. To buy my ticket home to Lotch.'

'Oh. I don't have money either. They give me everything I need.' Skir stared gloomily around his luxurious bedroom. 'Beeman could get some, I suppose. But he'd want to know what it was for.'

'Never mind, I'll think of something. Pity I can't ask for my wages off the paymaster. I must have earned ten gold bits by now.' Tansy fell silent. 'They'll be surprised to see me, back at Lotch. I said I weren't never coming back.'

Skir propped himself on one elbow to look at her. 'Were you miserable there?'

'Oh, no. I were happy at home. But when I left, I thought I were coming to Arvestel to work with the King's horses. My aunt sent word she had a place for me. I went off so proud. But when I got here, it were all a mistake. No girls in the stables, they said. Well, I didn't come all this way to scrub and sweat in the laundries. Might as well have stayed in Lotch and kept house for some old farmer. Or got married – same thing in the end. And then when I were riding, and helping out, I thought maybe old Ingle would sway something for me.' She looked down. 'But he never did.'

Skir had been thinking. 'I know how to get some money. There's a hunt tomorrow; I'll make bets – they're always trying to make me bet. It'll be easy.' He waved his hand around the room. 'I'll swap something from here.'

Tansy widened her eyes. Skir said uncomfortably, 'None of this is mine. I'm not rich. It's all – borrowed from the King, if you like.'

'So if I take money you've swapped, then that's stealing from the King.'

'No, no. Borrowing. Anyway, didn't you say you had wages owed? So the King owes you, really ... Oh, what does it matter? It's only *stuff*. Let's talk about something else. What will you do, when you go home?'

'I don't know.' Tansy lay back with her hands behind her head. 'Marry Morr, I suppose. He asked my brother Cuff before I came south, but I said no.' She sighed deeply. 'At least he's got horses. I'd get to ride sometimes. Before the babies come.' She looked gloomy.

'But you don't *have* to get married.'

'I'm sixteen. I can't live with Ma; she's with Cuff and his wife and there's no more room. My other brothers all got work, but there's nowhere to keep me. My Da died last summer, see. We lost the farm. It were a good big farm. We had the King's Herd graze there once. But it's all gone now.'

'I'm sorry,' said Skir after a pause.

'Anyway,' said Tansy briskly, 'I'll be glad to see the back of this place. I thought it'd be an adventure, but it weren't. Just hard slog, every day. And the other servants are all mean as cats. Even Aunty Fender. Nicest person I've met here is *you*.'

'Thank you very much.' Skir's heart thudded. He tried to keep his voice casual. 'I think I've seen you before. Around the stables, when I had my riding lessons.'

'I saw you, too. I saw you come off Thimble that day.' She began to giggle. 'Sorry. But you ain't a born rider, are you?'

Skir rolled over with his back to her. 'We should get some sleep. There's the quarter striking. It'll be morning soon.'

There was silence while the chimes died away, then Tansy whispered, 'I'm sorry. You're no rider, but then, I ain't no sorcerer. Everyone's different. You can't help it. Like my brother Dory. He's no hand with a horse either. And he's sweet, like you.'

Skir did not reply. *Sweet!* Somehow he seemed to have agreed to hide a laundry-maid in his bathroom for four days, barter and bet a vase into coins so she could pay her way home, and contrive to keep the whole thing secret from Beeman. And all this for a girl who thought he was *sweet*.

Tansy waited a few breaths, then whispered into the darkness, 'Thank you.'

But still Skir said nothing. He must have fallen asleep, thought Tansy, and a moment later she was asleep herself.

CHAPTER 5

Raid on Arvestel

'EASY, lads.'

Tugger's order was barely breathed. The four rowers shipped oars so smoothly that not a drop of water splashed into the river. Perrin nosed the boat into the reeds until it bedded itself in the soft mud. The silence was broken only by the cry of a wading bird. The air was warm, with the breath of summer; Perrin smelled trumpet-flowers and blush-blossom. There was only one moon, and it was waning, but even that was too much moon for Tugger.

'We'll lie up here tonight and tomorrow. Moondark tomorrow night. Perfect timing. Tonight's a recce. Wisp, you stay here.'

Perrin saw the flash of teeth as Doughty grinned. Tall, solemn Pigeon squeezed Perrin's shoulder with a bony hand.

'Watch the weather, Tug,' murmured Wisp. 'Smells like rain.'

'Wispy always smells rain. Not a cloud in the sky, but Wispy smells rain.'

The men stowed their gear under the canvas cover, and pulled their dark woollen hats low over their brows. Without a sound, they leaped onto the bank. Perrin followed; the reeds rustled as he landed, and someone chuckled softly. Tugger swung Perrin around, and smeared the dark paint more carefully across his face with his thumb. Then he nodded, and they were off, gliding between the trees in their usual order: Tugger, then Pigeon, Doughty, Perrin, and the twitchy Fello in the rear. Doughty muttered, 'Hey, Snake, any wild beasts nearby?'

Perrin grinned back at him. 'I'll let you know.'

It seemed like a quarter of the night had passed before they emerged from the woods. They'd circled the Palace carefully from the river; now they were on its eastern side. Almost imperceptibly Tugger signalled. Perrin still had trouble seeing his signals; sometimes Tugger seemed to communicate with his men through mind-speech. Perrin found himself on his stomach beside the squad leader. Tugger muttered, 'There it is, lad. Arvestel.'

The landscape was muted grey and green in the faint light of the single moon. The hills of southern Baltimar were like shallow bowls upturned on a tabletop with a silvery-green velvet cloth thrown over them. Beyond two low hills lay Arvestel, nestled in a valley: the Palace of ivory, the Royal Court, the soft, corrupt heart of the enemy. The towered Palace was all shining domes and slender spires; pennants drooped, colourless in the waning light. All around the Palace spread an embroidery of ornamental gardens: hedges and urns and clipped trees and fountains.

Tugger passed Perrin the glass. 'Patrols all around the Palace. Guards round the walls. They must keep those stitched-together beasts for the inside. See anything?'

Perrin peered. He was aware of all the men waiting,

listening, respectful. For the first time on this mission, he wasn't just the raw kid: he was the expert. He said, 'I can see something.' And they all took a breath, even Tugger.

'What is it? What is it?' That was Fello, quick and nervous.

'Steady,' murmured Tugger. 'Let me see, Snake.'

Perrin said, 'It's gone. Sorry. Looked like one of those half-men you were talking about. With claws instead of hands.'

Doughty swore softly. Perrin decided he'd better not push it too far. 'I can't see anything now,' he said truthfully.

'The Balts are holding the boy at the corner of the east wing, closest to us. See those two towers with the big flags? Below that, just above the first row of battlements. Those three long windows. That's our target, lads.'

Perrin passed the glass to Fello; they all took a turn, scanning the walls, checking the terrain. Perrin didn't have to worry about any of that, Tugger had said. His job was the beasts. The others would take care of everything else. 'But I want you in the room. You'll be with me. Clear? The boy's not far off your age. People like you. Might make life easier.'

Suddenly Perrin understood. 'He's not expecting us, is he?'

'We've tried to get word to him, but we don't know. There's a chance he might even be . . . hostile.'

'Hostile? To being rescued?'

'Captives can get attached to their captors. I've seen it happen. That's where you come in. Make friends. Persuade him we're here to help. Clear?'

Perrin took another look through the glass at the three corner windows. The others were muttering about hooks, and ropes, and signals; Perrin didn't listen. This time he really could see a patrol on the battlements. Three men. They looked ordinary enough, in the scarlet-and-blue uniform of Palace guards. Much smarter than the drab Rengani mud-brown. It wasn't what the Balt regular army wore, of course, but even the Balt battle gear was a tasteful shade of blue-grey . . .

Three men. Two with short swords, for close fighting. No shields. Not expecting any action, and why would they? What was the third man holding – a whip? Perrin squinted through the glass. It was a lead, a pair of leads. The patrol moved past a gap in the battlements, and Perrin grinned to himself as he saw the dogs. Two big black-and-tan hounds with square muzzles. They'd be vicious in attack, but they were just ordinary dogs; nothing he couldn't handle with his eyes shut. He'd never entirely believed Tugger's stories about the half-men, half-beasts, but it was still a relief to know that this was going to be easy after all.

On the way back to the boat, Perrin suddenly stopped short and cocked his head.

'Sst!' Fello alerted the others.

Perrin sang a low growl of chantment that made the hair stand up on everyone's neck. 'Surroan?' muttered Tugger.

Perrin, still singing, shook his head. He dropped to his haunches. 'Keep still,' he whispered.

A huge wild boar stood on the other side of the clearing. A big, heavy sow, with jowls flecked with foam. She raised her head and grunted.

Perrin lifted his voice. The sow swung her head toward him and squealed. She pawed the ground. Perrin couldn't see her eyes in the shadows. *Come on, princess. This won't take long, then you can go on your way.* He sang, low and sweet, and stepped toward the sow. She lowered her head – in submission, or ready to charge? Perrin heard someone's breath catch. For a long moment, he and the sow stared at each other. Then she swung her head away and trotted off through the trees.

'By the bones!' Doughty clapped him on the back so hard he nearly fell over. 'That was a close one! Lucky –'

'No luck about it,' said Tugger swiftly. 'Well done, lad.'

'It was nothing,' said Perrin modestly. It *was* lucky: lucky the boar was close enough that he could bring her closer without having to sing for long. He couldn't pull that trick too often, but knowing that tomorrow night was going to be so simple, he'd wanted to do something impressive. He was almost disappointed that Tugger wouldn't see him try his chantments on any man-monsters.

He just managed to stop himself from whistling.

The next day it rained. 'Damn you, Wispy,' muttered Fello. 'Can't stand to be wrong, can you?'

They spent an uncomfortable day crouched under canvas in the boat, well hidden in the reeds. Pigeon went out once, but didn't see anything unusual.

'Hunting party from the Palace. Just some fat Baltish kids fooling around.'

'Hope they run into that big boar from last night,' said Fello. 'Give em a fright. Did I tell you about that, Wispy?'

'Only about twenty times.' Wisp winked at Perrin, who sat quietly sharpening his dagger. Perrin recognised the subdued, tense mood of the men: it was the same before any battle. He reached into his knapsack and pulled out his finger-harp.

Now was not the time for rousing tunes or comic songs; he played the old ballads of Rengan that the men had learned as early as breathing, songs they'd heard as they lay in their mother's wombs. The steady drumbeat of rain on the canvas kept time, and the irregular drip of water as it slid off the brim of Tugger's battered hat made a counter-beat. Perrin kept his eyes on his fingering, but he saw Wisp raise a hand to his face, and Doughty turn away. He judged the moment Tugger was ready to say, 'That's enough,' and played a merry little jig to finish up.

The rain eased slightly around sunset, but didn't stop. 'No need to worry about moondark,' said Wisp. 'We got enough cloud to block ten moons.'

'And enough mud to drown a damn battalion,' growled Pigeon.

As the dial on Tugger's pocket-clock crawled toward midnight, the men grew quiet. Perrin was tense, but not afraid. The danger for him was the dogs, and he wasn't scared of them. Even if that big old boar-sow jumped out at them in the woods on the way, he knew he could handle her.

'Time, lads,' Tugger said softly. Perrin was the first to his feet.

'I'll have a swig of spiced wine waiting for you,' said Wisp. 'Good luck, lads.'

'We'll make our own luck tonight,' said Tugger sternly, but he laid a hand briefly on Wisp's shoulder.

'See you on the other side,' croaked Wisp. It was the traditional soldier's farewell, and Perrin lifted one hand to acknowledge it.

This time it was impossible to creep silently through the woods; the rain had turned the ground to slush. Doughty slid, and when he scrambled up, he was limping. 'It's not bad.' He shrugged off Fello's hand. 'It'll come good. I swear it, Tug, it's not that bad.'

'Stand on it,' said Tugger.

Doughty swore, and grimaced, and his leg buckled. 'Back to the boat,' said Tugger. 'Now. Send Wisp to catch up.'

The remaining four struggled on. Low branches lashed their faces, thorns snagged their clothes, and always the mud slid and sucked under their feet. At last they reached the place where there was no cover between them and the Palace gardens.

'Right, lads. Count of one hundred between. You first, Pigeon. Go, go, go.'

Perrin's stomach turned over. They were crossing the open ground alone, every man for himself. What was he supposed to do after that? He'd thought Tugger would look out for him. He hadn't listened to the briefings. It was too late to ask now. Pigeon and Fello were already gone.

'Ninety-nine, a hundred.' Tugger waved him forward, eyes down on his pocket-clock. 'Make luck for yourself, son. Go, go, go.'

And Perrin was off, running through the rain toward the dim, wavering lights of the Palace, bent double and gasping for breath as the wet ground slammed up beneath his feet. The rain was blinding. His dagger-belt was loose; it flapped at his side. He clutched it with one hand. Where were the lights? All the lights had gone out. No, there they were. He was veering south . . .

He slammed face-first into a hedge and the ground came up to meet him with a smack. Automatically he rolled, pressed himself flat. He groped for his dagger-belt, his hands slippery with mud and rain, and managed to pull it tight. *Don't panic, Perrin. All you have to do is creep through the garden.*

He crawled along the line of the hedge until he found a gap. But beyond the gap was another solid wall of greenery, parallel with the first. He blundered beside it; this one ran in a curve that took him right round the other side of the Palace. Another gap, a straight avenue, then bang, into yet another hedge. At last Perrin realised he was trapped inside a maze. Tugger hadn't mentioned a maze. Had he?

Back and forth Perrin crawled in the rain for what seemed an eternity, inching his way forward, sometimes forced back on his tracks. The hedges were too slippery to climb, and too dense to burrow through.

Then at last he was out, with a gravel path under his hands and knees. He rolled over and turned his face up to the rain. He guessed he'd only advanced twenty paces in all that time. The sky was black; the water fell out of it like stones. Far away, someone was shouting.

Someone was shouting. Perrin stumbled to his feet and set off again, head down, shoulder to the rain. The lights were close now, looming out of a sudden cliff of solid shadow. The Palace wall. What was he supposed to do? *Low, get low, behind this fountain.* He cursed the rain and wiped his hair out of his eyes. He couldn't see a damn thing.

There was a noise. Shouting again. Perrin tensed. It might be all right. It might be the shout of one patrol to another, calling, 'all's well'.

But he knew, even then, that it was all wrong.

He waited and waited, but no patrols came by. He heard voices, close to the Palace wall, but no more shouts. He glimpsed the flicker of lights. For no real reason, he started to run, crouching, toward the wall.

'Snake! *Snake!*'

Pigeon's long arms wrapped around him from behind and brought him to the ground with a thud. 'You frugging idiot,' he hissed in Perrin's ear. 'What are you playing at? I've been watching you march around that garden like you were on parade this full quarter of the night. Keep your head down. We're safe enough here. By the bones. As if things weren't bad enough.'

'What's happened?' whispered Perrin. Pigeon held him tight around the waist, so tight he could hardly breathe, and rocked him cheek to cheek.

'Fello's gone. Got stuck in that frugging maze and the patrol found him. Don't know where Tugger's got to; no sign of Wispy either. Shut up and let me listen.'

'Fello's captured?'

'Dead.'

Perrin swallowed. For a long time the two men were silent, rocking back and forth in the rain. Pigeon didn't seem to realise that he was clutching Perrin like a child with a rag doll. The rain beat down. Nearby, dogs barked, an excited clamour. Pigeon let out a long sigh, and released Perrin. 'Hear that? Come on, Snake. Go, go, go.'

Pigeon disappeared into the dark. Perrin gaped after him. *Go where?* On hands and knees he crawled after Pigeon. Now he heard other noises too: the scrape of metal on stone, the whirr of a rope through a pulley. Trust Tugger to get it right, even when everything else was turning to piss and mud. Tugger had pulled it off, climbed the face of the Palace with his pegs and toes, secured the rope and let it down.

Out of the rain Pigeon grabbed him again, shoved his mouth close to Perrin's ear. 'You're up. Go, go, go.'

He yanked the rope around Perrin's waist and tightened it, boosting Perrin up the wall. Confused, Perrin groped for foot and handholds. This wasn't the plan. *But the plan was all blown to pieces.* There were supposed to be four of them scaling the wall, two teams of two. Big Doughty was supposed to pull Perrin to the top. When he'd practised with Doughty before they sailed south, it was almost like flying; he'd pushed off lightly from the rocks as he rose effortlessly higher.

Tugger dragged him upward, rough as a sack of carrots; his hands and knees scraped on the stone, his hips banged into the wall. He couldn't see how high he'd come. Tugger stopped pulling. Perrin dangled at the end of the rope. If Tugger let go . . .

Desperately Perrin felt for a foothold. He managed to jam the toe of his boot into a crack, but then the rope jerked and he was yanked upward again. Not far now. He heard Tugger pant for breath. And dogs, the breath of dogs. Not barking. Heads down, intent on a scent close by. Didn't Tugger hear them too? A whine. He *must* have heard that.

In sudden panic, Perrin remembered: the dogs were his job. He started to sing. Rain poured down his face and into his mouth. Then the dogs heard. Their breathing changed, they whined; almost at the top, Perrin heard the irregular thump of tails. The dogs were right there.

With one last, rough heave on the line, Perrin reached the top of the battlements. And saw . . . not Tugger's black-smeared face, but strangers. Four men leering in triumph, holding the rope. Perrin saw this in the same instant he grasped the battlements and vaulted the top of the wall onto the walkway. He growled out a new chantment, and the dogs attacked.

They sprang just as the guards reached for Perrin. There was a flurry of teeth and fur, and screaming. Perrin rolled out of the way; a body fell, boots kicked wildly. The guards screeched commands at their dogs, but the animals were oblivious, obedient only to Perrin's chantment; they snarled and snapped and mauled their handlers. Perrin edged back from the tangle of dogs and men.

His groping hand came down on something warm and firm. It was Tugger. His body was crumpled beneath a window. His throat had been torn out.

Perrin's song dried in his mouth.

'Below! There're more below!' There was a clatter of boots, more yelling and barking. The dogs let go; Perrin heard them whine, and a confused scrabble of paws and boots as dogs and guards stumbled away. He pressed himself against the wall. He heard more shouts, then the whistle of arrows.

There was one moment of silence, then a roar went up. 'Got him!'

Perrin leaned against the wet stone, feeling sick. Fello, Pigeon, Tugger, all gone. He was alone.

The guards were gone, the dogs were gone. Alone. Perrin whispered, 'Go, go, go.'

He was standing near the corner of the wing, on the deserted walkway. A row of long windows were cut into the wall behind him. *Those three long windows. That's our target.* Perrin caught hold of the bottom pane of the nearest window and pulled with all his might. It wasn't locked, and the window slid up so smoothly that Perrin toppled into the room, tearing down a heavy curtain onto his head. He thrashed and lurched, a headless beast, a man-monster. He knocked into something, a little table or a chair, and felt it collapse beneath him like a nest of twigs.

'Don't move!' Perrin felt the prick of a sword-point through the fabric of the curtain, and froze.

The curtain was plucked off Perrin's head, and he blinked in the sudden blaze of light. There were lamps everywhere, glinting off silver and gold. It was like standing inside a treasure-box. He'd never seen anything like it: the flowers, the carpets, the gilt, the cushions. He staggered sideways.

'I said, don't move!' The sword pricked his back, and Perrin registered that the voice was female. Cautiously, he turned his head.

Two *kids* stood behind him. One, a slightly built, fair-haired boy in a white shirt and breeches, held the sword to Perrin's back with easy confidence. The other was a girl with shoulder-length red hair tied back; she was wearing a long grey dressing-gown with embroidered collar and cuffs.

'He's not moving. Put the sword down, Tansy.'

'Not till he throws his dagger down.'

Then Perrin realised he'd got it wrong. The one in grey was the boy, and the one with the sword was the girl. He started to laugh.

'Shut up!' said the girl fiercely. 'This ain't funny! A man was killed just outside that window.'

Perrin stopped laughing. 'I know.'

'Who are you?' asked the boy, quietly.

'He's come to kill you, that's what!' cried the girl. 'He's an assassin.'

'She's not your bodyguard, is she? I can see I'll have to revise my ideas about Baltish girls.'

'I ain't no bodyguard,' said Tansy. 'I'm a friend.'

Still smiling, Perrin whipped out his dagger. Tansy lunged, he dodged. They stood with blades poised, ready to spring.

'Who are you?' asked the boy again.

'I'm a friend too.' Perrin thrust his dagger back in its sheath. 'I'm here to rescue you.'

'Rescue me?' echoed the boy.

71

'*Res-cue you.*' Perrin almost spat the words out in frustration. 'Save you. Take you home.'

The two kids stared at him, and Perrin saw himself as they must see him: a wild figure splashed with mud, face blackened, drenched from head to toe. His knees buckled and he sank down on an enormous stuffed sofa.

'Call the guards,' he said. 'Get it over with. Three men dead. One injured. Who knows what's happened to Wispy, maybe the boar got him. The mission's failed. Go on, call the guards. Let them see Rengan's finest in action. Oh sweet bones of the everlasting gods.'

'I wish Beeman were here,' said Skir.

'Well, he ain't. Looks like he's abandoned you,' said Tansy.

'He wouldn't do *that*.'

At that moment there was a huge explosion. The room shook; Skir covered his ears. Paintings and mirrors crashed from the walls. Perrin rolled off the sofa and covered his head with his arms.

Tansy said in awe, 'The cannons on the roof.'

'They've never fired them before,' said Skir.

The tremendous boom sounded again; a vase of flowers trembled at the edge of a shelf, then smashed to the floor. Now they could hear whistles, shouts, dogs barking.

Perrin sprang up. 'They're coming back. They've worked out it's you we were after.'

The whistles shrilled close by. There were running footsteps inside the Palace, thundering up the stairs. Perrin looked at Tansy. 'Well? You going to help me save your boyfriend?'

'She's not –'

'He ain't my boyfriend!' Tansy's face turned scarlet.

'You going to turn me in then?'

Unconsciously, Perrin adopted the rhythms of her speech. It was a trick that came naturally to him, like mimicking the animals he tamed. Like trusts like. Already Tansy's distrust was wavering.

She hesitated. Then she thrust the sword at Skir and grabbed Perrin's hand. 'Quick. Into the bed.'

'I can't pretend I've slept through that!' protested Skir.

'Not you. Me and the Gani. You hold them off. We'll work out what to do with him later.' Tansy dived into Skir's bed, and Perrin burrowed after her.

Heart racing, Skir kicked the sword under the sofa's skirts. It hung over the fire for decoration; it had never occurred to him that it was an actual weapon until Tansy had pointed it out. He flipped a plump cushion over a muddy patch. The curtain! He bundled it up and shoved it after the sword. He was only just in time; the next instant, the doors crashed open and the room was flooded with guards, swords drawn, dogs straining at their leashes.

'What's going on?' Skir tried to make his voice deep and angry, but he could hear the squeak of fear, even if no one else could.

'Rengani assassins!' barked the captain of the guard. 'Why are all the lamps lit? Why's that window open?'

'I was trying to see what was happening out there – all the commotion –'

'That's dangerous.' One of the guards slammed the window shut.

The dogs sniffed and whined, straining to explore. Skir followed as they ran into the bedroom and snuffled eagerly round the bed. One put his muddy paws up on the covers and barked.

'Can't you control that animal?' said Skir. 'That's Gellanese silk.'

'Looks like they've found something,' said the handler.

But then the dogs turned away. One sat down and scratched himself. Another's tail thumped lazily on the carpet. They'd lost interest in the bed.

The handler rubbed his head. 'Don't know what's got into the dogs tonight. Damnedest thing, earlier, they turned –'

'Not in front of –' muttered the captain. He jerked his head toward Skir, then realised the boy was watching him. Belatedly he saluted. 'You hear anything suspicious? Your Highness?' he remembered to add.

'Well, there was a lot of noise. I got up to look. My tutor –'

'Yes, where is he?'

'He – he went to find out what was going on.' Skir clutched his dressing-gown round him. In fact Beeman's bed had not been slept in, and Skir had no idea where he was. 'Didn't you see him outside?'

The captain frowned. 'I'll send him back to you when I do see him. He's not supposed to leave you unattended.'

'There's nothing to worry about, is there?'

'No, of course not. Thought one of the Gani bastards had given us the slip, pardon my language, but it seems not.'

'A Gani couldn't get past you, surely?'

'No, Your Highness. No, we've got them all.'

'So you'll be calling off the search now?'

The captain hesitated. 'Well – yes.'

'And there won't be any more disruption? My protector, the King, won't be very happy if he hears my sleep's been interrupted.'

'No, sir. Should be all quiet now. Sorry we disturbed you.'

'I'll tell the King how conscientious you've been.'

'Thank you, sir. Goodnight, Your Highness.'

With salutes from the guards, the patrol withdrew.

Skir twitched the bedcovers. 'You can come out now.'

Tansy emerged. 'You talk to the King?' she said in awe.

'Never spoken to him in my life. But I'm a king myself, don't forget.'

'Not a *real* king, though,' said Tansy.

Skir stood open-mouthed, searching for a suitable reply to this outrageous statement. Perrin put out the nearest lamp and peered from the window. 'Looks as if they really have called off the search.'

'What now?' asked Skir.

'Put all the lights out,' said Tansy. 'Looks like a party in here, and anyone can see through that window. Where's that sword?'

Perrin said, 'What, you've shared a bed with me, and you still don't trust me?'

'That's the time to trust a man the least, my ma says.' Tansy caught up the sword and aimed it at Perrin's throat. 'Too right I don't trust you. But I reckon we can use you.'

'Are you sure you haven't done this before?' Perrin smiled, but Tansy scowled at him.

'I trained with my brothers. I could give you a fair fight. Want to try me?'

'No, thanks.' Perrin raised his hands in mock surrender and stretched out on the bed. 'This is like lying on clouds. What is it? Goose down?'

Skir returned from putting out the lamps. 'I guess if you wait a while it'll be safe for you to go.'

'Just him?' said Tansy. 'What about you and me?'

'What?'

'We're escaping, ain't we?' She turned to Perrin. 'Ain't that what you came for?'

Perrin sat up. He said crisply, 'Perhaps you didn't understand me. Our mission is in ribbons. Tugger's dead, so are Pigeon and Fello, maybe Wisp, too. Doughty and I will be lucky to get back down the river alive.'

'Down the river? You got a boat?'

'A boat. That's clever,' said Skir softly.

'So we just got to get out of the Palace and through the woods. We can do that. I know a way.' Tansy swung back to Skir. 'The Witch-Woman's got secret passages – Lorison showed me. There's one leads right out into the woods. There's a door in the green music room; I was meant to use it to get back to Madam after I took your – Anyway, never mind that now – think we can sneak out without them guards catching us?'

'The green music room isn't far,' said Skir. 'But –'

Tansy hugged herself. 'Long as Madam don't see us,' she whispered. 'I bet she got eyes in all them passages. But that's all right, you can protect us with your magic.'

'Tansy –'

'Good.' Tansy turned toward the cupboards. 'We already packed one bag for me, now we'll pack one for you. Lucky it's summer, you won't need much. Quick, get dressed. Where's that money you won?'

'*Wait*,' said Skir. 'I want to talk to Beeman.'

'Your precious Beeman ain't here. You got a Gani soldier sitting on your bed. You got to make up your own mind this time. *Get dressed.*'

'I want to talk to Beeman first.'

Tansy stopped pulling out clothes and seized him by the shoulders. 'You been telling me for two days how you hate it here. Ain't this your chance to get home?'

Skir screwed up his face.

'So? You want to get out of here. I got to get away from Madam. No more to say. I'm taking these boots. Lucky your feet ain't much bigger than mine. You got food, Gani, on this boat of yours?'

Perrin's hands dangled between his knees as he watched Tansy tear around the rooms, thrusting useful things into a rucksack. The boy tugged on some breeches. Perrin was very tired, and his head felt like lead, but he knew he wouldn't be allowed to rest for long. He whispered, 'Go, go, go.'

PART TWO

The Coast Road

CHAPTER 6

Penthesi

THE rain stopped at last. Perrin had almost given up hope of finding Doughty and the boat when he heard the rush of the river. The boy and the girl argued in whispers behind him; the boy was complaining about his feet. Thank the gods, they were nearly there. Now Doughty could take over. Doughty would know what to do.

Perrin was exhausted; he looked forward to hearing the bark of military orders again. Orders from Doughty were one thing, but he was damned if he'd take any more bossing from that laundry-maid. He wondered how the boy-king had come to choose a laundry-maid for a girlfriend. She *had* been useful, smuggling them out of the Palace. She'd led them through a maze of dark passages that stopped and started and wound back on themselves like a burrower's tunnel. And she'd been scared to death, too, that was obvious; she was so relieved when they emerged into the clean, damp air of the woods that she'd squeezed Perrin's hand nearly to pulp.

But there was no place for a girl on a mission like this, especially a Balt girl, even if she did know how to handle a sword. Well, she was Doughty's problem now. With Doughty and the boat, maybe, just maybe, they'd make it home after all. *Swordsman Perrin, survivor of a dangerous mission – rescued the boy-king single-handed – Hero of Rengan –*

They were at the edge of the woods. Perrin could hear the rustle of the tall reeds, and the lap and gurgle of the lazy river.

He stopped abruptly. There was a light on the water.

The boy and the girl came up behind him. The girl whispered, 'What's that?'

Doughty would never light a lamp. Never.

'Down!' Perrin ordered. He grabbed their arms and pulled them forward into the river as the shower of arrows whistled around them. The boy spluttered as his head went under, and the girl cried out. Perrin dragged them deeper into the current. Now he could see the boat was in flames, and soldiers were silhouetted along the bank, their bows raised and arms pulled back. Someone shouted, and more arrows rained down. The boy flailed in panic beside him, and the girl struggled against him; at last Perrin realised she was hissing, 'Let *go*!'

Promptly Perrin released her and turned his attention to the thrashing boy. 'Can you swim?'

'I learned on the farm,' said the girl, treading water beside him.

'Not you!'

The boy gulped and spluttered. 'A bit – no, not really –' He gasped as his head went under again; Perrin reached out to grab him.

'Stop *splashing*, you frugging idiot. Keep still and I'll tow you. We've got to swim, it's our only chance. They won't follow, they've got too much gear.'

'I can hold my breath . . .'

'Then hold it.'

Another shower of arrows shrilled around them. If they could shelter behind the burning wreck of the boat – *where was Doughty?* – they might be all right. The Balts couldn't swim, Tugger had assured him. Yeah, and man-monsters guarded the Palace, too, and here was the frugging laundry-maid paddling away beside him like a frugging otter, even with her knapsack on, hair plastered to her head. Still, safer in the water than on the bank . . .

The boy lay as limp as a corpse with Perrin's hand cupped under his chin; one slow stroke at a time, Perrin towed him toward the burning boat. The flames painted the river with dancing orange. They were nearly there; they were going to make it. The boat was burned nearly to the waterline; but he hoped there'd be something to grab onto.

Perrin saw the girl duck as yet another volley of arrows spat into the water, then his right hand blazed with searing pain, as if he'd caught a burning coal. He doubled over in the water, letting go of the boy.

'One down! One down!' came the shout. 'Sarge, I got one!' There were big splashing strides along the river's edge.

Moaning with pain, Perrin kicked through the water toward the wreck. The flames were dying; there was nothing left but a blackened shell. An oar floated past him, and he threw his arm over it; it bobbed and spun, and he swallowed a mouthful of water. It tasted like dead leaves. He rested his chin on the oar and kicked until he was on the far side of the boat; he wedged the end of the oar between the planks, and rested, gulping air as the cold, lazy current tugged at him.

His hand throbbed where the arrow-shaft stuck through it. His right hand; of course it had to be his right hand, his harp hand, his sword hand. He'd never been wounded before. He'd even come through the Battle of the Falls without a scratch. *Perrin's luck*, they said; men fought to stand beside him in the line. He knew he ought to pull the arrow out, and try to stop the bleeding, but he was in the middle of the frugging river! He felt faint; his mouth and nose slipped under the water. No – no. He mustn't drown, he didn't want to die here. *Like Doughty?* No, Doughty must be safe somewhere, hiding in the reeds on the other bank. They couldn't *all* be dead.

For the first time since the arrow had hit him, he wondered what had happened to Skir and Tansy. He couldn't see them. Maybe they'd drowned. At that moment, he didn't care; he had his own skin to save. He tilted his head back. The stars were always brighter at moondark. The clouds had melted away. Water filled his ears, blurring the noise of yells and splashes. *Breathe, Perrin. That's an order.*

Tansy saw Skir go under as the Gani writhed in the water; it took her a moment to realise what had happened. She duck-dived as the arrows sizzled around them; down into the cold, rushing water she plunged, down and down, until she thought her lungs would burst.

An image flashed through her mind: the luckpiece Wanion had given her, blazing into flame and then drenched with water. Fire then water. The Gani's boat was on fire, and now she was drowning. Wanion's magic was punishing her after all. Cold fingers pinched at her heart. As she came up she banged her head hard against something. Skir had stamped on the luckpiece, and now the Witch-Woman was stamping on her head. But she pushed out blindly with her hands and felt the wreckage of the Gani's boat. She gasped for breath, eyes squeezed shut, groping along the side of the boat with her hands. Skir couldn't save her now. Tansy clung to the wreckage with her fingernails, and waited for Wanion's death spell to claim her.

When Perrin disappeared, Skir had just enough presence of mind to gulp in another lungful of air and kick out hard, away from the hail of arrows. It was true he could swim a little; Beeman had insisted on trying to teach him, but the Baltimarans were horrified by the very idea, and it had been difficult to arrange lessons. The knapsack dragged him sideways, but Tansy had pulled the straps too tight – he couldn't wriggle out of it. Skir kicked and splashed blindly until he ran aground; he staggered to his feet and found himself some distance upstream, in the shallows by the riverbank, face-to-face with a Palace guard, his blue-and-scarlet uniform daubed with mud, waving a short sword in one hand and a blazing torch in the other.

'Don't move!' He was young, no older than Skir himself, and the sword shook in his grasp. He yelled, 'Sarge!'

Skir raised his hands. He felt oddly calm. 'It's all right. You mustn't hurt me. I'm the Priest-King of Cragonlands. I'm valuable property.'

The young guard took a wobbling step forward and ran his tongue over his lips. In the livid light of the torch, his face flickered copper and bronze. 'I said, don't move! One step and I'll run you through.'

'You know you can't do that.' Skir took a step back into the river. The water was up to his waist.

'Sarge!' bawled the guard, but the only response was a fierce, unearthly squeal from the direction of the woods. The young guard's head jerked round, just for a heartbeat, and silently Skir slipped under the water.

Skir let himself swirl in the current as long as he could before he risked snatching another breath. He was close to the boat. He dropped his head back into the water. He might not have the power of chantment, but he was well trained, first by the priests of the Temple at Gleve, and then by Beeman. One thing he could do was to hold his breath for a long, long time.

A hand grabbed the strap of his knapsack and hauled him closer, and his head reared up, spluttering.

'Ssh!' hissed Tansy. 'It's me.'

He could see her face dimly; it was starting to get light. They were on the far side of the charred wreckage of the Renganis' boat, hidden from the soldiers. Tansy's teeth were chattering, and one of her hands was thrust into a gap between scorched boards to keep herself afloat. Skir found a handhold and they trod water side by side.

'You all r-right?'

'I think so.'

'Ssh!'

Voices carried across the water. '– no time to find nets. Get some poles to drag the body in from the bridge.'

'– almost sorry for the poor kid –'

'More sorry for old Hooksey. Wouldn't want to be the one to make *that* report.'

'Did you hear what happened in the woods?'

The voices lowered, sober. Tansy could only hear the words *boar* and *two men*. Then the voices faded altogether. Everything was quiet. No shouts, no splashes.

'They think I've drowned,' whispered Skir.

'Thought I was going to, too.' Tansy's face was pale. 'That

was *her*. Wanion. We shouldn't never have hurt that luckpiece.'

After a moment, Skir said, 'They shot him, you know – the Rengani.'

But Tansy shook her head. 'He's holding on over there.'

Now Skir saw, in the strengthening light, a hunched shape attached to the side of the boat. 'Is he all right?'

Tansy shrugged. 'He ain't let go.'

Skir half-paddled, half-pulled himself along the side of the boat until he reached Perrin. The Rengani's head turned sharply and his teeth flashed white as he grinned. 'Well, well,' he said softly. 'Long live the boy-king. They've all gone off to fish your body out of the river. Good time to swim to shore, while it's quiet.'

'You're not too badly hurt?' asked Skir timidly.

Perrin held up his hand with the arrow shaft sticking through it; the flesh around the wound was swollen, raw and seeping blood. 'Think I can make it.' His voice changed. 'No such luck for Doughty.'

'Doughty? Your friend?'

Perrin jerked his chin. The boat dipped and swayed as Skir heaved himself up to peer in. A swollen shape bumped about in the water at the bottom of the boat; it looked like a mattress rolled up and tied with string. Skir lowered himself back into the river.

He whispered, 'I've never seen a dead body before.'

'Now you have,' said Perrin acidly. He'd lost count of the bodies, and parts of bodies, he'd seen since he joined the Army. Tugger, with his throat ripped out . . . Perrin bared his teeth in a mirthless grin. 'Well, can't hang around here all day, it'll be light soon. Better hold onto this.' He shoved the end of the oar at Skir.

'What about Tansy?'

'Your girlfriend isn't part of my mission. She'll have to take care of herself.'

'She's not my –'

Tansy had hauled herself hand-over-hand until she was beside them. 'I *can* take care of myself,' she whispered fiercely.

'Good,' said Perrin. 'Take Doughty's dagger. He won't need it any more.' And he struck out one-handed for the riverbank.

With more splashing than Perrin would have liked, the three struggled back to the shore. The sun had fully risen now, and already heat pulsed from it as if from an open stove. It was going to be a blazing-hot day.

Perrin crawled over the mud until he found solid ground to rest on, and examined his hand. By daylight, it didn't look too bad; he'd seen far worse on the battlefield. Just a scratch, really. If Tugger and the lads had seen him fussing over that last night, he'd never have heard the end of it.

But Tugger was dead.

Again Perrin pushed the knowledge away. Still, the boy was alive, and while he was alive, so was the mission. Perrin had orders to follow.

He found a flat rock, and turned his hand so the arrow head pointed to the sky. Swiftly he banged his hand down on the rock so the arrow-shaft was forced up through his palm. 'Frug!' He tugged on the arrow-shaft and it slid free with a gush of blood and liquid. The two bedraggled kids just stood there, watching. Skir's long hair was in rats' tails. There was a gash across Tansy's cheek, and a swelling bruise on her forehead. Perrin tried to tear a strip off the bottom of his shirt for a bandage with his teeth and one hand, but the cloth was too tough and he was shaking too much.

Without speaking, Tansy ripped a long band from the bottom of her own shirt and held it out to Skir.

He shied away. 'I don't know how.'

Tansy snatched back the length of cloth and said to Perrin, 'Give me your hand. Is it clean?'

'You tell me. You're the laundry-maid. Ow! That's too tight.'

'It's got to be tight. Can you walk?'

'I was shot in the hand, not the foot. Of course I can walk.'

'Get up then. I might be just a *laundry-maid*, but I got an idea.'

Skir gazed at her eagerly. 'What is it?'

'You still got that money? Well, I thought we might borrow something else from the King.'

Tansy led them through the trees to a low thorn hedge built close against the woods; beyond it, half-a-dozen horses cropped the grass. 'Ingle keeps the hunters in the Long Field, now the weather's warm.' Her voice was reverent. 'That's Warble, and Jasper, and Peak. The chestnut mare's called Sedge, she's a gentle one.'

'I like that big black stallion,' said Perrin.

Skir blanched. 'Can't we take the gentle one?'

'We'll need more than one,' said Perrin.

'You want to take Penthesi?' Tansy's eyes lit up, but she shook her head. 'He's the King's own hunter.'

'So he's the best.' Perrin stepped close to the hedge and sang out softly to the horses, a lilting call. The black stallion turned his head, and one by one the other horses pricked up their ears. Perrin held out his hand, singing. Tansy stared at him sharply.

Skir had wrapped his arms around his body, his eyes fixed nervously on the horses. They were an awful lot bigger than the ponies he was used to.

The stallion trotted up to the hedge, his tail swishing like a black flag, and whinnied at Perrin.

'Penthesi,' whispered Tansy. 'Curious as a kitten, Ingle says.' She held out her hand and the horse snuffled at her palm. 'I ain't got nothing for you now. But you'll get a treat later, I promise –' She reached up and stroked the velvety nose of the big animal.

The chestnut mare had followed Penthesi, and she craned her head over the hedge, staring at the three visitors with a rolling liquid eye.

Skir took an involuntary step backward, acutely conscious of the sheer size of the horses, their strong smell, the power of the muscled bodies that seemed barely contained by horsehide. He touched Tansy's shoulder. 'Someone's coming down the lane.'

'Time to go,' said Perrin briskly, and he scrambled clumsily over the low hedge, holding his injured hand close to his chest. He sang something, and the two nearest horses, Sedge and Penthesi, bent their front legs and kneeled in the grass.

Skir said to Tansy in sudden panic, 'I can't do this.'

'I'll help you. Come on, we gotta hurry.' She boosted him over the thorns and clambered over herself. Perrin had a hand on Penthesi's mane, but Tansy elbowed him aside. 'I better take Penthesi. He knows me, see. You take Sedge, she won't hurt you. Come on, Skir, get on behind me and hang on tight.'

Skir climbed onto the wide, slippery expanse of the big horse's back, clinging to Tansy for balance, and the stallion swayed and majestically rose, higher and higher, impossibly high. Skir moaned a little and shut his eyes as they trotted up the field toward the gate. Tansy crouched low on Penthesi's neck; Skir pressed himself hard against her. Perrin was just behind them, leaning lopsided over the chestnut mare's neck, one hand wound tight in the mane, his lips moving. The two horses broke into a canter as they approached the gate.

Then in a smooth, gathered movement, they leaped, and the next instant they were thundering down the lane. Skir's eyes flew open as the stallion jumped, and he glimpsed a blurred figure by the hedge, waving a cap, mouth open in an impotent shout.

Tansy headed them back to the cover of the woods, and slowed the big stallion to a trot.

'Was that old Ingle yelling at us?' Skir dodged a branch as they bumped along. 'He knows me.'

Tansy turned her head, one hand twined in Penthesi's mane. 'Ingle likes me. Maybe he won't tell.'

But even as she spoke, they heard the horns ring out. Ingle must have reported the theft of two of the King's horses to the Palace guard, but even Skir was surprised at the speed of their response.

'Doesn't like you as much as you think,' panted Perrin as he fought for balance on Sedge's back. They were near the edge of the woods now.

'Hold tight, Skir!' cried Tansy. 'Time for a gallop.'

'Aren't we already –' jerked out Skir in alarm, but then Tansy leaned over the horse's neck and urged it from a trot into a canter, and then a gallop. Skir fell forward and wrapped his arms even tighter around her waist; at any other time he would have enjoyed wrapping his arms round Tansy, but he was jolting too hard to even think about it.

They broke from the cover of the trees and the horses' hoofs thundered across soft turf. The shallow hills of southern Baltimar rolled gently away like the billows of a green sea, as far as the horizon. And Tansy was whooping – cheering! With the Baltimaran Army on their heels! Skir could just hear Perrin's slight chuckle as he encouraged his mare into a gallop, leaning low and holding hard with his one good hand.

And now they flew. The strong muscled machine of the black horse gathered power beneath them, and the ground blurred; the drumbeat of hoofs rang in Skir's head and vibrated through his body, and all he could do was hang on.

The hot summer sun rose higher on their right-hand side, turning the dull green hills to warm gold with lakes of shadow between, and the horses galloped, strong and free, even with the weight on their backs, glad to run, as if they knew that even the Baltimaran Army could never catch them.

CHAPTER 7

Widow's Cliff

THAT first day, it was like a glorious game to Tansy. She'd loved to play hide-and-seek, and hunt-the-bear, with her brothers when she was small: the breathless mix of terror and excitement as she peered out to see if it was safe to dash home, the glee when she outwitted the seekers. This was even better. The blood sang in her veins. For the first time since she'd come to Arvestel, she felt fully alive.

It was wonderful to be out in the open country. All around Arvestel were the Royal Farms, with low stone walls between the neat green meadows and pale yellow fields of ripening wheat. Copses of spander trees and birch were dotted here and there, and creeks tumbled down the gentle hills.

The two horses knew this country well; the Royal Hunt ranged across these farms. Penthesi and Sedge flew from one sheltering grove to the next, leaping the creeks and the low walls, always ahead of the slower, heavier horses of the Palace guards, but never quite shaking them off. Even the fact that they were the prey, not the hunters, couldn't spoil the wild joy of the chase. Tansy had always admired Penthesi from a respectful distance, but now she fell in love with him.

Her eyes shone as she urged Penthesi onward. Behind her, Skir clutched her waist and groaned occasionally, but that didn't bother her – as long as he didn't fall off, he wasn't much of a hindrance. Penthesi galloped, strong and joyous, a storm cloud driven by the wind. The chestnut mare, Sedge, followed him faithfully, with the Gani balanced on her back; Tansy had to admit he wasn't a bad rider.

But even the King's hunters grew tired at last. Over short distances, nothing could catch them, but they weren't bred for endurance, and by nightfall both horses were drooping and lathered with sweat. They'd left the Royal Farms behind, crossed Well's Water at a flying leap and were headed east, through the rich valleys of Middle Baltimar. Tansy pulled Penthesi up in the shelter of a birch grove and let him gulp fresh water from a stream.

'We ain't seen soldiers for a while. The horses need a rest.'

Perrin stretched. 'Excellent idea. I vote for an inn, a square meal and a soft bed.'

'We ain't even a day's ride from Arvestel!' said Tansy.

Perrin pulled a mocking face. 'It was a joke, sweetheart.'

The tips of Tansy's ears turned red, and Perrin grinned. 'There's a barn over there. Not as comfortable as an inn, but more suitable for fugitives.'

Tansy glanced at the shadowy shape on the hillside. 'You go and scout, Gani. Ain't you soldiers trained for that kind of thing?'

'But he's wounded,' said Skir.

'I'm all right,' said Perrin. Indeed, he and Tansy seemed as alert and excited as each other. He slipped from Sedge's back and skulked along the hedgerow that snaked across the top of the ridge.

Skir said anxiously, 'His name's Perrin.'

'I know what his name is.'

'Well, you can't keep calling him *Gani*. It's offensive.'

Tansy snorted. 'Then you tell *him* I ain't his sweetheart.'

Skir unclasped himself and half-slid, half-fell from the great height of Penthesi's back. Penthesi turned his head and blew mildly through his nostrils, as if pleased to be rid of an annoying beetle. Skir knelt by the stream and slurped up water. His arms and legs were shaking; he'd never been so exhausted. He felt as if every bone in his body had been crushed by a heavy roller, the insides of his thighs were raw, and his head throbbed. He could hear Tansy humming happily to the horses. Skir put his head down. In Arvestel, it would have been time for his bath, lemon-scented and steaming, and then into clean clothes for dinner: ginger broth with dumplings, roasted parsnips, honey pastries . . .

A twig cracked and Skir started backward. Perrin bared his teeth in a grin. 'Settle down, Your Highness, it's only me. The barn's dry. Full of hay, and no one in sight. The farmhouse is down in the valley. A big place. There's a huge, steep cliff hanging over it like a wave about to break.'

'Widow's Cliff,' murmured Skir.

'What's that?' Perrin cupped his ear. 'Speak up, young fellow.'

'This must be Widow's Cliff. It's north-east of Arvestel. It's exactly the direction they'll expect us to go, straight for the border.' He glanced over his shoulder, shivering. In daylight they could see the soldiers coming. Now dusk had fallen, anyone could be out there, and they wouldn't know until it was too late. He wouldn't be able to run; he could barely stand upright. Maybe it wouldn't be such a bad thing if they took him home . . .

Skir had never thought of Arvestel as *home* before. He felt a stab of guilt. Home was Cragonlands, he told himself; Cragonlands, not Arvestel.

Tansy said briskly, 'The horses'll catch a chill, sweating out here. Better get them under cover.' She slid neatly off Penthesi's back and patted him, crooning softly. The big horse lowered his head to nuzzle at her ear, and she laughed.

As soon as they were inside the barn with the doors safely shut, Tansy seized a handful of straw and began to rub Penthesi down, hissing between her teeth like the Palace grooms. 'Better rub down Sedge, too,' she said over her shoulder to Perrin, but he was struggling to light a lamp with his left hand.

Skir made a feeble motion to grab some straw and copy her, but it hurt too much and after a moment he collapsed onto the hay.

Tansy shot him a look. 'Hurts when you ain't used to it,' she said, kindly enough, but Skir felt the scorch of her contempt more keenly than his sunburn.

Tansy finished with Penthesi and started on Sedge, who leaned into her and whickered gratefully. Both horses had begun munching on the hay as soon as it was within reach. 'Starving, poor things,' murmured Tansy.

'Whereas *we* are only mildly peckish,' muttered Perrin with a flint between his teeth. Tansy took the lamp away from him.

'Shield it, so no one sees the light from outside,' he said.

'I might be just a laundry-maid, but I ain't stupid. There, that's got it.'

Perrin lay back in the hay and grinned at her. 'Temper, temper. You've caught yourself a fiery one here, Your Highness.'

Skir sat up. 'I told you before, we're not . . . It's not like that.' He looked sideways at Tansy, half-hoping to be contradicted.

But Tansy scowled down at Perrin. 'We told him plenty of times. If he ain't deaf, he must be thick in the head.' Perrin grinned cheerfully up at her and winked. She didn't see what he had to be so happy about, on the run, and all his soldier friends killed just the night before. It must be true then: the Ganis were just fighting machines, with no feelings at all. She kicked the hay close to his leg. 'Hey, Gani. Last night, did you know there was boars in the woods?'

'Yeah. We saw one. Yesterday – no, the day before.'

'Then why didn't you use them? If the boars had charged the soldiers before they started shooting at us, we could all have got away easy.'

Perrin shrugged. 'I didn't think of it.'

'Used them?' said Skir.

Tansy turned back to Sedge, grooming with long, steady strokes. 'You saw, in your room. He sent the dogs away. Just like he called Penthesi and Sedge to us in the Long Field. Didn't you hear him singing? He did some kind of magic.'

'*Magic?*'

'I charm animals.' Perrin yawned. 'I sing to them, and they obey me.' He put his hands behind his head and sang a lazy, lilting tune. In unison, both horses swung to face him and began to nod their heads up and down.

'Stop that!' flashed Tansy. 'They ain't your *toys*.'

Perrin stopped.

Tansy's face was pale. 'Don't *ever* do that again, you hear me! Ain't you got no respect? These horses got more brains and more . . . more heart than you could hope to have, Gani. If I ever catch you treating them like . . . like puppets you can play with, for your own *fun*, I'll knock your teeth clean out of your head. And don't think I won't.'

Perrin whistled softly and raised his left hand in a mock salute. 'Yes *sir*!'

Tansy glared at him, then turned back to Sedge and murmured something. Penthesi snorted, and Sedge nuzzled Tansy's hand. Perrin watched them, a slight frown creasing his brow. The laundry-maid seemed to think that the animals were her friends.

While Perrin watched Tansy, Skir had been watching Perrin. He said sharply, 'You're a chanter?'

'That's what they call it in the Westlands.'

'That's what they call it in Cragonlands, too.'

'Oh? I didn't know there were chanters in Cragonlands.'

'There's just one. Me.' Skir stared at him hard.

'Really?' said Perrin politely. He sat up. 'Plenty of sacks in here. They'll do for blankets. And there are always rats in a barn. Think we can risk a fire? I must say I prefer them cooked.'

'I can't eat rats,' said Skir.

'Either that or dine on hay like the horses, Your Worshipful Highness. What *do* they call you, in your kingdom?'

'Just Skir will do. We're not in my kingdom now. I can't eat meat. It's forbidden for the priests of the Faith.'

'Is that so? But as you just pointed out, you're not in your kingdom now. You'll be surprised what you can eat if you're hungry enough. After the Battle of the Falls — well, never mind. Let's just say, we would have been grateful for a nice juicy rat. Even a marmouse. You, Tansy? You're hungry, aren't you?'

Perrin arranged himself with his legs akimbo and a sack loosely open between his feet. He began to sing a low, sweet song, and there was a stirring in the hay.

'Don't,' said Tansy. 'That's as bad as playing with the horses. Worse, if you're going to kill them. It's tricking them. It ain't fair.'

'There's not much meat on them, but we have to eat. Unless you'd rather raid the farmhouse?'

'But that's stealing,' said Tansy.

'That's survival,' said Perrin crisply. 'We don't have the luxury of your Baltish scruples now.'

Cautiously, Skir flexed his arms and legs. He still hurt all over, but he thought he could move without groaning aloud. He said faintly to Tansy, 'I'll go. See if I can find something.'

But Tansy was glaring at Perrin. '*Baltish* scruples? What's that mean?'

'Private property is sacred?' Perrin raised an eyebrow. 'What's mine is mine? What can't be paid for isn't worth having? There's no ill that money can't heal?'

Tansy flushed, and her voice rose. She knew she was being insulted, but she wasn't quite sure how. 'But you own things in Rengan, too. You've got money.'

'Actually, my ignorant child, no, we don't. Our wealth is shared for the benefit of everyone.' He recited. 'Rengan's health is our common wealth.'

'But you must own things. Your land, your animals. Your clothes.'

'Animals and land, no. They're held in common, managed by High Command. Clothes – well, sort of. They're passed around. Mended, unpicked and remade. Except for the Army uniforms, of course. The Army gets the best of everything. This shirt's brand new, it's the only new thing I've ever had. And you're a fine one to lecture me about stealing, by the way, with two of the King's own horses over there in the corner.'

Tansy flushed. 'We ain't stolen them. Just borrowed. Soon as we're safe away from Arvestel, we can set them free and they'll find their own way home.'

'Ri-ight,' drawled Perrin. 'Of course we will ... Where's the boy – Skir?'

'He just said he'd go and find food. Don't you listen?'

'Oh dear,' said Perrin heavily, with a great show of folding up his sack one-handed. 'Now one of us will have to rescue him. Again.'

Tansy felt another surge of irritation. 'You do it, you're so good at it. Or does your hand hurt?'

'It's all right.'

'And if you find anything to eat, you can bring it back to share. Like in Rengan.'

Perrin smiled. 'Very good, Tansy, very good.' And with an elaborate bow, he was gone.

Tansy put the lamp out. She could see just as well by the moonlight that streamed through the chinks in the wall. It was chilly now, and she took her cloak from her pack. It was slightly damp, but the packs were good quality; they hadn't let in much water at all.

The smell of the horses and the sound of Penthesi and Sedge steadily munching hay was comforting. Letting them eat someone else's hay was a kind of stealing, too, she supposed. But horses had to be fed; that was more important. She didn't have any – what did the Gani call it? – *Baltish scruples* about that. And they *would* send the horses back, no matter what he said; she was no thief, and no idiot either. Not idiot enough to steal from the King ... She'd always thought Ganis were stupid, but this one was a smart-breeches. Twisting her words around and laughing at her.

But even the Gani couldn't spoil tonight. She was free, free of the Palace. And free of Wanion, too. Wasn't she? Tansy shivered as she fingered the bruise on her forehead and the gash on her cheek. She was lucky to be alive. Was the Witch-Woman finished with her? She'd never let herself be owned by anyone again; she'd die first. She'd never go back there, never. She'd follow Skir as far as he wanted; she owed him that. And she didn't care where they went. Cragonlands must be a good sort of place, if everyone kept fighting over it. Maybe she'd end up looking after the King's horses after all, but it'd be the King of Cragonlands, not the King of Baltimar . . .

Tansy stretched her arms up and sighed, as if a crushing weight had been lifted from her, and lay back in the hay.

Every sense alert, Perrin crept along the hedgerow down the hill to the big square farmhouse and the cluster of outbuildings. The moons were up. It was easy to see, and easy to blend with the shadows.

Perrin prowled close to the nearest building: a goat shed, judging from the smell. At the end of the path, in the farmhouse yard, he heard voices, the tramp of boots, a dinner gong. A door creaked, then slammed. A light moved about in the goat shed, and he heard bad-tempered bleats. And there was another sound. Somebody breathed in the shadows beside him: shallow breaths, frightened.

'Skir?' he whispered.

A hand grabbed his shirt. 'Ssh!'

Don't tell me to ssh, thought Perrin. *I'm the trained soldier.* A flash of memory: Tugger waiting with his back turned while the squad sneaked up behind him, calling each name as the long grass rustled. He'd never got one wrong. Perrin pushed the memory away and firmly closed the lid on it. Just survive the next few breaths, the next quarter of the day. Don't get stuck in the past, don't fret too far ahead. That was the way to stay alive.

Skir's grip on his shirt tightened. Then Perrin heard it too: the crunch of boots on loose stones. His heart quickened. Half-a-dozen men. Odd how the military march was the same, whatever side of the border. He pressed himself back against the rough plaster of the shed wall. These weren't Palace guards; this was the real thing. The Army – soldiers in battle-dress. The enemy. Perrin's stomach churned and his palms were slick with sweat. The corporal carried a lantern on a pole that swung back and forth in great arcs, illuminating the clean white sheds, the swept yard, the apple trees studded with tiny fruits.

'Halt!' cried the corporal, and the boots came to a ragged stop.

Typical Balts, thought Perrin. *No discipline.*

The men breathed hard, and someone coughed. *Out of condition*, thought Perrin automatically, then half-grinned in the dark. He answered back to himself as he would have done to his sergeant: *If the Balts are such a lousy crew, why do they keep beating us?* Skir stirred at his side, a small panicky movement, and he gave the boy's wrist a sharp warning squeeze.

'Who's that? What do you want?' It was an old woman's voice, surly and suspicious. A second lantern emerged from the shed to join the corporal's light on the path.

'Where's your master? We're on the King's business.'

'I'm the master here, laddie, so mind your manners. This is my farm. King's business, eh? The King never showed any interest in us before, unless it was to take taxes.'

'We're searching for fugitives, ma'am, dangerous prisoners and horse-thieves. Had a report they were seen riding this side of Well's Water. Two boys and a girl, one with red hair, one dark, one fair. Permission to search your property?'

'Couple of boys and a girl? Don't sound dangerous to me. Fine lot of soldiers you are, to go chasing after a couple of kids larking about. I've seen nothing, but I'll ask my lads at dinner. Now be off with you. I've chores to do, we're short-handed.'

'Permission to search then, ma'am?'

'No you don't. I don't want a lot of soldier-boys tramping about all over my property. Now get off my land before I take a pitchfork to your behind.'

Perrin peered around the corner of the goat shed and saw a thickset, beefy young man towering over the old woman. His fingers, thick as sausages, curled tight around his spear-shaft.

'I'm an officer in the King's Army and I give the orders!'

The old woman stood her ground. 'I know what I know. You got no right to be on my property unless I give permission. And I don't. You take one more step and I'll report you to My Lord Sabot. It's my taxes that pay for your fancy uniforms and your shiny swords, my lad, and don't you forget it. Now be off!'

There was a pause. For a dreadful moment in the silence Skir thought they'd hear his heart roar; he half-expected them to lunge around the shed and drag him away. Then, worse, he had an impulse to dart out, wave his arms, shout *Here I am!* He twisted his fingers into Perrin's shirt and squeezed his eyes shut.

The rhythmic crunch-crunch started up, the sound of retreating boots. 'We'll be back in the morning, missus!' yelled the corporal. 'And we'll bring your Lord Sabot himself!'

'You do that, laddie!' jeered the old woman, her lantern held high. 'If you can find him.' She spat onto the dirt. Then she made her way, slow and steady, down the path to the farmhouse.

Perrin nudged Skir in the darkness.

'Is it safe?' Skir whispered.

'Probably not. But I'm not going back to your girlfriend empty-handed.'

'How many times do I have to tell you, she's *not* my girlfriend.'

'You wish she was though, don't you?'

'No, I don't. I mean – well, I don't wish she wasn't –'

Perrin shrugged. 'She's a pretty girl, sort of, when she holds her tongue. And some men enjoy being bossed around. Not me. I get enough of that in the Army. But I can see why it might appeal to you.'

'It's none of your business!'

'She's a laundry-maid. You're supposed to be a king. Why don't you just click your fingers?'

Skir looked at him with dislike. 'I thought everyone was equal in Rengan.'

'Ah, but we're in Baltimar now.'

'Don't you think we've got more pressing things to worry about than whether Tansy and I are – are sweethearts?'

Perrin took pity on him at last. 'Let's see what the goats have left us.'

Fortunately for them, the old woman fed her goats on kitchen scraps, and they were able to salvage a decent haul: some carrot peel, a squashed quarter of fruit pie, cheese rinds and a handful of spinach leaves. Perrin also found one cranky nanny-goat that had been overlooked for milking, and squeezed out enough to fill a tin cup. They crept back to the barn in the moonlight.

'Baltish scruples saved us that time,' said Perrin. 'I owe you an apology, Miss Laundry-Maid.'

'Course she wouldn't want soldiers prying around,' said Tansy through a mouthful of fruit pie. 'Most likely she told the tax collectors she had a bad harvest last year, but she's got three barns stuffed with wheat. Happens all the time.'

There was a rustle in the hay, and Skir jumped. 'I wish we could bolt the door.'

Perrin grinned. 'The rats won't hurt you. Might just nibble your toes. They don't know you wouldn't do the same to them.'

Skir ignored him. 'We were lucky tonight,' he said. 'But we have to work out which way we're going.'

'Cragonlands is north,' said Tansy. 'I know that much.'

Perrin was silent. The rendezvous was at a place called Dody's Leap, right on the border. That's where Perrin's squad was supposed to hand over Skir to the second team, who'd take him not into Cragonlands, but further north to Rengan. Those were Perrin's orders; he wasn't going to stuff up anything else if he could help it.

'First,' said Skir nervously, not looking at Tansy, 'we should decide if we're all sticking together.'

Perrin reached for a spinach stalk. 'Tansy, you could take one of the horses. Fingers and his pals won't be looking for a girl on her own.'

'Fingers?' said Skir.

'Our friend the corporal. Hands like gloves stuffed with mincemeat, didn't you see?'

Skir shot a look at Tansy. 'You could ride home to Lotch.'

'Of course, Fingers *will* be looking for a big black stallion with the King's mark,' drawled Perrin. 'And I forgot – we're setting the horses free, aren't we?'

'Not yet,' said Tansy.

Skir said, 'But Tansy, if you'd rather go on alone –'

'I'll stick with you,' said Tansy. 'I ain't leaving you alone with *him*.'

'Well, if you're sure,' said Skir.

'I'll stay as long as you want,' said Tansy.

Skir's shoulders relaxed. He said, 'They'll be expecting us to head north-east, the way we're going now, on the road up through Suum and Tiff and Lotch. But we could ride due north through the forests, to the coast road, and follow that around Codlin's Gulf. It'll take longer, but there's not so many towns.' He saw Perrin's face and stopped. 'Do you have a better idea?'

Perrin laughed. 'No.' Dody's Leap was right on the coast; they'd reach it just as surely, maybe quicker, by Skir's route. As for what would happen when they got there – he'd worry about that later. He gave them a disarming grin. 'Baltimaran geography isn't my strong point. Tugger – our squad leader – showed us a map, but we were expecting to sail back around the coast, so I didn't waste any time studying it.'

'I never seen a map in my life, except the map of Da's farm,' said Tansy. 'I know Arvestel is south, and Lotch is north, and Cragonlands and Rengan is further north, but that's all. And the Westlands is over there somewhere, over the ocean, where all the sorcerers are.' She waved a vague hand at the barn wall in the direction of the sunset. 'All the sorcerers except you two.'

Skir said, 'Well, I've had ten years of geography lessons. I could draw a map of the Threelands in my sleep.' He scratched with a stick on the dirt floor. 'Here's Baltimar. This is Arvestel. We're about – here. There's the border with Cragonlands. This is Codlin's Gulf –' Without thinking, Skir scratched the Signs that spelled out the name.

'What's that?' said Tansy, leaning over his shoulder.

Skir scuffed out the Signs. 'Nothing.'

'It's witch-writing,' said Perrin at the same moment. 'Only sorcerers know it.'

Skir and Perrin exchanged a swift, mutually surprised glance.

'There are forests all along here,' said Skir quickly. And some villages – look, it doesn't matter.' He erased the rough map with his boot. 'As long as we keep north till we reach the sea.'

'Didn't expect you to be our navigator.' Perrin grinned. 'That'll give them a laugh at High Command. They enjoy a laugh.'

'Do you like being a soldier?' asked Skir.

'No,' said Perrin. 'I hate it.'

'Then why do it?' asked Tansy scornfully.

'I didn't have any choice. I was drafted at sixteen, like everyone else.' He stretched out his legs, clad in soldier's boots. 'So, we head due north. Not that we'll make it. We've no food, no supplies, nowhere to hide, and the whole Baltimaran Army on our tails.'

'Not the whole Army,' said Skir. 'They won't want to admit they've lost me.'

Perrin raised an eyebrow. 'You're right, you know. They'll try to keep it quiet as long as they can. They'll only send out their crack troops. Anyway, they're too busy defending Cragonlands to spare many men.'

'Just the crack troops? Nothing to worry about then.' Skir tried to smile as he massaged his aching knees.

'*You'll* be all right, whatever happens,' said Perrin sharply. 'It's me and the laundry-maid who'll be executed if we're caught. No one's going to harm a hair on your pretty red head... Speaking of which, we should do something about your hair. Cut it short at least. They can probably see it glowing from the border.'

'It's awful bright,' agreed Tansy, eyeing Skir critically.

'Cut it off then,' said Skir abruptly. 'Go on.'

Tansy sawed through Skir's pigtail with the dagger that had belonged to Doughty. When she was finished, Perrin said, 'Burn it. It'll stink, but we can't leave it lying around for Fingers to find.'

Tansy lit the lamp again. She lowered the hair into the flame, and it shrivelled into smoke. The acrid stench filled their nostrils, and the horses snorted and turned away.

Tansy held out the dagger to Skir. 'You better have this. I got the sword already.'

Skir shrank back. 'I couldn't use it.'

'I can teach you. Go on. You need something.'

'But I'm not allowed to –'

'Take it,' came Perrin's voice. 'What, you're not allowed to slice bread? Not allowed to cut through a branch in your way? Not allowed to cut a rope or a piece of cheese?'

Skir hesitated, then held out his hand. Gingerly he buckled the belt around his waist and slid the dagger into its sheath. Perrin chuckled, and Tansy glared at him.

'It'll be useful,' she said encouragingly, and Skir gave her a wan smile.

Exhaustion crushed him like a boulder. He spread his coat

over himself and lay back in the hay. He was still hungry, sunburned, dirty, rubbed raw, aching and bruised in every bone and muscle. He murmured, 'I'll never be able to . . .' His eyes flickered, then closed, and his head dropped.

Tansy watched him. 'He did all right today, seeing as he ain't much of a rider.'

'For a spoilt princeling, that young feller of yours has done pretty well,' agreed Perrin. 'We can use those sacks for saddles. But we can't go on riding without some kind of bridle. Although it doesn't matter, does it, since we're setting the horses free . . .'

'Oh shut up,' said Tansy. She patted Penthesi's flank. 'They don't want to go home yet. They're having an adventure – aren't you, my loves? Reckon I can turn that coil of rope up there into a bridle or two.'

Perrin nodded, stretched, and winced. 'What I wouldn't give for a hot bath! Or even a cold one.'

'Perrin,' said Tansy awkwardly, using his name for the first time. 'Show me your hand.'

Perrin held it out. 'What's the verdict?'

Tansy let it drop. 'It don't look good. I reckon a healer should see it.'

'So my hand's rotting, just to complete the perfect picture.'

'It ain't my fault.' Tansy reached along the coil of thin rope and began to measure lengths for a bridle. Perrin lay back and watched her fair head bent in the lamplight, her face severe with concentration as she unpicked and re-wove the strands of rope. Without looking up, she said, 'Skir and me ain't sweethearts, you know. So you can stop calling him *my young feller*, all right? I ain't going to tell you again.'

'All right,' said Perrin. 'He says the same, so it must be true.'

'Does he?' said Tansy. 'Then it must be.'

'It's a shame, really. I'm all in favour of young love. Ah well. Maybe things will develop.' Perrin smiled lazily as Tansy's face flushed pink. 'Or do you already have a young feller, is that it?'

Tansy laid down the rope and glared at him. 'You put one finger on me, Gani, and I'll smack you so hard your teeth'll rattle.'

'Fair enough,' said Perrin amiably. It was a new experience to meet someone apparently immune to his charms. Only Tugger – 'What's that?' he said abruptly.

They both froze, listening.

'Just cats,' whispered Tansy.

The howling died away. Perrin nodded. 'Wake me for my watch when you're sleepy. And don't forget to put the lamp out.' He rolled over, and before he'd taken three breaths he fell into a soldier's instant sleep.

CHAPTER 8

The Fastness of Rarr

SKIR started awake as Tansy shook his shoulder. He stared at her blankly for a moment before it all rushed back: the escape, the chase, the horses. He sat up, and just as quickly lay down again. Movement was agony. Slowly, painfully, he dragged himself upright. He could smell his own rank breath, the fetid stink of unwashed clothes and bodies and the overpowering odour of the horses. It was still dark; Perrin was moving around the barn. The horses snuffled and pawed the ground. Tansy whispered, 'Time to go.'

There was no breakfast, no basin of warm water to wash in, no tray of muffins and jam and hot reviving tea. Skir moved stiffly, trying not to fall behind the others. Tansy gave him an encouraging smile, and that straightened his bent back for a little while. As they crept from the barn, the cliff loomed over them, a solid, threatening slice of darkness against the pale sky. They led the horses across a field speckled with wildflowers to the shelter of the woods beyond. A bird whirred up from the trees and Skir jumped.

'This way, right, Skir?' said Perrin.

Skir nodded. 'This forest runs – it should run all the way to the River Shale, I think.'

'But the trees are too close together,' objected Tansy. 'We can't ride through that.'

'*Now* you want to let the horses go?' Perrin asked. 'After you sat up all night weaving that bridle?'

'Not all night,' said Tansy awkwardly.

Perrin narrowed his eyes. 'That's the beauty of the plan. Fingers knows we're on horseback. So he's less likely to follow us somewhere horses can't go.'

'So you're saying we really can't take the horses?' Tansy looked dismayed.

'*No.* But we'll have to lead them.' Perrin's head swung round. 'Speaking of Fingers – listen . . .'

A dull, rhythmic noise echoed up from the valley below: the tramp of soldiers' boots. A great many boots.

'Not just half-a-dozen men this time,' said Perrin softly. 'He's brought a whole platoon.'

Skir swallowed. Tansy's hand crept to her throat. The tramping noise swelled louder. Perrin kept his eyes on the valley road; he didn't turn around, but backed very slowly into the shelter of the trees, singing softly, and the horses followed him.

'Come on,' whispered Tansy, and Skir let her pull him into the forest.

There was no more talk of releasing the horses to find their own way home, and at times it seemed that they were the keenest members of the party, picking their way steadily through the trees, day after day, without complaint.

Tansy walked with Penthesi, and Perrin led Sedge. Every step was painful. The woods were eerily silent, except for the rustle of unseen animals. Skir glanced around nervously at every sound, expecting to see soldiers jump out from between the tree-trunks. He stumbled along in a fog of hunger and exhaustion and fear, wondering why he'd ever left Arvestel, torn between guilt over missing the Palace, worry about Beeman, and terror at being captured. A dozen times a day he'd look up to find the others had vanished ahead, and he'd break into a breathless, limping run to catch up.

'Skir ain't hardly eaten for three days,' Tansy whispered to Perrin; she glanced at Skir where he sat examining his blistered feet.

Perrin grimaced as he flexed his wounded hand. 'I notice you've got over your finer feelings. No problems now about strangling the bunnies and the birds I catch, let alone eating them.'

'I'm hungry,' said Tansy bluntly. 'Don't mean I enjoy it. But *he* still won't touch a morsel.'

Skir called out dully, 'I know you're talking about me. You may as well do it so I can hear.'

Tansy went to kneel beside him. 'You got to eat something. Or you'll fold up like a pea plant with no stake to hold it up.'

'No steak!' said Perrin. 'That's not bad, Tansy. By the bones,' he said longingly. 'A steak with roast potatoes and green beans and butter –'

'Shut up,' said Tansy crossly. 'Unless you can pull one out of your pack.' She rubbed Skir's shoulder. 'Won't you just try a mouthful of meat? Perrin's got a fat rabbit all ready to cook.'

Skir shook his head.

Perrin squatted beside him. 'Listen, you stubborn little

frugger. You'd better make it to the border, because if you die before we get there, High Command will have me executed. Now, what's more important, my life or a bunny's life?'

Skir wavered, Perrin saw, but then he said faintly, 'I'm not dying yet.'

Perrin threw up his hands. 'Starve yourself to death if you want to. But you won't be much good to the people of Cragonlands then, will you?'

At that, Skir's face closed up altogether.

At night they huddled by the warmth of the horses, on the chilled ground. No one slept much. Skir often heard Tansy cry out in her sleep. *No, Madam – please, no!* In the morning she would be pale and anguished, but she never spoke of her dreams.

She was in a grimmer mood each day, worried that the horses weren't getting enough to eat. At least her gashed cheek had closed up neatly.

As they set off on the fifth morning, Perrin stretched out his injured right hand for Sedge's rope bridle without thinking, and crumpled as if he'd been shot.

'Let's see,' ordered Tansy. She pulled away the grimy bandage and Perrin went white about the lips. 'That hand smells. Needs a healer.' She turned to Skir. 'Any towns near here?'

Skir gave her a glazed look. 'A town? If we follow the Shale upstream for a day or so . . .'

'Good,' said Tansy. 'We need food. The horses, too. But Perrin needs a healer first.'

'Even before oats for Penthesi? I'm touched.' Perrin tucked his hand gingerly away in its sling. 'But we can't risk it. Don't forget your boyfriend here – sorry, sorry, your *friend* – isn't some insignificant little horse-thief. He's the Priest-King of Cragonlands, hostage to the King of Baltimar. Fingers will be crawling over every town near Arvestel like maggots on dead meat.'

Skir said, 'When we reach Rarr, perhaps we should –'

Tansy stopped short. '*What?*'

'When we reach Rarr –'

'*Rarr!*' Tansy's face was green. 'You never said we were going to Rarr; you never told me that! That's where *she* lives, the Witch-Woman! Why didn't you tell me?'

'I didn't know – I didn't know she lived there,' stammered Skir.

'A Witch-Woman?' said Perrin. 'Sounds interesting.'

'Wanion ain't just any witch,' said Tansy. 'She's *the* Witch-Woman. Ain't you never heard of her? She tortures people, Ganis like you. I seen what she does, I *know* –'

'Be *quiet*,' said Skir. 'Stop shouting. They'll hear you in Rarr if you don't shut up.' He was trembling.

'Rarr,' said Tansy under her breath. 'Of all the places. *Rarr.*'

Perrin threw his arm around her shoulders. 'I'll protect you from the big bad witch.'

'*Oh* –' Tansy bit her tongue; she brushed him away and went to Skir.

'I'm sorry,' said Skir wretchedly. 'I didn't know.'

'That's all right.' Tansy was pale. 'She's watching me, see, watching me in my sleep. No wonder, if we're so close to her own place. It ain't your fault.' She reached for his hand and held it; Skir, surprised, squeezed it eagerly. After a moment Tansy glanced back to see if Perrin was watching, but he was leading Sedge over a fallen log. Penthesi rolled his dark eye at her reprovingly. Tansy frowned, squeezed Skir's fingers hard, and let his hand fall.

It was just after midday when Tansy caught sight of a dilapidated hut in a clearing beside the river. She drew her sword as she crept from the shelter of the trees, peered about, then beckoned to the others. 'Safe. There's grass for the horses, and we can rest in the hut. Tie up Sedge to the willow, Skir.'

'Must be an old woodsman's hut.' Perrin poked his head inside and blinked as his eyes adjusted to the dark. In a different tone, he said, 'Hello. I think someone lives here.'

'But it's falling down.' Skir joined him in the doorway. The hut was a single room with a fireplace against one wall; close to it was a bedstead piled with quilts. There was a table pushed against another wall, and bunches of dried leaves and flowers hung from the roof-beams. On the table was a cut loaf of bread and a wedge of cheese. Skir closed his eyes with longing. 'It's someone's house,' he said. 'We can't.'

'Rubbish. You've been in Baltimar too long, my friend. Go on, take it!' He gave Skir a little push.

Skir shook his head. Then, shamefaced, he darted into the hut and seized the bread and tore it apart with his teeth.

Perrin's face twisted in a cynical smile. He turned from the doorway to see Tansy stock-still in the clearing, with Penthesi's bridle in her hand. Skir came out of the hut.

A girl in a shabby pink dress had just walked up from the riverbank with a bucket of water in her hand. She stopped in the sunlight. Her mouth stretched into a grimace of fear. 'Who is it?' she called. 'Who's there?'

Perrin touched Skir's arm. He said softly, 'She's blind.'

Skir saw the girl's blank eyes, and knew it was true. A crooked band of scar tissue ran across her face, over her eyes; one eyebrow was missing, and the scarred skin was puckered and twisted like a skein of pink string. Skir held the bread guiltily, pointlessly, behind his back. 'Don't be frightened. We won't hurt you.'

'I'm not frightened. I want to know who you are.'

Tansy said, 'We're travellers. I'm Tansy, and this is my horse, Penthesi.'

The girl turned toward the new voice. 'A horse!'

She set down the brimming bucket and stepped forward as confidently as if she could see, with her hands held out. Tansy guided her fingertips to Penthesi's neck. The girl ran her hands over Penthesi's big, warm, muscled flanks, and smiled as he snorted in her ear.

'He's splendid.'

Tansy laughed. 'Isn't he? And this is Sedge.'

'Two horses!' The girl stroked the chestnut mare. 'Are they thirsty? It's hot again today, but there'll be rain tonight.'

'How do you know?' Tansy squinted into the sky, but it was simmering blue and cloudless.

'I can smell it,' said the blind girl. 'Who else is here?'

'My friend –' Tansy stumbled; she'd almost blurted out Skir's name. She shot Skir an agonised look; deceit did not come easily to her. 'My friend Perrin. And this is . . .'

'I'm Ren,' said Skir, from his full priestly name, Eskirenwey. He took the hand she held out; it was small but strong, as brown as a bowerberry, and roughened with calluses. The girl's hair and her skin and her mouth were all chestnuts and roses; if not for the ruined eyes and the scar slashed across her face, she might have been beautiful.

Perrin bounded up and clasped the girl's other hand, and she let go of Skir. 'The horses aren't thirsty, but we are,' said Perrin.

Skir felt a pang of furious jealousy as the girl turned her face toward the warm laughter in Perrin's voice.

'I'm sorry I can't shake your hand properly,' Perrin added ruefully, but the blind girl's fingers travelled swiftly over his bandaged right hand, and her face changed.

'You're hurt!' she said sharply. 'You'd better come in.'

It was crowded in the little hut when they were all crammed inside, but the girl moved about with brisk confidence. She poured water into earthenware cups and cleared spaces for them to sit. Skir tipped his stool against the wall and closed his eyes, resting his aching limbs and blistered feet. For the first time in days he felt safe, sheltered in the dim, fragrant hut.

The blind girl led Perrin to the single battered chair beside the fireplace. As she bent her head, unwinding the bandages so deftly it seemed impossible that she couldn't see them, Skir heard Perrin say in a low voice, 'We didn't ask your name.'

The girl's eyes flickered randomly left and right in surprise. 'I'm Elvie.' She touched Perrin's wound with her fingertips and he flinched. 'I have a salve that will help this, but I must clean the wound out first. No, no, don't help me,' she said, as Tansy sprang up. 'I know where everything is. Didn't they send you from Rarr?'

'No. We haven't come from Rarr,' said Skir, furious that he hadn't thought of asking her name, and determined to say something. 'We came through the woods from the south.'

Perrin pulled a face at him, a pantomime of outraged disbelief. Skir jutted out his chin to show he didn't care what Perrin thought. Then Perrin gasped in pain as Elvie probed his wound. Skir smirked. Tansy frowned at both of them. A strained silence fell as Elvie bent over Perrin's hand.

'This bandage should be burned, it's disgusting,' she said. 'You should have kept it dry. I'll give you a new one. How did you hurt yourself?'

'A hunting accident,' said Perrin.

'Why didn't you have it seen to?'

Tansy said, 'We're away from home. We thought it'd heal quicker than this.'

Elvie turned her face up to Perrin. 'Is the pain very bad?'

Perrin nodded, his face screwed up, then remembered she couldn't see him. He whispered, 'Yes.'

'I have something that will help.' Elvie slid a long, low box from under the bed where Tansy was sitting, and unlocked it with a key she wore around her neck. She lifted out a linen packet about the size of her thumb, then locked the box again and pushed it back under the bed. Tansy and Skir watched in puzzlement, but Perrin gave a low whistle.

'Is that rust?'

'*Rust?*' squeaked Tansy. 'That's forbidden!'

'Only to the poor,' said Elvie. She unwrapped the packet with careful fingers and held it out to Perrin, who took a pinch of red powder between his thumb and forefinger and inhaled it quickly through one nostril. A second pinch followed swiftly through the other nostril, and he sat back in the chair, breathing hard. A drowsy look came over his face.

Tansy said accusingly, 'You've done that before!'

'Only once or twice,' he said with a sleepy smile. His words were slightly slurred. 'All the soldiers do. 'M not an addict or anything. Don't even like it. But 's good for pain . . .' He breathed out a deep sigh, and his head lolled on his shoulder.

'Mmmm. Sleepy now.'

'He needs to rest.' Elvie straightened up. 'Are you hungry? I only have bread and cheese and jam, but you're welcome to share it.'

'We'll pay you,' said Tansy.

'You can pay me for the ointment. And the rust. That's fair.' Her voice was hard. 'But I'm offering you the food as my guests.'

'Thank you,' said Skir quickly. 'You're very kind. Tansy didn't mean to offend you. And I – I've already had some bread. I'm sorry.'

Elvie smiled. 'That's all right. There's another loaf in the crock.' She held out a hand to stop Tansy from helping her. 'Please don't. I have to keep everything in place; if things get muddled I'll never find them.'

Tansy and Skir tore into the bread and cheese, munching until their jaws ached. Elvie explained that she'd already eaten her midday meal; she sat beside Perrin until they'd finished. Then she said, 'There's not much room, but you can stay here tonight. Your friend needs to sleep, and you'll be safer here than in Rarr.'

Tansy and Skir exchanged a look of alarm.

'You're the runaways from Arvestel, the horse-thieves. Aren't you? Soldiers searched here two days ago. Don't worry, they won't be back. They're frightened of me.' Her face twisted. 'They think I'm a witch.'

'Because you're a healer?' said Skir.

'Because I work for Lady Wanion,' said Elvie.

Tansy jumped up; her plate smashed into a dozen pieces on the floor. 'You work for the Witch-Woman?' She drew her sword with a rasp and pointed it at Elvie.

'Tansy!' shouted Skir. 'Put that away!'

For a moment Tansy stared from one to the other; then slowly she sheathed the sword.

'Please, sit down.' Elvie knelt and groped for the shards of broken pottery. 'Everyone in Rarr works for the Witch-Woman in one way or another.'

'Let me do that.' Skir touched her shoulder.

Elvie returned to her stool. 'Lady Wanion owns this town. I grow herbs and I make rust for her. She sends me the chaka-weed from Cragonlands; she knows I won't cheat her, and she trusts me not to take any for myself.' A shadow crossed her face, and she gestured to her eyes. 'I got berry-juice in my eyes when I was young.'

'Ain't there no one to look after you?' Tansy's voice was tight with suspicion.

'My mother died last year. She was Wanion's rust-woman before me. Now I'm alone. I manage well enough. The villagers come to me for potions and salves and dyes, and they bring me what I need.'

Skir had spotted one last piece of broken plate beneath the table; in the darkness down there, he touched something hard, wrapped in fabric: a greasy cloth, so old it was almost rotted away. Gingerly he pulled the wrapping aside. The parcel was full of bones; they clattered softly inside the cloth. He drew in a sharp breath.

'Are you all right, Ren?' asked Elvie.

Skir scrambled hastily out from under the table. 'Did you say you had dyes? Hair dyes?'

Elvie took down a knobbly clump of root from a shelf above the fireplace. 'Sully-root will make your hair darker, if that's what you want.'

Tansy and Skir heaved Perrin's sleeping body onto the bed, then they boiled up the sully-root and took the cooled water outside to wash their hair. When they'd finished, Tansy's hair had become a strange red-brown, while Skir's chopped hair was a rusty black. Tansy surveyed him doubtfully. 'You look like you ain't seen the sun in a hundred years. And your eyebrows . . .'

Perrin stumbled out into the daylight, and laughed at them. 'It's always the eyebrows that give it away. Come here, Skir – I mean, *Ren*.' His voice was slurred.

Skir said in a low voice, 'Elvie guessed who we are.'

'Well, she didn't have to be a genius to work it out, after all the clues you two gave her.' Perrin dipped his thumb into the kettle and smeared it unsteadily across Skir's brows. ' 'S better.'

'What about *my* eyebrows?' said Tansy anxiously.

'Yours aren't so bad, they're dark enough anyway. It's Skir looks like a festival trickster.' Perrin grinned at her crazily; his eyes were still slightly unfocused.

'This hasn't helped at all.' Skir tugged a lock of hair forward to squint at it. 'One of us still has red hair, it just isn't me.'

'Could be useful. In a tight spot.'

Both the boys looked at Tansy. She said, 'You mean Fingers might kill me instead of Skir, by mistake?'

'Not kill,' said Perrin patiently. 'Don't forget, no one – no one's trying to kill Skir. It might even *save* your life.'

'So Fingers might kill *me* by mistake?' said Skir. 'I'm not sure this was such a good idea.'

'Any dye-water left?' asked Tansy. 'You can still see the King's mark on Penthesi, clear as day.'

Skir said to Perrin in a low voice, 'If you're feeling better, do you think we should move on?'

'What's the rush? Elvie said we could stay tonight, and the next, if we like.'

'But – is it safe?'

Perrin shrugged. 'No worse than the woods, and a damn sight more comfortable. What's the matter? I would have thought you'd enjoy a night indoors, Your Highness.'

Skir lowered his voice still further. 'Can we trust her?'

'Oh yes,' said Perrin at once. 'Definitely. Never wrong about that kind of thing.'

Tansy came up with the kettle in her hand and lowered her head close to theirs. 'You're only saying that because she gave you a pinch of rust. How do we know she won't run to the Witch-Woman when we're gone?'

Skir whispered, 'I found a packet of bones under the table.'

Tansy's eyes widened in horror. Perrin waved his hand dismissively. 'Plenty of healers grind up bones for ointments. Doesn't mean anything. They weren't human bones, were they?'

'I don't know,' said Skir. 'I don't know much about bones.'

'Maybe she's going to make broth out of them – how should I know!'

'*Human* broth?' moaned Tansy. Then she hissed, 'She ain't burned your bandage either, Perrin. I saw her put it in a box. She's keeping it for Madam.'

Perrin squeezed her shoulder. 'You may not have noticed, my turtledove, but it's high summer. She doesn't have a fire today. She's put the bandage away somewhere safe until she can burn it.'

Elvie's voice came from close behind them, and they all sprang guiltily backward. 'I work for the Witch-Woman,' she said harshly. 'But I've no love for her. I haven't told you how my mother died. Or how I got berry-juice in my eyes.' She turned and groped her way back inside the hut.

'Now you've upset her,' said Perrin. 'I told you we could trust her.'

Tansy was unrepentant. 'She can *say* anything. I reckon we should go. Get your bandage back and go.'

'And I say we should stay. Come on, Tansy! She's fixed my hand, given me a good sleep, dyed your hair and fed you. What more do you want? I give you my word. She's all right.'

Tansy turned to Skir. 'Looks like it's up to you.'

'Er –' said Skir, cornered. He wanted to believe Perrin; he wanted to sleep under a roof. And despite the bones, he liked Elvie. 'What do the horses think?'

'Penthesi kissed her ear!' said Perrin triumphantly, and the argument was over.

They spent that night in Elvie's hut. Tansy shared Elvie's bed, rolled as far away as she could get without falling off the mattress, and the two young men stretched out on the floor.

Despite Tansy's misgivings, Skir felt comfortable and safe for the first time since they'd left Arvestel. Elvie had given him a salve for his feet and a potion for his bowels. He had a pillow under his head, a belly full of food, and he'd washed properly, with soap, all over, before dinner. But now deeper worries stirred within him.

Suddenly Skir missed Beeman so much his chest ached. Where was he now? Had he been punished for Skir's escape? Beeman was his tutor, but he was also supposed to act as his jailer. Skir was uncomfortable with that fact, but it was true. In some ways Beeman was as much a prisoner as Skir himself, but as the Priest-King's companion, it was his duty to see that Skir didn't wander off, didn't put himself in danger, and didn't communicate with anyone outside the Court.

Of course, Beeman had stretched that final rule many times. Beeman had taught Skir to read, and he made sure that the celebration of Baltimaran 'victories' was balanced by news of setbacks and acts of rebellion by the insurgents in Cragonlands. Skir had always known Beeman's actions were risky, but all that would be nothing compared with the crime of allowing his pupil to be abducted by Rengani forces. Especially when it was discovered that the Rengani forces consisted of one reluctant soldier . . .

Tansy whispered, 'You still awake? You worrying about Elvie?'

'No. She can't do anything now – she's asleep.'

'What then?'

Skir hesitated, then in halting whispers, he told her what he feared.

Tansy was quiet, considering. 'I reckon, even if they have punished him, he'd think it were worth it, to get you home. That's what you got to remember. You can't help him now, if he is in the Pit. Even if they took you back, he'd still be punished for letting you go.'

'I'm not going back,' said Skir, certain for the first time. 'I can't go back.'

'No. So you just got to get home safe. For him.'

'I suppose so,' said Skir slowly. 'And what about you, Tansy? Are you all right?' It was the first time he'd thought to ask.

She was silent, and for a moment Skir was afraid she might be battling tears, but then she laughed softly.

'Sorry,' she said. 'I know it ain't right to laugh when we're in Madam's back garden, near enough, and we got soldiers after us and all, but – well, it's exciting, ain't it? This whole last year I was in Arvestel, I felt like I was suffocating. Shut in that laundry, same work, same faces. It were only with the horses I felt –'

'Free?'

'Yeah. That's it. And I feel like that now. Even with the Army on our tails. I can *breathe*.'

Skir rolled over. Elvie had left the door open for the night breeze, and in the oblong of dark he could see two crescent moons and one just past full, heavy in the clear soft sky like a ball of quicksilver about to drop. He heard the horses snuffle in the clearing, and Perrin's slow, half-drugged breath beside him, and a rustle of quilts as Tansy settled herself. As he watched, clouds rolled across the moons, and he tensed as he always did at the prospect of thunder.

But by the time rain began to patter on the roof of the hut, he and Tansy and the others were all asleep.

CHAPTER 9

The Captain's Luckpiece

BY morning, the swelling around Perrin's wound had gone down, and the horrible smell had disappeared. Perrin could even cautiously flex his fingers.

They sat outside in the clearing, breakfasting on tea and bread and honey, while, inside the hut, Elvie mixed more ointment for Skir's feet.

Perrin ruffled Tansy's hair. 'That weird colour actually suits you. It makes your eyes quite blue. I'll look for a blue scarf at the market today.'

Annoyed, Tansy batted his hand away. 'What?'

Skir was scowling.

'Elvie says it's market day in Rarr. I'll buy supplies.' Perrin stretched his legs luxuriously in the sunshine. 'We need blankets, and food, and oats for the horses.'

'You can't go. What about your hand? And people will know you're a Gani.'

'My hand doesn't hurt. Sedge can carry everything. No one'll know I'm a foreigner unless I want them to. Ask *her*.' He nodded toward the hut. 'She doesn't know. I'll bet you . . .' His smile broadened. 'I'll bet you a kiss.'

'That's a stupid bet,' said Tansy. 'You can't find out without telling her. Give me the money, Skir. I'll go to the market.'

Skir drew the heavy coin-purse from his pocket and weighed it reflectively. 'Wanion knows me, and she knows you. But she doesn't know Perrin.'

'I want to go,' said Perrin. His dark blue eyes were alight. 'This might be my only chance to see a Baltimaran market-place. All the riches of Tremaris laid out for my delight, and a pocket of coins to spend.'

'It's only a village market,' said Tansy. 'Skir, he'll just take the money and – oh, give it to him. I don't care if he does run off.'

'I'll let you have half,' decided Skir. 'That should do.' A day alone with Tansy and Elvie was worth paying for.

Tansy watched Perrin and Sedge disappear down the path; when she turned, Elvie was standing behind her.

'Oh! You gave me a start. Where's Sk – where's Ren?'

Elvie's blind eyes roved up and down and around. 'Rubbing his feet.' She put her hand on Tansy's arm. 'I make potions for love, too.'

'What would we need that for?'

Elvie smiled slyly. 'Which of them do you desire?'

'What? I don't – I don't like anyone that way.' But Tansy felt the heat rise into her face. True, she was drawn to Skir, but he was strange, destined for strangeness, a sorcerer, a king – even if it was only king of a funny little territory. Perrin was good-looking all right, but didn't he know it! She wanted to slap him twenty times a day. She shook Elvie's hand off her sleeve. 'We're in trouble. It ain't the time for thinking about that kind of thing.'

Elvie smiled. 'If love waited for the right time, there would be no love. But perhaps you don't need my potions. I think if you crooked your little finger, either one of them would follow.'

'No,' said Tansy abruptly. 'I don't need nothing from you. Thanks all the same.' And she stalked away toward Penthesi with her face still hot.

As Perrin led Sedge along the road to Rarr, it crossed his mind that he could do as Tansy had suggested: ride Sedge away and disappear. But where would he go? If he didn't bring Skir back to Rengan, High Command would have him hanged. Even as it was, there might be awkward questions; a sole survivor was always a suspicious figure. High Command might even blame him for what went wrong . . .

Perrin pushed that idea away into the dark box where he kept all his uncomfortable thoughts. The sooner he could hand over Skir to the rendezvous party at the border, the happier he'd be. Skir wouldn't be too happy in Rengan, though; High Command wouldn't hurt him, but they certainly wouldn't keep him in the kind of luxury he was used to at Arvestel. And as for Tansy . . . For the first time, Perrin wondered what would happen to Tansy. A Baltimaran slag, they'd call her. They might lock her up. Surely they wouldn't hang her?

That was another thought for the dark box. Perrin's mind veered in another direction. Suppose High Command decided he was a hero? Then it would be one dangerous mission after another, forever. He'd never be free . . .

Sedge nuzzled his hair to warn that they were almost there, and he'd better pay attention. Perrin reached up to give her a reassuring pat.

Rarr was large for a village, small for a town. It had six inns, a bell tower, and a market-square. There was a fountain, and a colonnade with brightly painted awnings above the merchants' stalls.

And over it all hung something that couldn't be seen from the woods: the Fastness of Rarr. It was the Witch-Woman's stronghold, a fortress of jagged grey rock. Half-a-dozen stone fingers thrust from a nest of dark, glossy forest. It cast its long shadow over the town, and wherever Perrin stood, it was there in the corner of his eye like a piece of grit, impossible to ignore.

And there was rust in this town. Perrin hadn't walked four paces down the main street before a man with red-rimmed nostrils stumbled from a grimy alleyway and gave him a groggy, unfocused smile. Perrin smiled back.

The next instant, a ragged child tugged at his arm. 'Want some, mister? Best quality, guaranteed. Straight from Cragonlands. Same fields *she* uses.' The child jerked its chin toward the grim, serrated towers that loomed over the town.

Perrin felt the weight of the coin-purse in his pocket, and the pleasant tingle in his veins that was the last of Elvie's pinch of rust racing through his body. He hesitated. Suddenly Sedge gave a great snort in his ear, and nudged him toward the bustling market-square. Perrin shook the child off gently. 'Not today.'

He led Sedge around the market, jangling the coin-purse in his hand. He couldn't find proper Rengani-style bed-rolls, lined with felt, with waterproof canvas on the outside, but he bought blankets, and leather straps to fasten them. Cooking pans, and another tin mug. A cake of soap; he wasn't going without soap any longer, and he knew Skir would appreciate it too. Tansy said she'd seen enough soap to last her whole life; she was quite happy just to splash herself in a stream. A razor would have been nice, but the Balts seemed to prefer facial hair and he was less conspicuous with stubble. More flints for the fancy silver tinder-box that Skir had filched from Arvestel; at least *he* had no Baltish scruples. A sack of oats for the horses.

He hesitated over saddles, but they were expensive. What they needed more than saddles was real food. Dried fruits, and hard-cake, and flour, and beans. Spices and salt. A round of cheese. A bag of carrots, and another of onions . . .

Perrin enjoyed himself, as he knew he would. There were no markets like this in Rengan. People bartered a little, a clutch of eggs for a bag of wheat, but it was nothing like this fistful of shining coins and all this – all this *stuff*. He was enjoying himself so much that he barely noticed the desperate, nervous faces of the stall-holders who begged him to buy their wares, or the woman with the twitching eyelid who brushed against him by the cheese stall, or the filthy child who'd followed him from the alleyway.

He wandered through the market with his spare change in his hand. He bought a blue scarf for Tansy, and hoped she wouldn't strangle him with it. He bought himself a comb at one stall, and stood for a while at another examining mouth-organs and finger-harps.

'You buying that harp, love?' wheedled the woman behind the stall, rubbing at her nose.

'I'll take it.' Perrin handed over the coins.

He was waiting for his change when he heard words that made his hair stand on end.

'– a boy with red hair? He's sixteen, but small for his age –'

Perrin froze. The voice came from just behind him.

'Yes, a black horse with a white star. There'll be a reward when the boy's found, a very handsome reward ... No? Thank you anyway. If you do see him, send word to me at the Hammer and Anvil. Just ask for the Captain.'

'Here you go, love.' The stall-holder poured a shower of little coins into Perrin's hand, and he shoved them impatiently into the purse. Ever so casually he turned his head.

The man was scanning the market-day crowd. He didn't look like a soldier. But he wore a sword, and his boots were a soldier's boots. His hair was long, and his clothes were – not fancy exactly, but good quality, made of fine grey-brown cloth. As Perrin watched, the Captain flung his cloak over his shoulder and strode away.

A very handsome reward. Perrin stood still, while Sedge chafed gently at the end of the bridle. He'd resisted temptation once today already. But how much rust could be bought with a very handsome reward? How many shining market wares? Could a very handsome reward buy freedom? He imagined a rain of copper coins, a riverful of silver, an ocean of glorious gold.

Perrin's heart beat once, twice, then he was running across the crowded market-square after the Captain, with Sedge clip-clopping behind.

'Excuse me.' He tapped the man on the shoulder and the Captain swung around. 'Excuse me – hello.'

'Hello.' The Captain looked Perrin up and down with an expression of mild surprise.

Perrin flashed his most charming smile. 'I couldn't help overhearing, and I wondered ...' He blurred his vowels and buzzed his s's, just like any Baltimaran. 'How much is a very handsome reward, exactly?'

'That depends,' said the Captain. 'If the boy's found alive, if he's found quickly, it would be a lot of money. A lifetime's money, let's say, at least.' He glanced at Sedge, weighed down with all the bags and bundles. 'Looks as if you've spent quite a bit yourself today.'

'I don't often get to market.'

'Ah.' The Captain looked at Perrin's bandaged hand. He rubbed at his eyes and said slowly, 'If you have anything to tell me, anything at all, I'd be pleased to hear it.'

Perrin hesitated. For an instant he seemed to see Tugger's shrewd dark eyes staring at him, appraising, judging. And he knew he couldn't do it.

Perrin shook his head. 'No. Wish I could help you. But I don't know any red-haired kid.'

The Captain took a step forward. 'Are you absolutely sure?' His voice was low and urgent.

'Yes, I'm sure.' Perrin stepped back. One or two curious people had turned their heads to watch; Perrin cursed silently. He said abruptly, 'Look, I said no! Now leave me alone, all right?'

The Captain raised his hands and stepped back as more heads turned. Someone gave a rust-sniffer's high, abrupt giggle. Perrin wound Sedge's bridle around his fist and pulled her away. The crowd parted to let them pass, and when Perrin looked back, there was no sign of the Captain.

He took Sedge to one of the inns and bought a flask of wine for later. He had just enough left for a mug of beer: smooth, mellow Baltimaran beer, not the gnats' piss you got in Rengan. Perrin swilled it slowly, regretfully, around his mouth. Then he untethered Sedge and set off on the road out of town. He was so busy thinking of the sacrifice he'd made that he didn't notice the dirty child who slipped along the road behind him.

'*Yes*, I'm sure he didn't follow me,' said Perrin impatiently.

The heat of the day had burned away and they were seated in Elvie's hut, by the fireplace. Elvie scattered herbs on the flames and the sweet scent of the smoke filled their nostrils. Perrin poked the logs. 'I told you, I didn't speak to him. He didn't even see me – why would he have followed me?'

'But you had a good look at him?' said Skir. 'You'd know him again?'

'Yes, yes. Long face, blue eyes, one of those hideous droopy moustaches. He had a grey-brown cloak, like a sea-eagle's wing, and high black boots, and long brown hair like a Balt noble.'

'Nobles don't wear brown,' said Tansy. 'They wear blue and green and purple.'

But Perrin's eye had been caught by something on Elvie's mantel. 'That's funny – he had one of these! One of these little dolls, pinned to his jacket, just the same as this.'

'It's a luckpiece,' said Skir. 'Everyone in Baltimar wears a luckpiece.'

Tansy's voice wobbled. 'Like this, Perrin? White, like this?'

'Yes, exactly the same. Why, what's the matter?'

Elvie sat with her hands folded in her lap. She said quietly, 'Lady Wanion gave me that luckpiece. She gives them to all her servants. All her bondsmen.'

'That Captain's working for Madam,' said Tansy. 'He's looking for Skir – for Ren. Oh, he's doing it for *her*!'

'It could be a coincidence,' said Skir in a small voice.

'It ain't no coincidence. You know it ain't.' Tansy swung

around to Perrin. 'You wipe that smirk off your face. You don't know nothing about it. It ain't nothing to smirk over. You ain't seen what I seen. I know about her luckbits because she gave me one, too. She tried to make me steal from Skir, so she could make her magic – that's how she does it, she takes something that belongs to a person, or – or part of a person . . .' Tansy swallowed. 'The part rules the whole. They say we won the war because of her magic. I didn't want to, but she . . .' Tansy choked.

Elvie said, 'The luckpiece binds you. You have to obey.'

Perrin said, 'But – all right, then, Tansy, where's your luckpiece now?'

'Skir burned it.' Tansy's voice dropped and she stole an awed glance at Skir, who shifted uncomfortably on his stool. 'He ain't scared of her. His magic's stronger than hers.'

Perrin and Skir looked at each other. Then Perrin put his arm around Tansy's shoulders. 'You've got two sorcerers to protect you now. So there's nothing to be frightened of.'

'But I disobeyed her! And it came back to me, like she said it would. Skir burned it, and drowned it, and stamped on it. And your boat burned, and we nearly drowned, and I hit my head –'

'Well then, it sounds like she's finished with you. Listen. This Wanion woman, the most powerful sorcerer in the Kingdom of Baltimar, isn't going to bother with one insignificant laundry-maid. She's too busy interfering in affairs of the state and meddling in wars to look for you. Anyway, we'll be gone before dawn, across the river and far away.'

Elvie turned her blind face to Skir in the firelight. In a low voice she said, 'Please. Before you go, will you burn my luckpiece, too?'

Skir was taken aback. 'If you really want me to.'

Tansy said, 'But – she'll burn you.'

'She has already burned me,' said Elvie harshly.

There was a silence. Elvie reached for Skir's hand. 'Please, do this for me. Break the bond. I don't want to serve her any more.'

'All right,' said Skir.

Perrin was still fiddling with the little doll; as he handed it to Skir, their eyes met. Skir took the luckpiece in both hands and held it above the flames. His pale face was lit with gold against the dark shadows of the hut; he looked solemn and filled with power. Despite himself, Perrin shivered.

Skir raised his hands and closed his eyes, remembering the ceremonies of the Faith. He and Beeman had practised them without the proper tools of office, but he knew the right words, the right expressions to wear, the right tone of voice. He pitched his voice low, and as he spoke, he knew that they were all silent, watching and listening, and he felt a tiny thrill of power. He said, 'This luckpiece has bound Elvie to the Witch-Woman, Wanion. Through day and night, through summer and winter, that bond has held fast. But now, with these words, and with the power of fire, I break that bond.'

He lowered the little doll to the flames and let it fall. There was a sizzle and a bright green flare, and the luckpiece shrivelled, blackened, crumbled. Skir struck the remains with the poker, blow after blow, until there was nothing left. Elvie stood and moved close to the fire, feeling its heat on her hands and face.

Skir said, 'It's done.'

'Thank you,' whispered Elvie, and briefly touched Skir's hand.

'Sounded better with words,' murmured Tansy. 'Wish you'd done the words for me.'

'Very impressive,' said Perrin. But he wondered vaguely, why didn't Skir ever sing any chantments? What kind of chanter was he, anyway? He yawned. 'Let's get some sleep. We want to be long gone by sunrise.' He pulled his shirt over his head. 'No one warned me spending money was such a tiring business.'

'It's not –' began Tansy, then saw that Perrin was naked. She took one look, flushing scarlet, and swung away. Perrin grinned at Skir and rolled his eyes, but Skir felt himself flushing too. None of them had been naked in front of the others before. Perrin sauntered across the hut and reached for a fresh shirt, as coolly as if he did this every day. Which, Skir realised, of course he did, in the barracks of the Rengani Army . . .

Skir was suddenly, hotly grateful that the others hadn't seen him washing. There was no denying it; though his voice had dropped, he was still a boy. But Perrin was a man.

Perrin slid between blankets on the floor. Tansy had already dived into the bed, hiding her hot face beneath the quilt. Elvie said to Skir, 'Are you going to sleep now?'

'I might sit up for a while and watch the fire,' said Skir.

Elvie hesitated. For a moment Skir thought she might offer to sit with him, and he almost told her he'd like that. But then she turned away. 'Don't leave without saying goodbye.'

'Don't worry, we'll wake you,' said Perrin, loud and cheerful, from the floor. 'Tansy'll probably tip you out of bed.'

Whatever delicate moment might have existed between Skir and Elvie was shattered. 'Good night then,' said the blind girl, and climbed into bed.

Skir settled himself in the chair by the fire and scowled

down at Perrin's blanket-wrapped body. He closed his eyes and conjured up again the fleeting touch of Elvie's fingers. The fire burned lower. Skir slept.

Penthesi nuzzled at Tansy's chin, rough and persistent. She turned her head, but he wouldn't leave her alone; again and again he nudged her, almost knocking her down with his urgency. *Tansy, Tansy, wake up,* he was saying. *There's danger, wake up!*

Tansy sat up in bed. For a moment she thought she was in Arvestel, in the tiny attic room she'd shared with Aunty Fender. Then she saw Skir, slumped in the chair, and Perrin's humped figure in the glow from the embers. She was too hot under the covers, with Elvie beside her. She swung her legs out of the bed.

Then she heard it, just like her dream: the whinny of the black stallion. *Danger.*

'Quick, quick, get up!' Tansy cried. 'Skir, Perrin, wake up!' She snatched her sword from under the bed.

Perrin scrambled to his feet. Skir tumbled off the chair. Outside, in the clearing, came a chink of metal against metal, a snapped twig, and the high, warning neigh of the horses. Perrin threw himself at the door and, in that heartbeat, all kinds of thoughts flashed through Tansy's mind: he'd betrayed them after all; he was running to Wanion to collect his blood-money; he'd condemned them all to a horrible death; she always knew you couldn't trust a Gani –

Then she saw him thrust the heavy bolt across the door, the big bolt that protected Elvie's box of rust, and a tide of relief surged through her.

Skir groped for his dagger. He gulped for breath, his mouth wide open in panic. Perrin looked around wildly. There were no windows, no other way in. Elvie shrank back against the wall, bed covers clutched under her chin, her blank eyes flicking madly back and forth. 'What's happening?'

'Fingers is here,' said Perrin. 'Balt Army.'

'Not Wanion?' said Tansy.

'No.'

The door shook as the soldiers hurled their bodies against it. Thud. Thud. The bolt would hold, but the wall was fragile. A few more blows and it would splinter apart. Perrin cried, 'Tansy! Bash a hole in the wall so we can crawl out. Save whatever you can.'

Skir grabbed the poker and swung at the wall on the opposite side of the hut.

'There's a loose board!' Elvie scrambled off the bed. 'Here, behind the clothes-chest.'

Thud. Thud. And a faint smell of smoke.

'They set the hut on fire!' shouted Tansy. Skir heaved at the loose board, his face contorted with effort. Thud. Thud.

Tansy shrieked, 'Perrin, help us!' But Perrin shook his head. He turned away to face the door. The loose board wrenched free, then another. Skir pushed Elvie through the gap.

Thud. Thud. And Perrin just stood there –

Then Tansy realised he was singing. She heard Sedge and Penthesi scream, and the yells of the soldiers as the horses' hoofs thrashed down. Skir shouted something, and she turned and began to hurl things through the hole, whatever was under her hands: the bag of onions, a blanket, a boot. The smell of burning grew stronger, and there was a crackle of flame in the thatch of the hut. Elvie and Skir were outside, grabbing whatever Tansy shoved at them and throwing it clear. The horses screamed again and again as they reared at the soldiers and struck them down with their flailing iron hoofs.

Perrin gripped Tansy's wrist and dragged her to the hole and pushed, and she was outside in the clear cool of night, the air fresh on her face. The hut was on fire, and the horses reared back from the flames. Perrin wasn't singing now. One of the soldiers saw them and shouted, and Tansy's sword was in her hand, and she'd never been so scared. 'Come on!' she yelled, and ran forward.

There were four soldiers – no, six – in full battle-dress, *as if they were facing the whole Rengani Fifth*, thought Perrin, *instead of a few raggedy kids*. One Rengani soldier, he corrected himself as he swung and parried, and a couple of raggedy kids. He moved as if in a dream. His body knew what to do. Swing and duck and thrust and turn, behind him, turn again, thrust and swing and parry.

From the corner of his eye he saw Tansy twist and throw one soldier to the ground as he tried to grab her. Skir slashed wildly, randomly, back and forth with his dagger, hemmed against the burning hut. The two soldiers who had him pinned there weren't trying too hard, they didn't force him back into the flames: probably under orders not to hurt him, guessed Perrin. But then, the men around Tansy weren't trying too hard either. Confused by her hair, shining copper in the blaze, they weren't sure which of the raggedy kids they were supposed to capture unharmed. One soldier went down with a surprised *oof!* and didn't move again. Good for Tansy, thought Perrin grimly, and he wondered briefly what had become of Elvie in all this. Then there was no more time to think.

Swing and thrust and pull and spin. The men kept coming,

and Perrin fought on, swift and methodical as he'd been trained. Nothing was real but the centre of his own body, his own sure right arm and his own two feet, smooth and easy, thrust and duck and parry and dance. There were grunts and blood and cries of pain, but Perrin barely noticed. Like chantment when it flowed true, he felt something greater than himself move through him – part of him and yet more complicated than he was. And the next, and the next, swing and thrust and turn.

Perrin stepped back and almost fell over a body lying face down. The grass was black with blood. Sedge screamed, and her eyes rolled white as Skir scrambled onto her back.

'Perrin! Come *on*!'

Perrin stared around. The clearing was strewn with bodies – three, four, five, all Baltimaran soldiers, some moving, some stilled. Tansy was high on Penthesi's broad back, with Elvie clinging to her; packs and blankets and food-bags dangled any old way. Skir leaned down from Sedge, his hand outstretched. 'Quick, I can't hold her –'

Perrin hauled himself up: he used his right hand, unthinking, and he gasped with pain. It was as if he'd closed his hand around a knife instead of Skir's fingers. Penthesi and the girls had already thundered away. Then Skir gave Sedge her head and they were flying along the river path, the road to Rarr. 'Not this way!' called Perrin. The bandage on his hand was red with fresh blood. The wound had split; he'd fought with it all that time and not even felt it.

'Not this way!' he shouted again. 'The Captain –'

Elvie yelled over her shoulder. '– the only road. Go fast!'

Branches whipped them as they galloped on. Skir clung to Sedge's mane with one hand, leaned over and was sick. Perrin saw that Skir's shirt was dark with blood, too.

'You hurt? Skir?'

Skir shook his head, and was sick again.

Tansy called, 'He killed someone.'

They galloped through the town, hoofs clattering on cobbles slimy with discarded food and filth. The market-square was stark in the moonlight, the colonnade deserted and the streets empty. The stark fingers of Wanion's fortress, with the moons behind them, cast multiple shadows across the town, like the bones of a skeleton's hand held over someone's face. The horses galloped through the bars of shadow, silver and black, as they sped away into the night.

Perrin groped for Sedge's bridle and turned her off the road. The fields here were freshly mown for hay and the high heaps of the new haystacks rose silver in the moonlight. 'Tansy! North.'

Tansy heard, and turned Penthesi to ride beside Sedge. They were already going fast, but now the black horse put his head down and ran like a colt, as if the two girls on his back didn't exist. Sweat spattered his flanks as he galloped across the meadows, up and down the billows of the fields. Sedge dropped back. Skir swayed, only just holding on. The wind tore at them. At last the fields that streamed away beneath them turned to wild grass, grazing land, dotted with trees. A herd of goats started away at their sudden approach.

Penthesi slowed to a canter, then a trot; his sides heaved. When he came to a creek, he didn't jump it, but stopped abruptly and lowered his head to drink. A glow ran along the horizon to the east, and the whole sky was fading to white. It was almost morning.

Tansy slid off Penthesi's back and helped Elvie to drop down. The blind girl sank to her knees in the long grass.

Automatically, Tansy yanked up a handful of grass and began to rub down the horse. 'Hush now, hush now, it's all right, it's over, it's over.' A sob caught in her throat.

Sedge limped up, her sides flecked with sweat and foam. Skir slithered to the ground, doubled over and vomited into the grass. Perrin jumped down and gripped his shoulder.

In the strengthening light, Perrin could see Skir's face, mud-coloured under his blackened hair. The front of his shirt was soaked with blood.

Skir croaked, 'I pushed the dagger at him. I didn't mean –' He gagged again, and pressed his hand to his mouth. 'It stuck . . . in him . . . and –'

'I was sick too,' said Perrin. 'After my first kill.'

Skir closed his eyes. He said thickly, 'Sorry.' He put out one hand, then stumbled to the edge of the creek. He lowered his hands into the swift water and watched as the thin threads of scarlet lifted and swirled away; then he tore off his stained shirt, soaked it and wrung it out, over and over, until the stream ran clear, and even after that he kept on dipping it and squeezing it out, until his hands were raw.

Elvie sat in the grass where she'd sunk down. She didn't turn her head as Perrin squatted beside her. 'Is he all right?'

'He will be,' said Perrin.

'Your house – it burned,' Tansy whispered. 'Like the luck-piece.'

'Yes,' said Elvie. 'We shouldn't have done that.'

'Someone must have followed me from town.' Perrin shook his head. 'I was so sure . . .' He remembered the scene he'd caused in the marketplace, when he approached the Captain; that was a mistake.

Elvie said, 'Someone in the town might have spied on you.

There are many in Rarr who would sell their own family for money for rust, let alone a stranger. Or Madam Wanion knew, when we burned the luckpiece.'

Or you sent word to Lady Wanion yourself, thought Tansy.

Elvie stood and brushed down her skirt; she'd slept in her faded dress, as she always did, but her feet were bare. 'I can hear birds. Is it dawn?'

'Yes. It's quite light now.'

'Then you mustn't stay. You must go on. Someone will see you.'

Tansy stared around at the blank horizon. 'There ain't no one here but goats.'

'Where there are goats, there'll be a goat-herder. You must go.'

'But you're coming with us,' said Perrin. 'We can't leave you.'

Elvie shook her head. 'No. I'll stay here.'

Tansy pulled Perrin aside. 'Maybe it's for the best,' she muttered. 'We don't know who told Wanion.'

'That wasn't Wanion tonight. It was the Balts, the Army.'

'You don't think the soldiers do her bidding too?' said Tansy. 'We can't take her. We got to get Skir home safe.'

'Yes,' said Perrin. 'Our precious Priest-King.'

Elvie raised her voice. 'I can't come with you. I would be a burden. Please, leave me. It's what I want.'

Skir came up; Tansy expected him to argue, but he didn't. He pulled out his coin-purse and pressed it into Elvie's hand. 'Take this.'

Elvie shook her head and let the purse drop into the grass. 'No. Someone will cut my throat for that. I have other ways to earn my keep. I'd rather leave my hands free.'

There was a moment's awkward silence. Then Tansy said roughly, 'Good luck.' She climbed onto Penthesi's back, and sat watching without a word as Perrin hugged Elvie, and Skir took both her hands in his.

'I won't forget you, Elvie.'

'And I won't forget you, Ren.'

When Skir swung back for one last look, Elvie was standing in the long grass, her faded pink dress warmed by the rising sun. She smiled bravely, and lifted her hand in farewell; but she was facing the wrong direction, waving her goodbye to no one.

CHAPTER 10

The Coast Road

THEY travelled steadily northward all that day, across plains starred with tiny orange flowers of goose-blossom. As the day grew hotter, more and more flowers opened, until it seemed they rode through a lake of fire.

The horses were weary, so they all walked, with Penthesi and Sedge carrying only the heaviest packs and bundles. Tansy and Perrin walked side-by-side. After a long silence, Perrin said, 'You fought well.'

She shot him a sideways glance. She wore the blue scarf, and her eyes were the same colour as the summer sky.

'I mean it,' he said. He wanted her to believe him; it was important that she did, and for the first time he doubted that she would. 'You fought like a soldier. Truly.'

She smiled uncertainly, and quickly looked away. 'I never had to do it for real before. It were always, you know, just playing.' Her voice was soft. 'It weren't like I expected.'

'I know.' Perrin thrust his hands deep into his pockets. 'I remember my first battle. Only two years ago, but it feels like a century. I was a kid of sixteen, a drafty. It was a shambles, that battle, at least it was to me. Noise, and steel clashing, and terror, and stink. I wet myself. I saw – well, never mind.' He looked at her. 'Last night was a good fight. You can be proud. It was a good victory, not too easy, not too hard. We earned it.'

As he spoke the words, he almost believed them; and it was true, the soldiers who'd attacked him had fought hard. But the men who'd fought Skir and Tansy had held back, tried not to hurt them. They would have been surprised that the kids had defended themselves so fiercely. Tansy had fought as hard as she could, she had fought well. Perrin said what she needed to hear.

Tansy nodded, and her chin went up. It was a secret dream of hers that if she'd been a boy, she might have been a soldier, a horseman on a proud charger like Penthesi. Until today, she'd thought she'd make a better soldier than Perrin, with his songs and his dandy ways. Look at what he'd bought in the market: a comb and a finger-harp! When he could have bought saddles and proper bridles! But now she realised there was more to being a soldier than she'd thought, and she wasn't so sure she'd make a good one.

All her brothers back home on the farm knew how to fight; every man did, up near the border, in case the war in Cragonlands spilled southward. As a child, Tansy had pleaded with Cuff to teach her, too. *Nay*, Cuff had said. *Da and us boys'll look after you and Ma, if it comes to that. Don't you fret on it.* But Tansy had begged, and at last Cuff had taught her to wrestle, how to use a boy's weight against him to tip him off his feet. She'd used that trick last night.

Then Nellip had helped her shoot straight, and Dory had shown her how to use a sword and throw a spear. She was only little then; she'd needed two hands to lift the wooden training sword. But she'd practised every chance she'd, even though Ma scolded her. Da didn't mind. *It's no shame for a lass to be handy with a bow, and a good thing if she can fight for herself*, he'd said in his soft voice, and smiled down at her. His girl. A lump rose in Tansy's throat.

'You all right?' said Perrin.

'Grit in my eye,' said Tansy.

All day Skir walked behind them. He didn't speak. He clutched Sedge's bridle tightly in his hand, as if he were drowning, and only that short length of rope kept him afloat. Every so often the mare would shove him gently with her nose, as if he were a foal; but Skir hardly noticed.

When they stopped at nightfall, Skir sat down abruptly in the grass and stared off to the horizon. He plucked up one blade of grass, then another, and let the evening breeze blow them away. He looked pathetically young, his hair plastered to his head, his eyes bruised and hollow.

Perrin sat down beside him. 'Give it time. You'll feel better soon.'

'No.' Skir's voice was low. 'I killed a man. I've defiled my priesthood. I can't be Priest-King any more. I can't do anything.'

'Don't be stupid. No one's going to care. It was self-defence. You fought well. It was a good clean fight.'

But the words that had worked so well for Tansy had the opposite effect on Skir. He looked at Perrin almost with loathing.

'*Clean?* What was clean about it? It was – awful. You're talking like a soldier. I'm not a soldier. I'm a Priest of the Faith.'

'Yes.' Perrin plucked some grass too. 'But I'm not a very good soldier.'

'And I'm not a very good priest.'

There was a short silence. Tansy built a fire and was busy with the cooking pot. Smoke drifted white above the ground, a cloud of unspun silk. The horses cropped at the grass nearby. Sedge gave a huge sigh, as if she were glad the day was over.

Skir said in a low voice, 'Maybe it was Tansy's witch. I killed her little dolls, so then I killed a real person. Do you think she could do that, make that happen?'

Perrin looked away. He said, 'You don't have to tell anybody, you know, if that's what's worrying you.'

'But it *happened*. I did – what I did. I can't undo it.'

Perrin glanced at him curiously. 'You want to tell them, don't you? You sound relieved. Don't you want to be Priest-King?'

Skir flushed. 'It's not that. I –'

'Here, eat this.' Tansy squatted beside them with the cooking pot. 'Careful, it's hot. It's porridge, with wine in it.'

'You used the oats? The horses' oats?' Perrin raised his eyebrows.

'Penthesi and Sedge won't grudge us. Not today.'

Perrin told her, 'Skir doesn't want to be a priest any more.'

'It's not a question of wanting. There are rules.' Skir stood up. 'I took a life. I've broken the Faith.'

'Have some porridge, Skir. You'll feel better if you eat something.'

'I'm not hungry. I wish I was dead!' He stalked away across the plain toward the red and purple streaks of sunset, kicking his way through the tiny closed-up flames of goose-blossom.

'You'd better go after him,' said Perrin. 'He won't want me to see him cry.'

'He ain't crying!' said Tansy. 'Sorcerers don't cry.'

'Oh yes they do,' said Perrin. 'You poured that good wine into porridge? That's enough to make me cry. Give me the spoon.'

For several days, they veered back and forth across the plain, dodging a farmhouse here and a herder there, careful to keep out of sight. Finally, they reached the ocean. At the top of the cliff Tansy halted Penthesi and simply stared. She tasted salt in the air, and the wind blew her hair into stiff spikes. Far below, the waves crashed and roared against the rocks, but she was dazzled by the wide belt of turquoise, a breathing jewel that spread from land to sky.

'What's the matter? Never seen the sea before?' Perrin's hand was still bandaged, but it was healing cleanly, and he could hold the reins in his fingertips. He wheeled Sedge so he could see Tansy's face. 'Big, isn't it?'

'Don't tease me,' said Tansy, unable to drag her eyes from the great wide sparkling sea. 'It's grand.'

'I sailed right across there.' Perrin flung his arm out to the western horizon. 'It took a whole year. We went to all the little islands, and the people came racing to the harbour like we were gods.'

'You would have liked that,' said Tansy with a sniff, and they grinned at each other.

'What do you think, Skir?' said Perrin.

Skir sat behind Tansy; he could balance now without holding onto her waist, and he sat stiffly upright, withdrawn from her, still wrapped tight in his misery. He said, 'I've seen the sea before.'

'Ain't it grand?' said Tansy. 'It's beautiful.'

Skir gazed dully at the ocean. 'I suppose.'

The north coast of Baltimar wound east to west along the long shore of Codlin's Gulf. It was a mostly deserted region, a bare wilderness of salt-scrub and windswept grasses. As Skir had predicted, there were only two or three small towns scattered along the whole length of the shore: isolated fishing villages, cut off from the rest of Baltimar. The so-called coast road was no more than a rutted track, stony and overgrown with weeds.

Day after day the three rode along the cliffs and across the hard-packed sand without seeing any sign of life but gulls and crabs, until one morning Perrin abruptly halted Sedge, and Tansy had to wheel Penthesi aside so as not to run into them.

'Careful, you lackwit!'

'What's that? Over there.'

At the top of the next rise, high on the cliffs, stood a huge grey haystack. But it was far bigger than any haystack: it was an immense, weathered pile of driftwood that towered over their heads. Whole trees had been thrust onto the pile; branches poked out randomly, stripped bare, grey and eerie as ancient bones. Tansy urged Penthesi nearer, then cried out so suddenly the stallion half-reared and Skir almost fell off.

'Don't go near it! It's witches' work.' Tansy's hand groped automatically, uselessly, round her throat for a luckpiece.

'Out here? Are you sure?' said Perrin. 'What is it, little dollies tied to the branches?'

But when Sedge came nearer and he saw what Tansy had seen, he gave a low whistle and turned away.

Skir looked sick. 'What is it?'

'Shore fire,' said Perrin. 'Tugger told us about them. Meant to ward off the western chanters. Keep the Singer of the Westlands at bay, stop her from bringing her Rising here.'

'Rising? What's that?' said Tansy.

'The revolution of the chanters. Chanters will take over all of Tremaris, if the Singer has her way. That's why my parents ran away from the Westlands. They –'

Skir interrupted; he'd heard enough about the Rising. 'What about the – that thing inside the pile?'

'Punishment.' Tansy's face was pale. ' "The Witch-Woman will send you to the shore fires," that's what they say. This is Wanion's work.'

'Whoever that was,' said Perrin, 'they've been dead a long time.'

Tansy twined her hands into Penthesi's mane to stop them shaking. The two horses trotted away swiftly, as if they too were glad to leave the gruesome sight behind. For a long time after, the three young people sensed the high, brooding presence of the bonfire on the clifftop behind them, and they all breathed easier when the shoreline curved and it dropped from view.

'Sedge has a loose shoe,' said Tansy when they stopped that night in a hollow in the dunes. 'We need a smithy.'

'I don't think we'll find one,' said Perrin. 'Even if we could risk going into a village.'

Tansy looked at him hopefully. 'Can't you fix it?'

'Don't have the right tools.' Perrin helped himself to a slice of hard-cake.

'I mean, can you sing something?'

'Sing what? You need an ironcrafter for this sort of job.'

Skir asked abruptly, 'Can we still ride her?'

'Yes. But it ain't good for her hoof. You better ride her alone, Skir, you're the lightest, and don't carry nothing.'

Skir picked at his toes without looking up. 'I can't,' he muttered.

Tansy and Perrin exchanged an exasperated glance. Tansy said, in a bright, encouraging voice, 'Course you can manage her! You're nearly as good as me now. Old Ingle wouldn't know you. Just let her favour that right foreleg. You'll be all right.'

Skir's face set in a sullen frown. 'Just don't blame me if something goes wrong.'

'Nothing'll go wrong,' said Perrin. 'By the bones! I know you're not happy, but do you have to make us *all* suffer?'

'Sorry,' said Skir stiffly, and he rolled himself in his coat and pretended to go to sleep while Tansy and Perrin hissed and whispered together about him.

It was long after midnight when Tansy woke and saw a glow on the horizon. She whispered, 'Perrin?'

'Yes.' His voice came quietly out of the dark. 'I can see it too. They've lit the shore fire.'

For a few moments they were silent, watching the eerie flicker of the flames against the sky.

Tansy whispered, 'Why?'

'The fires are meant to keep chantment at bay. Maybe the soldiers we fought at Rarr heard me sing and told your Lady Wanion one of us was a chanter.'

'And Skir.'

'Yes,' said Perrin after a pause. 'And Skir.'

'So she knows – she knows where we are?'

'I only said maybe.'

'But you let our fire go out . . .'

'Better cautious than a corpse, as the commander likes to say. Don't worry, Tansy. Go back to sleep.'

'No. I'll keep watch now.' Tansy sat up, shivering, and

wrapped her blanket round her shoulders. She thought Perrin had fallen asleep, but after a long time he spoke again.

'Don't tell Skir.'

'No,' said Tansy. She kept her eyes fixed on the distant orange glow until, just before dawn, it died away. Only then would she let herself sleep again.

The next day Skir rode Sedge alone. After midday they came to a patch of shingle that led down onto a long stretch of hard sand. Tansy and Perrin slipped from Penthesi's back, and pebbles skittered underfoot as they led him down. Skir hesitated at the top. He squeezed his legs gently. 'Go on, Sedge.'

Sedge flicked her chestnut ear questioningly, then set one hoof on the shingle. The stones shifted. Sedge put another hoof down, then another. Too late to turn back now. It was all right, thought Skir with relief, and then the world swung sideways. Sedge screamed in pain and fright as the shingle rushed up to slam against Skir's face. He rolled over, winded, and stared up at the wide blue sky.

'Are you hurt?' cried Tansy.

'I – I don't think so.' With infinite care, Skir raised himself on his elbows.

'She was talking to the mare,' said Perrin.

Dazed, Skir looked around. Sedge was down. Tansy was at her side and feeling up and down her legs as she soothed her. The chestnut tried to struggle to her feet, but kept collapsing, and at last Tansy gathered her head into her lap.

'Her leg's broken.'

Skir closed his eyes. 'Stupid, stupid, stupid! I told you I couldn't do it, I *knew* I'd mess it up.'

Tansy spoke past him to Perrin. 'Can you heal her? Can you *make* her heal?'

'No.'

'There must be something, some magic to help her!'

Perrin squatted beside Sedge. 'There's only one thing I can do.'

'What?' Tansy looked up eagerly, but Perrin kept his gaze fixed on Sedge as he rubbed the mare's nose.

'I can sing her to sleep, Tansy. That's all.'

'To sleep? You mean – you mean she won't wake up?'

'Yes.'

Penthesi whinnied, and Sedge lifted her head to answer, a soft, bewildered nickering.

'She knows, Tansy. She knows there's nothing else to do.'

Tansy bent her head over Sedge's neck, and said nothing.

Skir said, 'But it's only her leg! Can't we bandage it?'

'That wouldn't do no good.' Tansy spoke without bitterness or blame, just a terrible sadness. 'Perrin's right.'

'Poor old girl,' murmured Perrin, stroking Sedge's velvet nose. 'Poor old girl. Stay there, Tansy.' And he began to sing a chantment, a crooning song like a lullaby, and Skir felt the hairs rise on the back of his neck as they always did when Perrin sang.

Penthesi lowered his head, as if he knew exactly what was happening. Skir patted his neck, and the big horse snorted into his hand, then turned back to watch Sedge.

The chestnut lifted her head; she heaved a great breath, then laid her head calmly in Tansy's lap while Perrin's chantment drifted over her. Tansy whispered something that Skir couldn't hear; she was crying.

Skir walked away to the water's edge where foam hissed

and died on the sand, and each wavelet smoothed the beach like the caress of a gentle hand.

When he returned, Sedge was dead. Perrin sat beside the big, motionless body. Already flies had collected around the soft dark nose and the sealed eyes. Skir sat on the sand.

'Where's Tansy?'

Perrin gestured down the beach to where two tiny figures, girl and horse, walked slowly side by side.

'It was my fault,' said Skir leadenly. 'I killed her. I wrecked two dolls and now I've killed two living beings. First the soldier, now Sedge. It's Wanion's magic coming after me.'

Perrin hesitated, tempted to agree, then he shook his head. 'No, Skir. Not everything in the world revolves around you. You didn't kill Sedge. I did. With my chantment.'

Skir was silent for a moment.

'Have you sung that chantment before?'

'Yes.'

'When?'

'When I had to.' Perrin brushed the sand from his hands and stared hard at Skir. 'And what about you? What kind of chantment do you sing?'

Skir stiffened. 'I'm not supposed to talk about it.'

'Really? Not even one chanter to another? It's just that, in all this time, I haven't heard you sing one chantment.'

Skir frowned at the sand. 'The Priest-King's power is sacred. It's only to be used for the defence of Cragonlands.'

'But I thought you couldn't be Priest-King any more. You've defiled your office. So now you're just an ordinary chanter. Like me.'

'I'm Priest-King until the Temple releases me.' Skir's frown deepened.

'You haven't been very successful at defending Cragonlands, have you? The Balts invaded, what, twenty years ago? And you haven't exactly shaken them off yet.'

'The insurgents –'

'Your precious insurgents wouldn't have got far without the Rengani Army behind them, my friend.'

'We don't need any of you.' Skir's face was scarlet. 'Why can't you leave us alone?'

'Why don't you make us, if you're such a mighty chanter?'

'Because I'm not!' cried Skir. 'I'm not a mighty chanter. I'm not any sort of chanter. I can't do it. All right? Are you satisfied now?'

'Ah,' said Perrin softly.

There was a silence while they both stared away at Tansy and Penthesi walking along the beach. Skir kicked the sand. As they watched, the girl and the horse turned, and began to walk back toward them.

Skir said wretchedly, 'I'm supposed to be an ironcrafter. The Priest-King is always an ironcrafter. When you said that, about fixing Sedge's shoe – I thought you knew, I thought you were making fun of me.'

'No.'

'Ironcrafters can move the earth, shake the ground, make the mountains quake. But I can't. I never could.'

'So why did the priests choose you?'

'I don't know! They made a mistake. I suppose they couldn't find anyone. There has to be a Priest-King ... Beeman said I might grow into my gift, he said it sometimes happens that way.' Skir glanced at Perrin. 'Is that true?'

Perrin shrugged. 'I've never heard of a gift that didn't show itself in childhood.'

'I knew it,' said Skir savagely. 'I know the songs, they taught me all the chantments, but it never – the magic never –'

'If it doesn't come, it doesn't come,' said Perrin. 'You can't force it.'

'It doesn't matter anyway,' said Skir dully. 'They won't let me be Priest-King any more. All those years I spent learning the rituals, wasted. Bettenwey will have to find someone else . . . He's the High Priest. Or he was – I don't even know if he's still alive . . .' He pushed his fingers into the sand. 'Maybe he'll give it to you.'

'No, thanks,' said Perrin.

'But you're a chanter.'

'Not a chanter of iron. Only a chanter of the beasts.' Perrin swept some sand into a pile and crumbled it with his fingers.

Tansy and Penthesi trudged toward them; Tansy leaned into the big horse's body.

Perrin looked up. 'You all right?'

Tansy nodded without speaking; her eyes were red and swollen. Perrin put his arms around her, and the two of them stood there for a long moment in silence.

Skir stood too and brushed sand from his hands. 'Perrin?' he said.

Perrin looked over his shoulder. 'What?'

Skir flung back his head. 'I want you to sing to me like you did to Sedge. I want you to – to sing me to sleep.'

No one spoke. Tansy disengaged herself from Perrin's arms, and they stared at Skir. The silence crackled with tension, like the pause between a lightning flash and its roar of thunder. At last Tansy said softly, 'You ain't serious.'

'I'm perfectly serious.' Skir spoke louder. 'You heard me. I want to die. I've been training all my life to do one thing, and I can't do it. I'm supposed to be a chanter, but I'm not. No, Tansy, that's right, what do you think of your mighty Priest-King sorcerer now? I killed that soldier and now I've killed Sedge. Wanion's cursed me. I ruin everything . . .' He swept his arm around to encompass the beach, the sea, the body of the dead horse, Tansy and Perrin and Penthesi. The waves roared. 'It's too hard!' cried Skir. 'I'd rather be dead!'

His words rang out in the empty sky.

At last Perrin said, 'Songs of the Beasts don't work on people.' His voice was cold and distant.

'Why not? We're animals too, aren't we?'

'We're different. We speak, we have language, the Power of Tongue.'

'Penthesi speaks, in his own way. You understand him, so does Tansy. And some people don't speak –'

'Skir, the chantment won't work.'

'Just try it.'

'No.'

'But I'm *asking* you to. Maybe I won't mess up my next life. You tell him, Tansy.'

Tansy stared at him. 'I ain't asking Perrin to kill you!'

'There you are,' said Perrin crisply. 'Tansy doesn't want you to die. Happy now?'

'Just try!' shouted Skir.

'I won't do it, you lackwit,' said Perrin. 'Clear?'

Skir swung his fist, but Perrin dodged the blow easily. At the same instant, his fist flew out and crunched into Skir's face. Skir thumped backward onto the sand. After a moment he sat up, holding his nose. Blood seeped between his fingers.

'Perrin!' shouted Tansy. 'What did you do that for?'

Perrin winced as he nursed his knuckles. 'Just trying to knock some sense into him.'

Tansy stamped her foot. 'A few days ago you were ready to die for each other and now you're punching each other in the head! And next to poor Sedge's body, too. Ain't you got no respect?'

A muffled moan came from Skir. 'What am I going to do?'

'I'll tell you what to do. We're going to Cragonlands, taking you home, just like we planned. Ain't that right, Perrin?'

'Right,' said Perrin. 'Taking you home to Cragonlands.'

'We ain't come all this way for nothing. And here's you two squabbling like ducklings over a crust. You forgotten we got Madam chasing after us, and half the Army, too? You ain't dying, Skir, not after we went to so much trouble to keep you alive. Tip your head back, that'll stop the bleeding. Come here, you stupid boy, you're shaking.'

Tansy put her arm around Skir, and he didn't pull away. He leaned into her as earlier she had leaned into Penthesi and Perrin, and she felt the heat of his skin against her body. He was as hot as a child who's been a long time crying. He held his sleeve pressed hard to his nose. She kissed his hair roughly. 'It's all right. It's all right.'

Perrin spat onto the sand. 'Save it, kids. We'd better move on. It'll be dark soon, and we can't camp anywhere near *that*.' He nodded to Sedge's body. 'It'll stink by morning.' He heaved the packs and bundles onto Penthesi's back, took the horse's bridle and stalked away down the beach.

Skir and Tansy pulled apart. Skir cautiously felt his nose. Tansy snapped a handful of sea-grass and scattered it over Sedge; the mare's once glossy coat was dull now, and her legs stuck out as stiff as poles. Tansy paused over her. 'Funny, ain't it? How she ain't *here* no more.'

'Yes,' said Skir, and all at once he was in the clearing by Elvie's hut, with the dagger in his hand, and there was the soldier jumping out at him, and it was so sudden, so quick, the feel of the dagger as it went in, the noise as it came out. The young soldier's eyes going wide, his wispy yellow moustache, his open mouth, his crooked teeth –

As if Tansy sensed his thoughts, she turned to him. 'You're a priest. You got any words to say, words for the dead?'

Skir pulled himself upright. Of course he knew what to say. This was one part of his role that always felt right and true: he spoke well, and he knew it, and he knew that others knew it too. He tasted the solemn power of the words, even there on the beach, under the wide sky, without the echoes of the Temple to give them strength. Though somewhat muffled because of his swollen nose, the familiar speech flowed without a stumble.

'Sedge, our sister in faith, we honour you in death as we honoured you in life. From earth and air, from fire and water, you were born. To earth and air, to fire and water, you will return. As the rain joins the river, your spirit joins the Great Spirit and becomes one with it. You are not lost. You have come home.'

He bowed his head, and the gulls cried overhead. Tansy blinked.

'Did you think that up yourself?'

'Me? No! It's ancient, as old as the Temple. Maybe older. We say those words when a priest dies.'

Tansy nodded. 'Well, it was beautiful.'

Skir said, 'Tansy, are you angry with me for not being a chanter?'

Tansy was quiet. Then she reached for his hand and squeezed it. 'I ain't happy that you lied to me. But I ain't angry. You can't help what you are, no more than anyone.'

'I suppose that means Perrin can't help being obnoxious,' said Skir savagely.

That made her laugh. Skir thought, I should kiss her now. Right now, while we're alone, while she's holding my hand. Now, after I made her laugh, while she isn't thinking what an idiot I am.

But it was too late. Tansy wiped her nose on her sleeve, and sighed. 'Better catch up with Perrin and Penthesi, I guess.'

'Yes,' said Skir. At least they were still holding hands as they walked together, both grateful for the silence and the falling dusk.

CHAPTER 11

Dody's Leap

THE next day they loaded Penthesi and set off along the beach, hidden from the road by the swell of the dunes. The sand was baked hard, and the sun glared overhead. They walked mostly in silence. Skir had two black eyes. Tansy suspected that Perrin might have actually broken his nose. How would the Cragonlanders punish someone who broke their Priest-King's nose? Because whatever Skir said, sorcerer or not, he was still the Priest-King.

Tansy squinted against the rising sun as she walked with Penthesi. It was as if Skir were two people: the self-assured priest, master of words, who had spoken over Sedge's body; and the miserable boy who scuffed his boots in the sand ahead of her, his head twisted against the sun's glare. And because of that, Tansy's own feelings were a muddle between awe and respect on one hand, and a kind of exasperated, protective fondness on the other. Tansy remembered Elvie's sly smile as she'd questioned her about the boys.

And what did she feel about Perrin? He was two people, too. There was the arrogant obnoxious smart-breeches that Skir complained about, but there was also the gentle man who'd stroked the mare's nose as he sang to her . . .

Penthesi snorted, and looked mournfully around for Sedge. Tansy murmured, 'I know, my sad boy. You loved her, didn't you? You'll miss her, poor Sedge.'

Perrin stalked ahead. 'Look!' he called over his shoulder. 'We're almost there.'

Now they could all see the brown folds of the mountains of Cragonlands, floating on a thick haze of green: the dense forests of needlewood that marked the border.

Skir said nothing; he stared ahead, tenderly touching his swollen nose.

'Cheer up!' said Tansy. 'You're nearly home.'

'If they still want me,' muttered Skir.

'Least Wanion can't catch us there –'

'Sh!' Perrin held up his finger for silence. Swiftly he scrambled to the top of the dunes to check the road, and just as quickly slid down again. 'Soldiers.'

Tansy put her hand automatically to her sword-hilt, just as once she would have clutched at her luckpiece. 'How many?'

'A company. A couple of hundred men.'

'Which way are they coming from?'

Perrin gestured ahead; the troops were between them and the forest.

'Solk's Wood,' said Skir dully. 'The road leads to Solk's Wood. It's a garrison town. Crawling with soldiers.'

Perrin's hands curled into fists. 'Then why didn't you –' With an effort, he controlled himself. 'It might have been useful to know that earlier,' he said through gritted teeth.

There was nowhere to hide. The beach was wide, and empty; only the soft mounds of the dunes, scattered with clumps of sea-grass, stood between them and the approaching soldiers. They could all hear the faint clink of metal, the tramp of boots, growing louder every moment, and there was nothing they could do but wait for the troops to pass. Tansy felt a trickle of sweat run down her nose. Penthesi shifted from hoof to hoof, not understanding why they'd suddenly stopped, and Perrin reached up to pat and shush him.

Perrin looked very handsome with his tousled dark hair and his clear, angry blue eyes. Angry with Skir, thought Tansy, and felt a stab of protectiveness. While the others stood tense and alert, Skir had slumped onto the sand; his head drooped between his knees as the sun beat down on the back of his neck.

The tramp of boots grew louder and louder. Tansy could hear the rhythmic beat of a marching chant, without being able to make out the words. Da-dee-da-dee-da-dee-dum, da-dee-da-dee-da-dee-*dum*. The shuffle and clatter of shields and spears and breast-plates built to a roar; Tansy's hand tightened on her sword-hilt. Then, to her surprise, she found her other hand in Perrin's cool, dry grip, and he was smiling at her. It was a smile of encouragement, one soldier to another, and Tansy returned it uncertainly, her feelings more confused than ever.

And then, before she had time to realise it, the noise of the troops was fading. The marching chant diminished to a grumble like a dying thunderstorm, and was gone.

'They've passed,' said Perrin, and let go of Tansy's hand.

'Listen,' said Tansy. 'We oughta send Skir on ahead. Skir and Penthesi. They'll be safe in the trees, they can wait for us there. Don't matter so much if you and me get caught, long as Skir's all right.'

But Perrin shook his head. 'Better if we all stick together.'

'No it ain't. Safer if we split up, specially now we know there's soldiers around.'

'I said no, Tansy!' Now the clear angry blue light was turned on her. 'Not when we're so close.'

'That's right,' said Skir. 'Talk about me as if I'm not here. As if I don't exist.'

'Oh, stop feeling so damn sorry for yourself,' snapped Perrin. Then his head whipped around; he had better hearing than a dog. 'Hoof-beats.'

Tansy's heart skipped. 'The Captain?' she whispered. 'Wanion's man?'

Perrin had scrambled up the dune to look. 'It's him. Browny-grey cloak. Coming fast.'

'That's it then.' Tansy made a step for Skir with her hands. 'Gallop for the woods, hard as you can. Don't lose Penthesi. Perrin'll find you later.'

'But I can't gallop Penthesi! I couldn't even manage Sedge.'

'Quick,' said Tansy. '*Quick!*' She hoisted Skir onto Penthesi's back. Penthesi barely waited for Skir to find his seat before he was off, thundering away along the curve of the beach.

'Tansy!' Perrin grabbed her shoulder. 'I said no! We can't split up now!'

'Too late.' Tansy watched them go. 'Safer this way. Gotta be.'

'Yes, but –'

'But what?'

'All our supplies are in the saddlebags,' said Perrin lamely. 'Oh well. Come here.'

'What are you doing?'

'Putting my arm around you. If the Captain looks over the dunes, he'll think we're a courting couple. By the bones! Anyone'd think you'd never been walking with a boy before.'

'Is that what they call it in Rengan?' said Tansy tartly. 'Walking?' After a moment she began to giggle. 'You forgotten I'm wearing boy's clothes?'

'Oh,' said Perrin. But he left his hand where it was, resting lightly on her waist; and Tansy let him.

Numbly, Skir gave Penthesi his head; he didn't think he could control him even if he wanted to. It was all he could do to hang on while the bags and bundles bumped against him and the sand blurred below. Penthesi put his ears back, and his hoofs thundered. Presently the big horse seemed to decide that it was time to leave the beach; he leaped and scrabbled up and over the dunes.

'Hey! Whoa!' said Skir, in alarm, staring around to see if the soldiers or the Captain were in view. But Penthesi had chosen well. They were in a narrow valley where a stream ran down to the sea, hidden from either side.

Penthesi streaked across the meadows toward the thick hedge of green below the brown haze of the mountains. Skir managed to keep his balance. The rhythm of the gallop swung through his bones; he wasn't going to topple off. The woods were closer. The border forests were all one colour, the dull, unrelieved grey-green of needlewood. The trees waited, still and silent, as Penthesi galloped toward them, and a chill ran down Skir's spine.

Then, suddenly, they were at the edge of the forest. Penthesi halted, his sides heaving. In the silence, Skir heard the drumbeat of distant hoofs.

Skir squeezed his legs in panic. 'Go on! Go on! He's coming!'

Penthesi snorted. Clammy sweat broke out all over Skir. He wished he'd never let the others out of his sight. The forest was dark and tangled; the heavy branches of needlewood brushed the ground. Then Skir realised what the problem was; Penthesi was waiting for him to get down. It would be easier to walk between these trees than ride. He slid off Penthesi's back and wound the bridle around his fist.

Pushing between the branches was like shoving against an endless leaden curtain. Each downward-hanging branch was laden with stiff, prickly needles, a dead weight that resisted being moved aside. The sunlight that struggled down between the needlewoods was murky and shifting; Skir couldn't see the sun or tell which direction they were walking. The needles snagged on the canvas of the saddlebags, and soon Skir's arms were covered in tiny nicks.

After a while Skir stopped and listened. Nothing. 'We'll wait here,' he murmured. 'That's what we'll do. Sit tight.' Penthesi regarded him with one solemn, liquid eye. Skir felt like crying. Were they far enough into the forest? Would they be safe? Priest-King of Cragonlands, heir to the Circle of Attar, leader of his people? He couldn't even walk through the woods. He was useless, a fraud, an impostor. Without Tansy and Perrin to look after him he wouldn't have lasted half a day. He'd be better off dead . . .

It was true. The words seemed to take on a weight of certainty: a cold, stony logic, like a rock in his stomach. Everything would be better if he were dead. Cragonlands would be better off: the priests could choose a new Priest-King, one with the powers he was supposed to have. Beeman and Tansy and Perrin would all be free –

A twig cracked in the forest, and Skir started violently.

Formless terror flooded through him. He wanted to be dead, but not caught by Wanion, with her skin-peelers and her finger-slicers.

Skir threw himself onto Penthesi, and the horse smelled his terror. Even before Skir could urge him on, Penthesi crashed away deeper into the forest, with the Captain crashing after them.

To Skir, the chase stretched endless as a nightmare. He blundered through the trees, whipped and scratched by needles like a thousand metal pins, sliding around on Penthesi's back, his feet tangled in saddlebags and bundles. Sometimes the Captain was so close that Skir heard his horse whinny, and the crash and crunch of hoofs on fallen needles. But then Penthesi sped away, and Skir could hear only the pounding of his own heart and the rasp of the stallion's breath. Once they waited while the sun shifted a handspan across the sky. But then came a horse's snort, the metallic clash of branches, and the hunt was on again.

Perrin's hand didn't remain on Tansy's waist for long. An unspoken urgency drove them to walk faster and faster, hand in hand, and then they began to half-run, in silence, along the sand.

Tansy panted, 'We oughta cross the road. Cut through the fields.'

'No,' said Perrin. 'Keep to the beach.' He put on a spurt of speed so that she had to run outright to keep up with him. They splashed across the stream that Penthesi had jumped and kept running, feet squelching in their wet boots.

'No sign of Skir.'

'Nor the Captain. He must've passed us.'

'Unless he's waiting.'

They both ran faster, Perrin with long, loping strides and Tansy's feet flashing beside him. They didn't speak, just ran steadily, side by side, while the sun glared on the tops of their heads, then slowly began to slide down the sky behind them.

Then Perrin stopped dead. 'There.' His voice was low and savage.

Tansy stared. The beach curved around to meet the forest in a tumble of rocks. The mouth of a creek flowed out between the steep sides of a wooded gully, forming a narrow, sheltered inlet. In the tiny harbour lay a boat.

'It's all right,' said Perrin. 'They're not here. They're upstream, at the bridge. At Dody's Leap. Come on.' He began to climb the slope into the forest, springing from one tree to the next, steadying himself against the rough bark of each tree trunk.

'Perrin! Perrin, wait! I don't –' Tansy followed, her face creased in bewilderment.

'We have to find Skir and Penthesi before they do,' called Perrin over his shoulder. 'I told you not to send the horse away. You're going to need him.'

'What? *I'll* need him?' Tansy caught up with Perrin at last at the top of the gully, which had deepened beside them into a steep-sided ravine with the creek running along the bottom. She seized his sleeve and held fast. 'Perrin, *stop*. What's going on?'

'The rendezvous team, the second team. They're waiting for us at Dody's Leap. For me and Skir. To take Skir back to Rengan. That's what the boat's for. Don't look at me like that. I've got it all worked out. They won't get *you*. You'll take

Penthesi, just like we said in the beginning, remember? You can ride him home to Lotch, or wherever you want. Don't *look* like that. You'll be safe, Tansy. We just have to find the damn horse.'

Tansy stared at him. 'You're taking Skir to Rengan?'

'Those are the orders. Hand over the target at Dody's Leap.'

'But – you're supposed to be rescuing him. Taking him home. If you take him to Rengan, that ain't a rescue. That's kidnapping.'

Perrin shrugged impatiently. 'I only know my orders.'

'But what do they want him for?'

'To be Rengan's hostage instead of Baltimar's, I suppose. High Command didn't confide the details in me – I'm just a humble swordsman, remember.' He ran his hands through his hair. 'What? Stop looking at me like that. I told you, I'll see you get away safely. I won't let them hurt you. What's the matter?'

'What's the *matter*?' Tansy's face was white. 'You lied to us! You been lying all along! You said we were going to Cragonlands, you promised –'

Perrin spoke over her. 'But you're going to be safe –'

Tansy cried, 'I thought we were together – all of us together. I trusted you, and all the time you –'

'I had *orders*. I never said –'

Tansy choked. She put out her hands blindly in front of her to ward him off, and then she was running, slipping and stumbling on the carpet of fallen needles, deeper into the forest.

'Tansy! Tansy, *listen* –'

Perrin wheeled around. He heard voices, not far off. Rengani voices. The bridge must be nearer than he'd thought.

He hesitated, peering through the trees. They were here, they were close by. All he had to do was walk a few steps toward the bridge; the Rengani Army would close up around him like a fist ... He shut his eyes for an instant. Then, just as if he were on a parade ground, he turned on his heel, and took off after Tansy.

She hadn't got far. He was almost close enough to touch her. 'Tansy . . .' She spun around and wildly swung her fist at him. He caught her wrist before she could hit him. Their feet slipped on the needles. 'Tansy, wait –'

She cried, 'I hate you!' Her face was blotched and swollen with tears.

A horse's scream rang through the forest.

Tansy gasped, 'Penthesi!' She shook her wrist free and tore off toward the sound, back toward the gully. Perrin followed, close on her heels.

Tansy burst into the clearing. Penthesi was rearing at the very edge of the ravine, his front legs thrashing the air, nostrils flared, eyes rolling in terror. Skir cowered on the ground beneath his flailing hoofs; sacks and bundles, all their precious supplies, slid off the horse's back and spilled down into the gully: the bag of oats, the bed-rolls, the cooking pan.

'Skir, get back!' Tansy darted forward. 'I'll take his head –'

'Let me sing first.' Perrin thrust out his hand. 'Good boy, good boy . . .' He sang a chantment, rather breathlessly, and Penthesi shuddered and lowered his head, blowing through wide nostrils. Tansy grabbed his bridle, dancing back out of reach of his hoofs. A flurry of small stones skittered over the edge.

Skir sat up, feeling Perrin's song slow his own drumming heart. 'The Captain's close. But this ravine marks the border.

The other side is Cragonlands.'

Perrin nodded. 'We can't use the bridge.' He shot a look at Tansy. 'We'll have to cross here.'

Tansy threw back her head and glared at him as she hung onto Penthesi's bridle. Her grey eyes were huge in her pale face. 'We? Who's we, Perrin?'

Perrin reached out and gripped her by the shoulders. 'All of us together, just like you said. We're all crossing into Cragonlands. You, me, Skir, Penthesi. All right?'

For an instant they gazed at each other; then Tansy nodded. Perrin let her go and turned to Skir. 'But we can't use the bridge because Rengani soldiers are crawling all over it.'

'Rengani?' said Skir faintly. 'But –'

Perrin swung back to Tansy. 'Can Penthesi jump it?'

'All stirred up like this? You must be joking.'

'Pity you're *not* an ironcrafter,' said Perrin to Skir. 'You could just –' He brought his hands together to mime the sides of the ravine drawing close, then parting again.

'Sorry for the inconvenience,' said Skir bitterly, stabbed once more by his own uselessness.

There was a noise of snapping twigs and distant shouts. Tansy's eyes widened. 'That ain't the Captain. That's more'n one, that's soldiers!'

'Then we have to cross. Now.' Perrin glanced around. 'There! Where the gap's narrow.'

He pointed to a place where the sides of the abyss leaned close together. From the ledge on their own side to the lower clifftop opposite was about the distance of a long, but not impossible, jump. 'But the other side doesn't look very safe. The edge is crumbling away.'

Tansy looked. 'I can jump that easy,' she said at once.

'Let's see you do it then,' said Perrin, and again the challenging look flared between them.

Tansy thrust up her chin, gathered herself and sprang. She landed in a heap on the far side; a small cascade of stones rattled down the cliff-face.

'Easy as jumping a creek,' she said. 'Long as you don't look down.' She held out her hand to Penthesi. 'Come on, darling boy. Step over.'

But Penthesi wouldn't budge. He was hemmed in by the trees.

Tansy looked at Perrin. 'No room to jump.'

'He'll jump if I tell him to,' said Perrin grimly. 'Or we'll leave him behind.'

'No!' said Tansy. 'You said all of us. All of us, right?'

'Right,' said Perrin softly.

Tansy peered down into the depths of the ravine, swallowed, then nodded; *far more concerned*, thought Skir, *with the damn horse's safety than she had been with her own*. She held out her hand again. Without looking at Perrin she said, 'Sing him over then.'

Perrin sang. The chantment made Penthesi's ears prick, and he whinnied. He took one step back, then a step forward. Perrin frowned, stopped singing, then began a different chantment, livelier, more rousing. Penthesi tossed his head and pawed the ground.

Skir was aware of a gathering of muscle, and then the leap: a black blur and a rush of wind. And Penthesi was across, shaking his head as if even he couldn't believe what he'd done, and Tansy threw her arms around his neck and kissed him.

'My turn,' said Perrin. He chewed his lip, kicked off against the side of the cliff, and jumped. He landed hard, half over the brink of the ravine, and his legs thrashed in mid-air, dislodging loose stones from the crumbling edge. Tansy grabbed his arms and hauled him up.

'What, no kiss?' panted Perrin. 'Well, it was worth a try.' But he jammed his hands into his pockets to stop them shaking.

Tansy said in a low voice, 'Reckon that scared you more than the fight at Rarr.'

'Reckon it did,' said Perrin. Their eyes met. 'No going back now.'

Tansy said fiercely, 'There wasn't never any going back.' Her face flushed, and she looked away. 'Now Skir,' she said abruptly.

Skir stood hunched, arms folded. The three figures on the other side seemed very far away. Faintly he heard Perrin say, 'Come on, darling boy.'

The malice drifted past without touching him. Skir advanced to the edge. It was a long way down, much higher than his window at Arvestel. Somewhere far below a creek dashed over rocks.

He only had to step off the cliff. Just one step.

'Don't look down!' Tansy's voice seemed to come to him through a long tunnel. 'You can do it.'

Much sharper was the yell from behind him: 'Over here!' Boots crunched through needles.

Skir swayed. This was his chance, to plunge into nothing. He tried to lift his foot, but he couldn't move. *Useless.* He couldn't even do this.

Then the strangest thing happened: he heard Beeman's voice, warm and clear, as if he were right there in the forest.

Skir!

The three figures on the other side of the ravine wavered

before his eyes; he seemed to see Beeman standing there with them, shaking his head.

Skir, you spend altogether too much time thinking about yourself.

'I can't help it. I'm not brave like Tansy.'

You think it's brave to die? Courage is to go on living.

'I killed that man –'

And if you step off this cliff, you'll have killed another.

'The Witch –'

Superstitious rubbish.

'I'm a fraud. I'm not a chanter like Perrin.'

If there was a mistake, it was the priests' mistake, not yours. You don't have to be a chanter to make use of chantment.

A shiver ran through Skir. He felt light and tingling all over, as if someone had taken a blanket off his head; he was filled with a strange exultant calm. His eyes flicked open and he looked at Perrin. 'Sing me across,' he called.

Perrin's eyes widened. 'I can't. We've already had this discussion.'

Tansy cried, 'Help him, Perrin, just try!'

'Do it!' commanded Skir.

Perrin shot him a look of surprise. 'All right.'

Skir stared straight ahead. Perrin's song began. The chantment quickened, and Skir felt the power of the magic reach for him, and pull. His knees bent beneath him, charged with a strength he didn't know he possessed. Perrin's voice tugged, a wind yanking a kite. *Yes*, thought Skir, and he jumped.

As he flew, he sensed, without seeing it, the void that whistled below. He hung in mid-air, poised between earth and sky, between life and death. For a single heartbeat, the chantment held him, and then the crumbling ground slammed into his face and his chest. Pain radiated from his swollen nose; hands grabbed him and pulled him to his feet. He was safe. He was alive, in Cragonlands. He had crossed the border; not just the border between two lands, but the border between one life and another.

Perrin kicked at the cliff's edge. Stones and chunks of earth rattled to the bottom of the ravine. 'Break it, quick, so they can't follow!'

This was another task that an ironcrafter could have accomplished in moments, but Perrin refrained from saying so. Tansy and Skir stamped at the lip of the abyss. Penthesi struck with his rear hoofs, and the clatter of rocks rose to the thunder of a small avalanche.

Tansy said over and over, 'I knew you could do it, I knew it!'

Skir wondered if she was talking to him or to Perrin, but then her voice faded. A dark tunnel closed around his eyes. His knees buckled and there was roaring in his head. An arm gripped his shoulders. Skir swayed, and tried to lift his head. There was something important he had to say – very important – but the blackness bore down.

Across the ravine, far away, in another country, in Baltimar, was a cloaked figure on horseback. Someone shouted his name. Then the blackness closed over him.

'Put him on Penthesi,' panted Tansy. She held Skir's feet, while Perrin dragged him under the arms.

'Very funny. I can hardly hold him, let alone lift him. He's damn heavy for such a little runt . . .'

Tansy dropped Skir's feet. They were well back from the ravine's edge, hidden behind curtains of needlewood. Tansy wriggled forward through the branches.

'The Captain's riding away,' she reported. 'He's gone.'

'What about the Balts?'

'Still crashing around. Wait. There's something — wait.' The needles clashed softly as Tansy vanished.

A few moments later she returned with needles in her hair and a long scratch on her cheek. 'There's more coming along the bottom of the ravine, about half-a-dozen. Your lot. Ganis.'

'They must have heard all those rocks fall, and come up from the bridge to take a look.' Perrin scrubbed his hands through his hair. 'This is a rotten place to hide. All right for us, but Penthesi . . .'

He didn't say *we should have left him behind*, but Tansy heard it in his voice. She said, 'Pity they can't all see Skir lying here looking dead. Then they'd leave us alone.'

'Tansy,' said Perrin slowly. 'You're a genius. Do you trust me?'

'After today, what do you think? I don't trust you no further than I can spit.'

Perrin grinned. 'That should be just about far enough.' His face was radiant. 'This is going to be magnificent.'

There was only just enough time. Tansy scrambled down to where the cliff jutted out in a rough, wide shelf and lay down in a hollow in the rock.

'Closer to the edge,' hissed Perrin. 'They have to see your hair. Don't move, I'm sending Penthesi down.'

There was a brief silence, then Tansy heard the hesitant

steps of the big horse, and his uneasy breathing as he descended to the ledge. Perrin's chantment, very faint, sounded from above. Of course it had to be faint, so no one else could hear it, but what if Penthesi couldn't hear it either? Tansy felt a wave of fear. Penthesi gazed at her with a troubled expression. He lowered his nose to nuzzle her, and she stifled a gasp as his breath tickled her neck.

'I'm all right,' she whispered. 'Good boy. Just do what Perrin tells you. We both got to trust him.'

Penthesi knelt above her, then lowered his massive bulk on his side. There was just enough room for her to lie in the hollow beneath him. His head lolled over the edge of the rock shelf. He wouldn't be able to lie like that for long, no matter what magic Perrin sang. Nor would she, come to that. Her breath came in shallow gasps. When she breathed in, her chest pressed against the hot, crushing weight of Penthesi's body. If Penthesi rolled even a finger-span, he'd mash her to pulp . . .

Tansy closed her eyes. Perrin's song was soft and sweet as a lullaby. Bright stars flared behind her eyelids, firebursts of lightning, whorls of flame.

Voices. She froze, listening hard. Men's voices floated from the other side of the ravine. High, excited voices. They'd seen them.

'There! Sarge! Down there!'

A low whistle. 'Shame. Nice-looking animal.'

'What's that, Sarge? Underneath.'

Silence. Then: 'Red hair. Kid's got red hair.'

Someone swore. 'Any sign of the others?'

'Nah. The girl wouldn't have made it this far. And if the Gani was dumb enough to jump the border, a patrol'll pick him up.'

A nasty laugh. Tansy forced herself to breathe slowly, to control the flush of anger that threatened to burn her face. It was stiflingly hot beneath Penthesi; sweat trickled down her eyebrows. Her nose prickled. Tansy prayed to every god she could think of, not to let her sneeze. She missed the next few words.

'– retrieve the body?'

Tansy held her breath, heart pounding.

There was the sound of a gob of spittle hitting the forest floor. 'What for? Kid's no good to anyone dead. We're still pretending we've got him tucked up in Arvestel. No one's going to find the poor bastard here. Leave him to the birds.'

Someone shouted: 'All right, men! Keep searching the woods for the Gani.'

Muttered laughter. 'He's long gone, mate. Long gone.'

Tansy heard a whistle, then a sharp cry. The hiss of arrows. A barked command, a clatter of stones. The Renganis down in the ravine had been watching the Baltimaran soldiers. There was a sudden din of shouts, the harsh metallic swish of weapons being drawn. Penthesi shifted uneasily above Tansy as the noise rose and drowned out Perrin's song, and Tansy bit her lip to stop herself crying out.

But now, thank the gods, the sounds faded as the fight shifted further down the ravine. As the noise grew more distant, Perrin's chantment became louder, and Penthesi raised his head. He rolled laboriously onto his knees, then stood, snorting his disdain for the whole human enterprise.

Tansy scrambled from under his shadow. Her arms and legs shook so violently she couldn't stand.

Perrin hissed down to her, 'All right?'

She nodded, but she couldn't speak. She couldn't let him

know how frightened she'd been as she lay in that hollow, with only his frail song between her and the deadly bulk of Penthesi.

'It worked,' said Perrin. 'Your lot have chased my lot back to their boat. Everyone thinks Skir's dead, for now, anyway. Can you hold Penthesi's head, Tansy? I can't see where he should step – that's it. Give me your hand.'

Perrin clasped Tansy's wrist and hauled her up the steep slope, steadying her with both hands. At the top they stood close to each other in the dappled sunlight of late afternoon. Perrin searched her face with his eyes.

'All right? Truly?'

It was the first time Tansy had seen anxiety in those dark blue eyes.

'All right,' she said.

'Have you forgiven me?'

'I don't know yet.'

They stared at each other, on the verge of anger, or something else; then Perrin laughed, and released her. He said solemnly, 'Now then. Skir's dead. Will you tell him, or shall I?'

PART THREE

Cragonlands

CHAPTER 12

Over the Border

I'M HOME, Skir told himself. *This is my homeland*.

His head was aching, and his nose still hurt, but every breath of crystal-cold air seemed to cleanse his lungs and clear his clouded brain. He stared about, trying to match what he saw to his blurred memories.

As soon as Skir had recovered and they emerged from the forest, it was obvious that they'd crossed the border into a different country. Instead of sunny meadows and tall trees, there were stony uplands and dusty mountains, bleak with light. Skir had forgotten the quality of the light: the harsh, metallic sunlight, the brightness of the sky and the shifting veils of cloud around the peaks faintly dusted with snow.

Tansy had been raised among soft grassy hills and gurgling streams; it was hard for her to see the beauty in this rough, unforgiving landscape, though she tried for Skir's sake. The barren land seemed to shoulder her away: not exactly hostile, but supremely indifferent. If Baltimar was swathes of billowing green velvet, then Cragonlands was coarse brown sacking, dumped indifferently down.

They walked. In half a day, Penthesi's coat and their own clothes were grey-brown with dust. They followed a winding road along a valley floor, with low mountains slumped on either side. Cragonlands was a tired country, worn out by fighting.

Squares of pale green flourished here and there on the lower slopes: gardens of chaka-weed, carefully tended by farmers who were now too poor to grow their own food. Instead, the rust-lords paid them to grow chaka-weed, to spread precious dung around its roots, to dribble water over it, to harvest the tender shoots with fingers that bled from chaka-thorns, and to hope that the poison that lurked in the berries didn't seep under their broken skin. Skir thought of Elvie's blind eyes, and other memories returned: a crowded cottage, a boiling pot, the sludge carefully scraped from its rim and dried in the sun to red powder; children with blackened, swollen stumps for hands. If the priests hadn't chosen him, he might have been one of those children.

'Only place in Tremaris that's poorer than Rengan,' said Perrin. 'Makes you wonder why they bother fighting over it.'

'You know why,' said Skir. 'For rust. But I'll put a stop to that.'

'*You'll* put a stop to it?'

'Somehow. If they let me stay,' said Skir. Perrin glanced at him; his eyes were brighter, and there was a glow in his cheeks. Skir quickened his pace, and Perrin dropped back to let him take the lead.

They passed a broken, blackened bridge, and twisted fragments of metal that had been a cannon. The slopes were pock-marked from shelling, scarred and scabbed with black. There had been battles here, years ago, all up and down the border. Now the centre of the conflict was in the north, along the border with Rengan. That was where Perrin had done his fighting.

They walked through a ruined village with few trees and little shade. The houses were mud-brick cubes, roofed with clay tiles; many had been smashed by the fighting. Tansy was startled to see children peering from darkened doorways.

'People still live here!'

'Nowhere else to go,' said Perrin.

'Why don't they fix the houses?'

'They have.' Skir pointed out the makeshift repairs. The villagers had converted the remains of an armoured cart into a roof, stitched Baltimaran Army flour-sacks into a shade-cloth, piled stones together to make a wall. He was proud of his people, their courage, their ingenuity. *Courage is to go on living.* He almost wished someone would recognise him, so he could tell them how he felt. He wished, too, that his homecoming could be the way it ought to be: the triumphant return of the leader from exile, shaking the mountains in rage and vengeance. That was what his people deserved – not this sneaking home with dyed hair and a dirty shirt, as if he were ashamed . . .

He realised with a start that his shame, for what he'd done, and what he was – or rather, what he wasn't – had disappeared. It was as if it had tumbled into the ravine along with their supplies. He still regretted killing the soldier at Rarr, regretted it with his whole heart, but the crippling guilt was gone. And with every step deeper into Cragonlands, Skir was more convinced that he had come to the place he belonged.

They spent the first night in the open, huddled beside the shelter of Penthesi's big, warm body. They ate the last of their food, the scraps they'd carried in their pockets. Everything else was lost.

Skir stared at the familiar pattern of the stars. There were only two moons, both in crescent, and he could see the constellation of the Eagle clearly. He'd never seen that in Arvestel; it was too far south. He felt sick with excitement, and fear, and longing, and impatience. Soon he'd be in Gleve, back in the Temple. Home. But would they let him stay, could he still be a priest? If they threw him out, he might find his home village, the family he could barely remember. What would he do there? He knew so many things, all of them useless. He might go to Rengan with Tansy; Perrin said they needed horse-trainers. He drifted into a dream in which he helped Tansy to break wild colts . . .

In the morning he woke stiff and sore, ready to tell Tansy his dream. But she and Perrin were still asleep. They were leaning into each other under one cloak, with a dusting of snow on their shoulders.

Skir lay down again and drew his coat around him. So that was how it was. He felt as if he'd just noticed something that he should have seen long before. All this time he'd taken it for granted that Tansy was his. Not that she was in love with him, but that she and Skir somehow belonged together, with Perrin on the outside . . . And under his nose things had shifted. Well, he wouldn't let it stay like that; he could make it change. He believed that now.

That day they saw Baltimaran soldiers. They marched in columns beneath blue-and-scarlet banners, or rode in twos and threes on horseback. There was nowhere to take cover, so the three shuffled in the dust as the Cragonlanders did, stooped, heads down. 'We're cousins, walking to the next village,' said Perrin, but no one stopped them. No one asked them anything. The soldiers glanced at them with the casual contempt of the victorious for the conquered, and passed by.

'We're walking like we've been flogged,' said Skir bitterly.

'If they think we look too uppity, we'll *be* flogged,' said Perrin. 'Look down, Tansy. You too, Penthesi, you're a sad old horse.' And Penthesi dropped his head and limped along like a broken-winded old nag.

They walked through one dusty village, then another. The air was bright and cold. They were hungry, but Skir's purse of Baltimaran coins was of no use here. They had nothing to barter, and in any case the villagers looked so poor that perhaps they had no food to offer.

'We must find a temple,' said Skir. 'The priests give hospitality to travellers. Look for a red roof, and bells outside.'

Late in the day, in the fourth village, there was a temple. It was low to the ground, no higher than the tumbledown huts that clustered around it, but its roof-tiles were red, and three bells were arrayed outside on a heavy iron frame.

Skir picked up the little hammer and tapped each bell in turn, and as the last and deepest echo died away, a priest appeared in the doorway. She was about thirty years old, with a thin, lined face. She wore blue robes, and her hair was hidden under a blue cap held in place with a twisted circlet of wire. Her eyes went straight to Skir.

He said, 'We're sorry to trouble you, but we're travellers. We beg food and shelter.'

The priest looked them over, unsmiling. 'By the tenets of the Faith, we must share what we have, little though it is.' She stepped aside. 'My name is Lora. Come in.'

'What about our horse?' said Tansy.

'Bring him, too.'

'We've trained him well,' said Perrin with his most engaging smile. 'He eats less than we do.'

Lora did not smile back. She led them through the wide double doors into the temple yard. As soon as they were inside, she closed the heavy doors and bolted them.

'You do us a discourtesy,' she said at once. Her words were aimed at Skir. 'You bring danger here, and we are defenceless.'

Skir's jaw dropped, but he recovered almost immediately. 'Are strangers no longer welcome in the temples of the Faith?'

'Strangers!' Lora stared at him with her pale blue eyes. 'We turn no one away. But you, My Lord, are no stranger to any temple.'

'Do you know who he is?' said Perrin.

'Of course,' said Lora scornfully. 'If your brother walks into your house, even after ten years away, do you not know him? Should we not know our Priest and King, though he left us so long ago?'

'I didn't leave you,' said Skir. 'I was taken away. It wasn't my choice.'

'We don't want to put you out,' said Tansy sharply. 'We just need some food and a place to sleep. We'll be gone by morning.'

'A place to sleep!' muttered Lora, as if Tansy had asked for the three moons on a platter. She never took her eyes from Skir's face. 'Forgive me, My – My Lord.' The title seemed to catch in her teeth. 'But you cannot stay here. This temple is already under suspicion. If you bring the soldiers here, they will burn it to the ground.'

Tansy began hotly, 'But we –'

Skir put his hand on her arm. 'We have no wish to bring you danger, Lora. If you can spare us some food, we'll leave at once.' He spoke calmly, with authority.

Perrin thought, *By the bones, for once he does sound like a king!*

Even Lora faltered before Skir's steady gaze. 'No, wait. Someone will come tonight who can take you to Gleve.'

'Make up your mind!' said Tansy. 'Can we stay or not?'

'Tansy, remember we're guests here,' said Skir. 'Thank you, Lora. Please have someone bring us food. We'll wait here.'

'Very well, My Lord.' Lora dropped her eyes and walked away.

Perrin let out a long breath. 'Well done.'

Skir shrugged. 'I've had years of lessons in how to talk to – people like her.'

'Officer material,' said Perrin.

Skir half-smiled. 'It's only people like you I don't know how to deal with.'

The temple yard was a square, with a square pool of water in its centre. Skir and the others sat in the shade of a walkway on woven carpets and ate dry bread and yoghurt and chopped fruit. There was hay for Penthesi, but not much.

Perrin said, 'I want to ask you something. At Dody's Leap, when I sang the chantment to you, did it work? Or did you jump by yourself?'

Skir scraped yoghurt from his dish. 'The chantment worked. But only because I – I let it in. I wanted it to work, so it did.'

Perrin looked away at the square pool, narrowing his eyes against the light. 'So if I *had* sung you to sleep on the beach that time, it would have worked after all?'

'Only if I'd wanted it to.'

Tansy said, 'Was that what made you faint? The magic coming into you?'

Skir had his own ideas about why he'd passed out at the edge of the ravine. He sensed it had something to do with the Faith: a darkness had settled him briefly, instead of forever; the merest taste of death, to remind him what he had chosen, and what he had given up. But he wouldn't speak of that in front of Perrin. He shook his head.

Tansy said hastily, 'Let's not talk about it. Perrin, why'd you ask about that anyway? Do you want to know if you could . . . if you could force someone to do something . . . against their will?' She slowly turned pink.

Perrin said, 'There are some things that aren't worth having, unless they're given freely.' He and Tansy exchanged a long look.

Tansy, flushed scarlet, scrambled up and went to see to Penthesi.

Perrin leaned back against the rough mud-brick wall with his arms behind his head. 'Think she loves me?'

'Tansy doesn't love anyone except Penthesi,' said Skir.

'She loves you,' said Perrin.

Skir managed to gaze at him steadily, though his heart had flopped over in his chest.

'Yes, she loves you,' drawled Perrin. 'Like a brother.'

He slid it in as smoothly as a knife between the ribs. Skir said, 'I think Tansy has enough brothers already, don't you?'

'Definitely,' said Perrin.

Skir leaned forward. 'You don't deserve her.'

Perrin's smile faded. 'I know.' There was a pause. 'Has she told you –'

'No,' said Skir coldly. 'She hasn't told me anything.'

'Good,' said Perrin.

The two young men stared at each other, neither of them

willing to be the first to look away. For the first time, Skir thought, Perrin had let his cynical, mocking mask drop; he looked young and vulnerable and somehow naked. But in a flash the mocking mask returned; Perrin laughed, and broke their gaze. 'Hey, Tansy!' he called. 'You want this last slice of melon?' He unfolded himself and prowled away, leaving Skir to feel somehow cheated.

That night a man arrived to take them to Gleve.

Diz towered over all of them, and met Penthesi eye to eye. He had a fearsome moustache, a mane of curling black hair, and a fierce stare. He dropped on one knee to Skir. 'My Lord, we must go quickly. The Balts don't know you're here yet, but it won't be long. The news is spreading though the province like fire.'

'Please, stand up,' said Skir. 'And you mustn't call me Lord. If the Baltimarans don't recognise me yet, they soon will if you carry on like that.'

'Forgive me, My –' Diz swallowed. 'I'll wait outside while you farewell your companions, then we must be off.'

'Whoa there!' said Perrin. 'Who said anything about farewells?'

Almost in the same instant, Skir said firmly, 'These are my friends, the ones who rescued me. Without them, I'd be dead. We travel together, or not at all.'

Skir and Perrin's eyes met; they were both startled.

Diz looked doubtful. 'Even the girl? The Baltimaran?' He spoke as if Tansy wasn't there.

'All of us,' said Skir.

Tansy flared, 'You can trust me.'

'And the horse?'

Tansy grasped Penthesi's bridle. Skir saw her flush, and knew that if she had to choose, she would choose Penthesi. He said, 'The horse comes too.'

Diz scowled.

'Good,' said Perrin briskly. 'All settled. How do we get to Gleve?'

'Across the mountains, a secret way, off the roads. It is safe, but the journey is hard.' He glared at Tansy. 'She might find it difficult.'

Perrin laughed, and clapped Diz on the back; he couldn't reach his shoulder. 'My friend, if you think anything is too tough for Tansy, you're in for a pleasant surprise.'

The journey to Gleve took another half-turn of the moons. Diz was not a talkative man, and his silence spread to the others. They trudged on, lost in their own thoughts. In any case, the mountains robbed them of breath; they had little left for conversation.

Diz knew his way like a bird or a mountain goat; they followed no track that Perrin could see. Diz led them up stony screes and across barren valleys, dry and cold and glaring with sun; he led them as high as the snowline, where gnarled trees reached out from the steep slope like arthritic hands. He led them through an unlit tunnel that threaded deep into the mountain, where Penthesi shied and baulked, and Tansy and Perrin needed all their persuasion to coax him through the narrow passageway. When they emerged at last, the shock of the light drenched them like a bucket of icy water.

Sometimes, far away, Tansy glimpsed another Cragonlands:

a splash of green at the bottom of a valley where irrigated farms squeezed life from the dirt; a thickly wooded slope, basking in sunlight and protected from the cold wind by a fold of the mountains; the deep-blue sparkle of a river, fringed with trees and little cubes of houses.

But Diz kept them well away from any villages or towns. He would not let them light a fire, even on the coldest nights; he would not let them leave behind even a footprint that might betray them. He would not lead them against the horizon, in case their silhouettes showed against the sky; he would not let them sleep all at once. Even in the most isolated places, someone always kept watch.

Diz was part of the Cragonlands resistance. 'One of the insurgents,' said Skir, but Diz drew his terrifying brows together and spat on the ground.

'That's what the Balts call us. Not what we call ourselves. Nor rebels, like the Ganis say. We fight for our own land, against the invaders.' It was the longest speech Diz ever gave.

Diz and his companions were the reason the Baltimaran Army, for all their boasting of victory, could not really claim to have conquered Cragonlands, even after so many years in occupation. The resistance had destroyed the bridge and the cannon they'd passed near the border. The Rengani Army helped them in an uneasy alliance, hoping to gain control of the supply of rust, and thus obtain a powerful weapon against the Baltimarans. But the resistance was wary of Rengan too; they knew the Renganis would invade Cragonlands if they had the chance.

Diz spoke to Perrin more often than the others. He was in awe of Skir, and Tansy was one of the enemy, no matter what she did. But in Perrin he recognised a fellow soldier and an ally, and he gave all the credit for Skir's rescue to the Rengani. When Diz farewelled them on the last night at the hidden rear entrance to the Temple at Gleve, he bowed low to Skir, gave a grudging nod to Tansy and patted Penthesi. But he embraced Perrin like a brother, and Perrin was sorry to see him vanish into the darkness.

The Temple at Gleve was the same shape and layout as the little village temple where they'd rested, but far more impressive. It was higher, three times as high as the buildings of the city that surrounded it, and to enhance its grandeur it was built on a hill that towered over the whole valley. The nine bells outside it were huge, twice the height of Penthesi, and plated with gold, and the roof-tiles were a dazzling scarlet. Bright banners flew from the arches of its portico, and its doors were rimmed with glowing bronze. To see the Temple at Gleve, no one would think that the priests and servants of the Faith were secretly persecuted, or that the Temple was the spiritual heart of a vanquished people.

They learned later that the Baltimarans had deliberately refrained from damaging the Gleve Temple; they'd preserved it in the same spirit in which Skir had been 'invited' to enjoy the King's hospitality at Arvestel. If the invading Army had destroyed their Temple, the Cragonlanders might have risen up in mass rebellion overnight. But by seeming to preserve and even support the Faith, the Baltimarans hoped to win over the people they had defeated.

The priests were shrewd enough to turn this desire to their advantage. Gradually they'd insisted on total control over the Temple grounds, beginning with the sacred inner rooms, then the priests' quarters and courtyards, until the entire Temple precinct was forbidden to the Baltimarans. Only the highest-ranking officers were invited to the Temple, and they had to come alone, without escort.

The priests took advantage of their privacy to shelter resistance activity. They treated insurgents hurt in the fighting, they taught the Signs, they supplied the resistance – though not with weapons. It was whispered that they even made rust and sold it in secret to fund the rebels. The Baltimarans suspected the priests, yet could prove nothing. But it would only take one careless action to smash the whole fragile arrangement.

The Temple's secret door was opened by a timid-faced female priest in blue robes. 'Welcome home, My Lord.'

But she spoke to Perrin, not Skir. Perrin flashed her his disarming, crinkle-eyed grin. 'Thank you. But your Lord is standing behind me.'

'My Lord, forgive me,' stammered the priest. She stood back to allow Tansy to lead Penthesi into the dark passageway. 'I couldn't see . . .'

'It doesn't matter,' said Skir. 'It doesn't *matter*. By the bones, show Tansy somewhere to put her horse and let's get on with it.' He twisted his hands together; now that the moment was finally here, he was shivering with nerves.

'This way, follow me. The horse . . . Errett will show you to the stables.' She beckoned to a man standing in the shadows.

'I'll go and settle him in,' said Tansy. 'Where will you be?'

Skir looked around at the warren of corridors and darkened rooms. The priest held a lamp, and shadows leaped and trembled on the high stone walls. Skir said, 'I don't know where we are.'

'The throne room is this way.' The priest gestured. 'Bettenwey is waiting.'

'So he is alive?' *Well, obviously*, Skir added to himself in a savage undertone. 'Come on then.' He strode away into the dark, and the priest scurried after him with her lantern.

Perrin touched Tansy's hand. 'Don't be long.'

He hurried after Skir and the priest, but they set such a rapid pace that he couldn't catch them. He was always one corner behind, just glimpsing the priest's blue robes as they whisked around another bend, or vanished through another high, brass-studded door. He was aware of people watching in the dark, peering from doorways. He could hear whispers and soft footfalls, but he could see no one clearly. The Temple seemed to be thick with invisible, phantom inhabitants.

At last Perrin turned a corner and found himself in a high, wide room. Compared with the darkness of the rest of the Temple, it blazed with light. The priest bowed and withdrew, and Perrin walked slowly forward between pillars lined with bronze. The floor was laid with dark mosaic tiles that reflected the lamps set high on the walls, so Perrin seemed to walk between pools of shimmering fire. The walls were hung with sheets of dull metal, etched with strange symbols – not the Signs, as Perrin quickly realised when he tried to read them, but mysterious designs that swirled like dust in the wind, or the clouds that streamed from the mountain tops, or the curls of a river along a valley floor.

In spite of himself, Perrin was awed by the Temple. He'd never been anywhere so vast – except Arvestel. It was strange to think that Skir was Lord of this place. He realised that, through all their journey, he'd never taken Skir and his fretting seriously; he'd thought of him as a spoiled kid, a naïve drafty. Only now, seeing this place, did he appreciate that Skir's responsibilities were real.

At the far end of the room stood a group of high-backed

chairs, placed apparently at random: for a throne room, Perrin thought, there was a remarkable absence of thrones. It was a great cold bare hall that glimmered with broken light, filled with mirrored flames, and echoing with voices and footsteps. It took Perrin a moment or two to find the small, slight figure of Skir. The dye had faded at last, and his red hair reflected the fire that hung from the walls. He faced a man who rose from one of the high-backed chairs as Skir entered.

Perrin had expected the High Priest to be a doddering old man. Instead he saw a smooth-faced man of about forty, with dark intelligent eyes, a strong nose, and quick, decisive movements. His head was hairless, polished like a copper bowl, and he wore a thin strand of twisted bronze wire across his forehead. He advanced toward Skir with his hands outstretched to clasp those of the Priest-King. As if they were equals, thought Perrin; but then, he realised at once, Bettenwey had been in charge here for a long time.

'My Lord Eskirenwey. Be welcome in your home.' Bettenwey pressed Skir's hands in his, then embraced him chest-to-chest. Skir pulled away uncomfortably, and Bettenwey turned to Perrin. 'I bid you welcome, too, Swordsman. And where is your Baltimaran friend, the one called Tansy?'

'You know everything about us.' Perrin stepped forward to shake hands. Bettenwey smiled, and Perrin saw a shrewd man, a clever man, no fool. Of course, that didn't mean he was a friend. He wondered if Skir realised that.

'I don't know quite everything.' Bettenwey motioned them to sit. Again, the gesture struck Perrin: who was master here?

Skir said, 'Tansy is seeing to her horse. Or rather, the horse we borrowed from the King of Baltimar.'

'Ah, yes.' Bettenwey settled back in his chair. 'You must tell me the tale of your adventures another time. Please sit, My Lord. Etiquette forbids that we should sit in your presence if you do not. Would you make boors of us?'

It was a light reproof, but still a reproof, and Skir felt it like the sting of a slap. It was on the tip of his tongue to order Bettenwey to his feet again, but he bit back the words. Instead, he forced a smile as he sat down. 'I've lived without etiquette since I left Arvestel. It's been a refreshing change to have only friends around me.'

Bettenwey inclined his head. 'Baltimar's daughter, Rengan's son, and the Priest-King. For that reason alone, a remarkable journey. Remarkable, and unexpected. Your superiors, Swordsman Perrin, were very considerate. If we had known that our Priest-King was wandering unprotected through Baltimar and the border territories, think of our concern.'

'The Renganis didn't inform you of their rescue plan?' Skir turned a puzzled gaze to Perrin.

Perrin's heart skipped. So Tansy hadn't told him. Tansy, who couldn't tell a lie, had kept the truth from Skir for his sake. He said quickly, 'Rengani High Command wanted to take the Priest-King hostage for themselves. But I helped Skir to come home instead. He was not unprotected.'

Perrin saw Skir frown, then smooth his face. His swift glance at Perrin said, *We'll talk about this later.*

'A loyal friend.' Bettenwey measured Perrin with his eyes. 'Though not loyal to his own people.'

'I can't win, can I?' said Perrin mildly. 'I'm sure you wouldn't have been pleased if I'd taken Skir to Rengan. But because I've brought him here, you don't trust me.'

Skir said loudly, 'He's loyal to *me*. That's what matters.'

And again Skir and Perrin glanced at each other, startled by their own words.

Bettenwey said, 'And the girl? She is loyal, too?'

'Tansy? I've never known anyone more loyal in my life,' said Skir, and Tansy came into the room in time to hear him say it.

'Here is Baltimar's daughter herself. I trust the horse is comfortable? Good. Please, Tansy, join us, sit down. May I have your hands?'

The four of them were seated in a circle; leaning forward awkwardly, they could just about touch hands. Bettenwey gripped their fingers strongly, flung his head back and proclaimed, 'Three strands in the rope. The strength of the Threelands is in you all. You have brought back Our Lord to us, and for that you will always have our thanks.'

Skir pulled his hands away, and clutched the arms of the chair. There was no one else in the room but Bettenwey and Perrin and Tansy, nothing but flickering shadows and pools of deep dark. He must speak now; he must confess.

But already the moment was lost. Bettenwey rose to his feet. 'Forgive me, My Lord, my new friends. You are tired and hungry, and I have kept you here talking. We will speak again tomorrow. Supper and your beds await.' The High Priest clapped his hands and a silent servant appeared and gestured to them to follow.

'Goodnight,' said Perrin, standing up.

'Goodnight,' echoed Tansy.

Skir rose, and hesitated. Would he go with Tansy and Perrin, or join Bettenwey in the priests' quarters? Somehow he knew that this choice was a crucial one; that his whole future hinged on it. For a moment it seemed obvious that Perrin was right: if he chose to say nothing, Bettenwey and the rest would accept him as Priest-King as they always had. It would be easy . . .

But then he remembered. How could he have forgotten? There was more to being Priest-King than saying the right words and wearing the Circle of Attar. He had no chantment in him. He couldn't be Priest-King even if he wanted to . . .

And Skir knew that he did want to. Ever since he'd crossed the border, he'd grown more certain, and now, just as he was about to give it up, he realised that he wanted it very much indeed. He felt like Tansy, fighting for the first time after rehearsing all her life. It wasn't what he'd expected; he wasn't sure he liked it. But he knew he could do it, and do it well.

And yet he didn't want to leave Tansy and Perrin alone together. To let Perrin have her was to admit defeat. He wasn't ready to give up . . .

Bettenwey was waiting for him. 'My Lord Eskirenwey. We have kept your old room as you left it. Do you remember the way?'

Skir looked at the others. Perrin wore his lazy grin; Tansy watched him anxiously. After what seemed like a long silence, but lasted only a breath, Skir said, 'Thank you, Bettenwey. I'll follow you.'

CHAPTER 13

Broken Fire

SKIR'S room was just as he'd left it five years before, though it seemed much smaller than he remembered. There was the narrow bed with its warm orange coverlet, the round rug, even the shelf of toys: a bat and ball, a spinning top, a box of marbles. It could have been any child's room. But on the other wall, a row of hooks hung with ceremonial robes declared that this was also the room of the Priest-King of Cragonlands.

Skir ran his hand down an embroidered edge. Even his vests in Arvestel were more delicately stitched than this rough ribbon, but he touched it reverently. The robes were small; they wouldn't fit him any more.

Bettenwey watched him. 'Memories?'

'Yes,' said Skir. 'Lots of memories.' He dropped his hand. 'Bettenwey, I must talk to you.'

Bettenwey raised a hand to silence him. He checked the corridor outside, then shut the door firmly. 'We must be careful, even here.'

'Just like Arvestel,' said Skir. 'Beeman always –' He stopped.

'Your tutor sent us regular reports on your welfare,' said Bettenwey. 'But we have had no word from him since the beginning of summer.'

Skir's heart sank. 'Isn't there any way we can help him?'

'We could not extricate you, My Lord. I fear there is nothing we can do for your tutor.' Bettenwey sounded regretful, but not overly upset.

That's one thing I can do. I'll go back and rescue him myself, thought Skir. *If I'm not allowed to be Priest-King any more.* He said in a rush, 'Bettenwey, there is something I have to tell you. On the way here we were attacked by Baltimaran soldiers. During the fighting, I – I killed one of them.'

Bettenwey sighed. 'That is very sad, very regrettable. Unfortunately accidents happen in times of war. I am sorry if you have suffered over it, My Lord.'

'No – no. That's not the point. I mean – I've taken a life. A Priest-King who breaks the Faith – well, he can't go on being Priest-King, can he?'

A strange expression flickered over Bettenwey's face. He seemed almost annoyed. 'Not at all. As I said, this is a time of war. You fought to defend your own life, did you not? There must be a ceremony of cleansing, of course. I will arrange it for tomorrow, if you wish. But in the long term, it need not interfere with your duties.'

Bettenwey stared at Skir with his bright dark eyes, his hands clasped inside his sleeves. Skir was bewildered. He had agonised over this for so long, and the High Priest had brushed it aside as if Skir had done nothing more serious than accidentally step on a beetle. Perrin was right all along: no one cared. In a vivid flash of memory, Skir saw the young soldier's face. He told himself fiercely, *But I care!*

Bettenwey said blandly, 'Is there anything else, My Lord?'

'Yes,' said Skir. 'You know there is. How can I be Priest-King? I'm not a chanter. You all thought I might grow into it, but I haven't. I'll never be able to sing the chantments of iron. I should never have been chosen. I'm a fraud.'

Bettenwey closed his eyes, and sighed. Then he said, 'Sit down, Skir.' It was the first time he'd used the familiar form of Skir's name.

Skir sat on the bed. Bettenwey drew up a chair, closer than Skir would have liked, and stared into his face. 'Listen to me. We will have this conversation once, and once only, then we will never speak of it again. Do you understand?'

Mutely, Skir nodded.

Bettenwey spoke slowly and deliberately. 'There was no mistake. You were chosen as Priest-King, and that choice cannot be unmade. You are Priest-King until the day you die. There is no release, no escape, no loophole. Do you understand?'

'But I didn't mean –'

'I said, *Do you understand?*' Bettenwey's face was dark as thunder. 'You are not *supposed* to have any power. The Council of Priests rules Cragonlands, as it has always done. If you prove yourself worthy, one day, you may participate in the decisions of the Council, but until that day your role is purely ceremonial. If your guardian did not make that clear to you, then he has done both you and us a grave disservice.'

'But the chantments –' stammered Skir. 'The magic –'

Bettenwey gave a short, sharp laugh. 'Trickery, that's all. There is no magic in the Threelands. Chantment comes from the Westlands, it does not belong here. We may have a use for the Singer of All Songs and her chanters in time, but that is none of your concern.'

Skir was reeling. None of this made sense. The ground had opened beneath his feet and he was falling, falling. *No chantment – trickery – purely ceremonial – a grave disservice –* He forced himself to listen to Bettenwey.

The High Priest said, 'Has it occurred to you that your arrival may not have been convenient for us?'

'Not – not *convenient*?'

'We have plans afoot, complicated plans. It may be possible to use your return to our advantage, but we have little time to work with. Why did you not send us word from Baltimar? We could have given you instructions. You should have stayed in hiding until we were ready. Now there are whispers the length and breadth of Cragonlands. The Baltimarans are suspicious. They have tightened patrols along the border, too late to catch you, of course, but it has caused us problems. Three of our agents have died as a result of your thoughtlessness. Do you wish to be cleansed of those deaths, too? You have acted like a child, Skir. You think only of yourself. You do not understand the least part of how the world works.'

Skir stared into Bettenwey's dark, furious eyes. All trace of warmth was gone. Skir was aware of a dull ache in his stomach, a deep throb of anger. He said tightly, 'Would you rather I hadn't come back at all?'

'Yes, frankly. Your sneaking back here has created all kinds of trouble for us. And to cap it all, you bring that Rengani petticoat and a Baltimaran whore with you!'

Skir stood up. 'Get out of my room.'

Bettenwey rose to his feet. For a long moment they stared at each other, then Bettenwey bowed coldly. 'My Lord.' With a swish of robes, he swept from the room and slammed the door.

Skir sank onto the bed and buried his head in his hands.

'Welcome home, My Lord!' He began to laugh, and the laugh became a hard, hiccupping series of sobs. After a time, the candle by his bed flickered and died, and the darkness reared up to engulf him.

'It's all right,' said Perrin to Tansy as soon as they were alone. 'He's going to confess to the High Priest. Couldn't you see it in his face? He wanted to do it in private.'

'Oh . . .' Tansy let out a long breath. 'I thought he didn't want to be friends with us no more. Too grand for us now.'

'If they make him give all this up, I wonder if they'll pay him compensation?'

Perrin wandered about the room they'd been given. It was a large, square room in the priests' wing, not far from the stables, pleasantly, but not luxuriously, furnished. A pair of shuttered double doors faced an internal courtyard. There was a low table on which a simple supper had been laid, and several chairs. Two wide beds were set against opposite walls. Perrin dived onto one of them. 'A bed at last! Do you know the last time I slept in a proper bed?'

'I ain't slept in a bed since Elvie's,' said Tansy.

Perrin stopped bouncing. 'I wonder where she is now.'

'Gone back to Wanion, I'll bet. She were tougher than she looked, that one.' Tansy picked up a leafy stalk from an earthenware plate and regarded it doubtfully. 'We meant to eat this? Or is it just decoration?'

'They don't seem to go in much for decoration round here. Now what I want is a place to wash.' Perrin prowled across the room and flung open a door.

'Aah!' he said, with deep satisfaction. 'A bathroom. *And* a jug of warm water. Not as good as a tub, but it'll do. Excuse me.'

Tansy picked at the supper plate, but she had little appetite. When Perrin emerged, pinkly scrubbed and fresh-shaven, she said rather wistfully, 'Think Skir'll come along to say goodnight?'

'I doubt it.' Perrin sat beside her, towelling his hair. 'He and that High Priest will have plenty to talk about. Don't look so grim, Tansy! We've got food, and comfy beds, and a bathroom – a *bathroom!* Enjoy it while it lasts – who knows where we'll be tomorrow. One day at a time, that's my motto.'

'I know,' said Tansy. 'I wish I was like you.'

Perrin laid down the towel, suddenly serious. 'Don't wish that, Tansy. I wish I could be more like *you*.'

'Me? Why?'

'Because you're brave, and loyal, and quick-thinking.'

'You're quick, too,' said Tansy. 'And brave.'

Perrin laughed. 'But not loyal. Even Bettenwey could see that. I envy you. And Skir, too. I wish I . . .' He went on slowly, thinking it out as he spoke. 'I wish I knew what to think, how to feel, how to act. I do things because I can, not because I should. But you always know what's right.'

'Not always,' said Tansy. 'I didn't know if I should tell Skir about you taking him back to Rengan. I didn't want to lie, but – I didn't want him to think bad of you.'

'He knows now. I told him.'

Tansy's face lit up. 'Oh – good! That's what I wanted. Did he – was he angry?'

'He'll get over it. Let's not talk about Skir. Let's talk about me.'

'How you only think about yourself?'

They both smiled. Perrin touched her hair, then took his

hand away. Their heads were close together now, the dark and the fair.

Perrin said softly, 'I'm not thinking about myself now.'

'I ain't so sure about that,' said Tansy dryly.

'Be brave, Tansy,' whispered Perrin.

She leaned across the space between them, and kissed him.

In the morning, Perrin flung open the double doors and let the fresh cold sunlight stream into the room through the ironwork grille. He came back to sit on the edge of the bed.

'Hello,' he said softly.

'Hello.'

'Still hate me?'

'Hmmm.' Tansy reached up to touch his face. 'Let me think about it.'

Much later, they had begun their breakfast of hard-boiled eggs and stewed peppers and hot coffee when there was a rapping at the door. A servant announced, 'Rise for My Lord Bettenwey.'

Automatically, Tansy and Perrin scrambled up, but when the High Priest entered he motioned to them to be seated.

'Please, go on with your breakfast. I will not trouble you for long.'

Tansy was frightened by Bettenwey. Timidly she said, 'We was wondering if Skir – if the Priest-King could have breakfast with us.'

'Is he still the Priest-King?' asked Perrin casually.

Bettenwey looked at him coolly. 'Of course. Why would he not be?'

'That's what I told him. I knew it'd be all right.' Perrin looked smug.

'Unfortunately, My Lord Eskirenwey's arrival, though of course welcome, was – ill-timed.' said Bettenway. 'This is what I wish to discuss with you. I'm afraid I must ask for your patience. My Lord Eskirenwey's return cannot be announced until the appropriate moment. Until that moment arrives, we must keep his presence here secret. I'm sure you understand.'

'All right,' said Tansy doubtfully.

'Hold on,' said Perrin. 'How are you going to keep it secret from people who visit the Temple?'

'My Lord Eskirenwey has agreed to remain in his room until further notice. I'm sure that his friends will also respect the necessity for discretion?'

Perrin whistled. 'You're locking us in? Indefinitely?'

'For a short while only.' Bettenway stood. 'I knew I could rely upon your intelligence.'

Tansy jumped up. 'What about Penthesi? He'll fret if he don't see us!'

'The horse will be well cared for.'

Perrin said, 'Can't we at least see Skir?'

'I'm afraid that will not be possible.' The High Priest withdrew toward the door. 'Your co-operation is appreciated. Please regard yourselves as our honoured guests.'

The door closed behind Bettenway. Perrin looked at Tansy. 'Honoured guests, my backside. Prisoners, more like.'

Tansy said, 'Gives me shivers up my spine, that Bettenway. Near as bad as Lady Wanion.'

'He's a smart man.' Perrin prowled across the room and yanked the door open; a pair of armed servants barred the corridor. Perrin saluted them, and shut the door. 'Just checking . . .' He threw himself down on the rumpled bed and patted the space beside him. 'You know, it might not be so bad, being locked up in here all day.'

'You mind your manners,' said Tansy, reaching for her coffee cup. 'I ain't finished my breakfast.'

The next few days passed in blank misery for Skir. He was more of a prisoner here, in the only home he could remember, than he had been at Arvestel, among strangers. At least at Arvestel he was free to walk outside; he'd had his painting, conversations, music, light and air and luxury . . . All the things he thought he despised about Baltimar turned out to be the things he missed most.

No. What he missed most was Beeman.

After their argument on the first night, Skir and Bettenwey maintained a cold civility. They were never alone together. They had one disagreement, in Skir's only secret meeting with the Council of Priests, when he learned that Tansy and Perrin were locked up too. He insisted that they be freed, at least within the Temple walls, and Bettenwey backed down. They would be permitted to move about inside the Temple precinct, so long as they spoke to no one.

Skir longed to see them, especially Tansy. He felt like a shadow of a person, drifting around his sparsely furnished room. Outside the Temple, with Tansy and Perrin, he had been real. How long could Bettenwey keep him here? What was he waiting for?

Then one day Skir found out.

Starved for company, he had struck up a tentative friendship with the servant who brought his meals. At first Ulia was too awestruck to speak, but gradually she began to tell him scraps of gossip from the kitchens. 'There are rumours all over Gleve, My Lord. Some say you're here in the Temple, and some say you're dead.'

Skir shovelled eggs onto his fork without comment. He had begun to wonder if Bettenwey planned to murder him in his bed. Then both rumours would be true. 'Have you seen the two who brought me here?'

'The two foreigners? Yes, I've seen them, My Lord.' She gave a sly smile. 'He's a charmer, that lad, isn't he? Reckon I might have more news of them, come tomorrow. You wait and see.'

Perhaps Perrin would use the Signs to send a message with Ulia, thought Skir. But the next day it was a priest who brought his breakfast tray, the same timid-faced woman who had let them into the Temple.

'Where's Ulia?'

'She cannot wait on you today, My Lord.'

'Why not? Is she ill?'

'She – she has been whipped, My Lord, on the High Priest's order.'

'*What?* What for?'

'She was weak, and disobedient. She spoke with the foreigners. She plotted to help them meet you, against the High Priest's specific instructions.'

Skir threw down his knife and fork. 'And she was whipped for that?' He dragged on the dark blue tunic that marked him as a high-ranking priest and jammed the twisted copper wire, the Circle of Attar, onto his head.

'What are you doing, My Lord?'

'I'm going to speak to Bettenwey,' said Skir grimly. He pounded on the door. 'Take me to him at once.'

The servants who guarded him lowered their staffs and looked questioningly at the priest.

'It is forbidden, My Lord,' she said.

Skir glared at her. 'You'd follow the orders of the High Priest rather than the orders of your Priest-King? I'll be Priest-King here long after Bettenwey has gone to his next life, and I have an excellent memory. Take me to him now, or you'll regret it.'

The woman twisted her hands together. 'My Lord – the High Priest is taking the morning prayer.'

'Then I'll wait in his rooms.'

Her eyes darted nervously down the corridor.

Skir said, 'I'm not going to run around all over the Temple. And you can't stop the Priest-King from seeing the High Priest.'

A moment later Skir was marching down the corridor after the priest with the two servants at his heels, and a moment after that he'd banged the doors closed and shut himself in Bettenwey's empty room.

The High Priest's quarters were far larger than Skir's own, almost as big as Skir's sitting-room at Arvestel. It gave Skir a perverse satisfaction to see that Bettenwey was even more untidy than he was. The bed was unmade, robes and shirts lay crumpled on the floor, and a big table by the wall was strewn with parchment scrolls. Skir paced up and down. It was a relief just to have a larger space to walk about in.

He glanced at the scrolls that lay on the table. Temple business, tedious matters of protocol, the minutes of boring committee meetings . . . Then he froze in shock. He re-read the Signs, unable to believe what he saw. But there was no mistake.

When Bettenwey returned from the morning prayer, Skir was standing by the window with the scroll in his hand. 'Shut the door,' he said.

'My Lord, may I ask why you are in my room?'

'Shut the door. What is this?'

'Those papers are records of Temple business, and no concern of yours, even if you could read them.'

'Surely Temple business *is* my business. And I can read them. Fascinating stuff.'

Now it was Bettenwey's turn to freeze. 'My Lord?'

'Beeman taught me to read the Signs. You must have known that.'

'He was not instructed . . . I don't believe –'

Skir read from the scroll. 'Operation Broken Fire. The operation will take place on the first day of autumn.'

Bettenwey tried to snatch the parchment from Skir's hand. 'That is private; it should not have been left lying about.'

'I'll bet,' said Skir grimly, holding the scroll out of reach. 'Careless of you. Still, no one can read it except me, and the Council. Do they know about this?'

'The formal approval of the Council of Priests has not yet been sought.'

'Because you know they'd never agree to it. What is Broken Fire? Some kind of explosive? How many people do you think will be killed by this scheme of yours?'

'Some casualties will be unavoidable.'

'I thought the priests helped the resistance with sabotage, destroying roads and bridges. Not mass murder!'

A look of irritation passed over Bettenwey's face. 'My Lord

Eskirenwey, if you are going to spy upon matters that don't concern you, you should at least attempt to understand the situation.'

'True.' Skir folded his arms. 'You explain it.'

Bettenwey took a deep breath. 'Your disappearance from Arvestel has brought about a crisis in relations between Baltimar and Rengan. The Baltimarans can no longer sustain their military involvement in Cragonlands. They are willing to compromise over territory with Rengan on condition that the border skirmishes cease.'

Skir stared. 'They're going to end the war? But that's good!'

'No, you fool. They plan to carve up Cragonlands between them. There will be secret talks between the Baltimaran Colonial Administration and the Rengani High Command to work out who gets what. The talks will be held at the White Pavilion in the Old Quarter of Gleve, beginning on the first day of autumn.'

'But that's . . .' Skir calculated. 'Four days from now!'

'Three days,' corrected Bettenwey. 'And I am going to stop them.'

'You're going to blow them up,' said Skir. He crumpled the scroll in his hand. 'And then – *then* you'll announce that I've come back. That I did it.' Skir's face was white with anger. He recited from the parchment: '*There may be unavoidable civilian casualties.* You mean it could kill other people – not just the soldiers and the politicians at the talks, but people living near the White Pavilion, innocent people, citizens of Gleve! I won't have mass slaughter committed in my name.'

Bettenwey clenched his teeth. 'Eskirenwey, do you not see the opportunity presented here? This is the chance we have waited for all these years. We will strike at the Baltimarans, who invaded us –'

'Baltimarans like Tansy.'

'And at the Renganis, who have exploited us –'

'Renganis like Perrin.'

'The symbolic importance of the blow cannot be under-estimated. This is only the first step. It will begin a mass uprising. The people of Cragonlands will throw off their oppressors. At last we will have true independence. With the help of the chanters.'

'What chanters? There's nothing about chanters here.'

'We will send for chanters from the Westlands to help us. They have built their power in the years of the Rising. Now it is time for the Singer to show what she can do.'

'But you said chanters don't belong here! Why would they help us?'

Bettenwey bared his teeth in a wolfish smile. 'Oh, I think they will. They don't belong here, but we can use them.'

'Just as you want to use me,' said Skir bitterly. 'Well, I won't do it.'

'Do what? My Lord Eskirenwey, it is not necessary for you to *do* anything. This plan will proceed with or without your co-operation.'

'I won't allow it.' Skir crumpled the scroll with both hands. Bettenwey stepped forward and gently prised it from his fingers.

'My Lord,' he said, almost in a whisper. 'I suggest you think about this carefully. Very carefully indeed. I told you once before, accidents happen in times of war. It would be dreadful if one were to happen to you. Now please, return to your room. I have work to do.'

CHAPTER 14

The Evening Prayer

'IT ain't good for Penthesi, cooped up in the stables all the time,' said Tansy. She and Perrin sat in the thick shade in one of the inner courtyards. A priest walked briskly past and frowned at them; the Cragonlanders disapproved of idleness, and even more of idle foreigners. Tansy stuck out her tongue at his blue-clad back.

'Being cooped up isn't good for us, either,' Perrin pointed out. 'Or Skir.'

'I wonder why Ulia didn't turn up today,' said Tansy. 'Hope she ain't in no trouble.'

'Probably just too busy. She'll come tomorrow.'

'We got to talk to Skir. Got to find a way.'

Perrin gave her a searching look. 'Do you want to tell him about us?'

'No,' admitted Tansy. 'But I guess we should.'

'You do realise he's got a crush on you?'

'No he ain't! Don't be daft.' But Tansy's face had flushed pink. 'We're friends, that's all. I always said that.'

'I know that's what you *said*. That's what he'd say, too – but that doesn't make it true.'

'Surely Bettenwey'll let us go soon,' said Tansy, changing the subject.

Perrin pulled a gloomy face. 'Let us go – where? I can't go back to Rengan, you can't go back to Baltimar. And I'm sure Bettenwey won't let us stay in Cragonlands.'

'It ain't up to him. That's for Skir to say.'

'If you haven't noticed, Skir doesn't actually run this place. Bettenwey does, and I'll bet you five gold pieces he has us shooed over the border faster than Penthesi can gallop. *Which* border, that's the question ... There's only one solution. You can head north and become a horse-breaker in Rengan, and I'll go back to Baltimar and be a wandering minstrel.'

'You'll need another finger-harp, for the one you lost at Dody's Leap. And the Baltimarans would arrest you, too.'

'I'll grow a beard.' Perrin stretched his arms above his head and said abruptly, 'Speaking of music, let's go to the evening prayer and listen to some. It's almost sunset.'

The dawn and evening prayer ceremonies were held in a great hall. As in the throne room, the pillars were cased in beaten metal, and the floor was tiled; but while the throne room was enclosed and lit with torches, a room that belonged to the night, the Hall of the Faith, was open on two sides to allow the sun to stream in at sunrise and sunset, and the air danced with motes of gold. The people of Gleve flocked there to hear the twice-daily prayers and to make their own devotions, and the hall thrummed with shuffling feet and the rustle of bodies as men and women kneeled and rose and kneeled again.

Perrin and Tansy found their usual place in the gallery at the back of the Hall, where they were permitted to observe. With little else to do, they'd fallen into the habit of attending the prayer ceremonies, and had enjoyed them more than they'd expected. Tansy leaned over the rail with her hands clasped. Bettenwey stood in the ranks of priests on the platform. He was slightly built, flanked by burlier men, but his gaze seemed to pierce every person in the Hall. He glanced up at the gallery and his eyes glittered a warning at Tansy. Tansy shifted uneasily.

When Bettenwey stepped forward to speak, the murmurs and rustles died away. Even the smallest children fell quiet. The sounds of Gleve drifted over the Temple walls on the late summer air: the last calls from the market, the rattle of carts, the plaintive bleats of backyard goats begging to be milked.

Bettenwey's voice rang out like the deep chime of a temple bell, with the rich singsong intonation of well-worn ritual. Tansy remembered the night Skir had burned Elvie's luckpiece, and the words he'd spoken over Sedge. She shivered. It must have been Bettenwey who taught him to speak like that.

'Sisters and brothers of the Faith, hear my prayer.'

The response rippled through the crowd: 'Our brother, we pray with you.'

'Earth beneath our feet, air upon our faces. Water in my left hand, fire in my right.'

The impassive priests placed the ceremonial vessels in Bettenwey's outstretched hands and he raised them high.

'We give thanks for life and breath in this day that has passed. We pray for warmth and safety in the night to come. By light and by dark, we uphold the Faith.'

'We uphold the Faith,' came the murmur of five hundred voices, and Tansy found herself whispering, *uphold the Faith*. Perrin sat with his head bowed as the music of the exchange flowed through him.

A single bell clanged, slow and rhythmic.

'Sisters and brothers, take hands.'

All through the Hall, men and women reached out to clasp the hands of the strangers or loved ones beside them.

'Sisters and brothers, give your strength in this time of hardship. Sisters and brothers, take strength now from one another. Let us pray together for better times. Let us create those better times together.'

And the crowd responded, 'We will work together.'

The bell ceased, and the crowd stood in silence, heads bowed and hands clasped. Tansy watched Bettenwey as he watched the crowd, judging the moment to break the silence: too short, and its solemn power had no chance to build; too long, and people would cough and fidget. At precisely the right moment, Bettenwey's voice rang out.

'Sisters and brothers! We give thanks –'

The High Priest paused, then frowned. There was a disturbance at the back of the Hall, under the gallery. Tansy leaned over, but all she could see was a wave of movement that compressed the crowd as someone tried to force their way forward. Blue-robed figures streamed along the edges of the Hall to the site of the scuffle. Bettenwey spoke, and now his voice was both nervous and angry.

'For friends who know how to be silent, we give thanks! For those who give help *when it is asked of them*, we give thanks! For these and all our blessings, we give thanks.'

Perrin hung so far over the rail that he was almost upside down. The crowd had held back the person trying to push forward; now blue-robed priests flowed into the spaces in the crowd and clustered around a tall man. He had long brown hair tied back, and a drooping moustache; a grey-brown cloak was draped over his shoulders. For an instant, his eyes met

Perrin's. Then one of the priests threw a blanket over his head, and he was borne, struggling, away.

'Tansy!' whispered Perrin sharply. 'It's him – the Captain! Wanion's man!'

'*Here?*' Tansy jumped up.

'Sisters and brothers of the Faith!' Bettenwey's voice rang out loudly. Slowly the hubbub in the Hall subsided; the crowd, which had bunched into knots and tangles, smoothed out again into its former lines, a little more ragged than before.

'Sisters and brothers, we ask for these three things ...' Bettenwey continued the ceremony, but Tansy and Perrin were running downstairs from the gallery and out into the courtyard.

The would-be assassin was surrounded by blue-clad figures. The Captain struggled silently beneath the blanket as the priests half-pushed, half-carried him across the courtyard and inside, into the warren of rooms in the priests' quarter. Perrin sprinted after them, with Tansy at his heels, and they plunged into the cool dark of the priests' wing.

They could hear furious voices. Someone had taken the blanket off the Captain's head.

'I must see him!'

'– disrupting our prayers – disrespectful –'

'– the High Priest –'

There was a final, convulsive struggle in the half-light as the Captain threw them off. Like a beast at bay, he faced a circle of wary, dishevelled priests ready to pounce again. Everyone was breathing hard. The Captain glared beyond the circle to Perrin and Tansy. When he spoke, it was to them.

'They won't let me see Skir.'

Tansy yelped; her hand twisted into Perrin's shirt to hold

him back. But Perrin edged forward, holding the man's gaze, as he would have approached a wild dog. The Captain had steady blue eyes.

Tansy cried, 'You stay away from Skir! Don't you dare hurt him!'

'I want to speak to him, that's all. And I'm sure he wants to speak to me.'

One of the priests said, 'It is not permitted.' He snapped his fingers at a passing servant. 'When the evening prayer is ended, fetch the High Priest. Tell him Beeman has come.'

'He already knows,' said the Captain dryly. 'Didn't you hear him in the Hall, praying for me to mind my own business?'

Tansy gasped. '*You're* Beeman?'

Perrin began to laugh. Tansy's grip on his shirt tightened, but Perrin said softly, 'It's all right, Tansy.'

Tansy cried, 'Why didn't you say nothing, at the border?'

'I did. I called to Skir, I was sure he heard me. But then he fainted and you dragged him away.' Beeman gazed at them intently. 'You're his friends. You brought him here.'

'Probably more accurate to say that he brought us.' Perrin's dark blue eyes flickered to a door on the right of the corridor; Beeman understood. The priests were muttering together, craning anxiously for Bettenwey; just for a moment, their attention lapsed.

'Now!' shouted Perrin, and darted for the door. Beeman ducked beneath someone's arm and followed. Tansy pelted after them; she banged the door in the priests' startled, furious faces and dropped the bolt.

'Can you take me to Skir?' panted Beeman, but Perrin shook his head.

'No good. He's locked up.'

'Penthesi?' gasped Tansy, and Perrin veered around the next corner in the direction of the stables. Everyone was at prayer; the Temple was nearly deserted at sunset. Servants and priests had just begun to stream out of the Hall of the Faith. One or two people turned to stare as they ran, but Tansy and Perrin were familiar figures around the Temple by now, and unseemly behaviour was almost expected from them. Running through courtyards was nothing; if they'd torn their clothes off as they ran, hardly anyone would have been surprised. As for Beeman, he pulled his hood over his face – another foreigner in their midst.

The Temple stables were large and well-appointed. Once, fifty horses were kept there for the priests to travel the breadth of Cragonlands; since the Baltimaran invasion, there were only half-a-dozen ponies left to pull carts to the market. One of the ponies whinnied and stamped as Tansy, Perrin and Beeman approached, and when they arrived in the stable-yard, Penthesi poked his head through the half-door as if he were waiting for them.

They all slipped inside Penthesi's stall, and Tansy closed the top half of the door. The stall was spacious, but with a large horse and three people inside, it felt cramped.

Beeman threw himself down on a bale of straw. 'Thank you. Most uncivil behaviour, I thought, especially after all I've done for them.' He looked up. 'What are your names?'

'I'm Perrin and this is Tansy.'

'Let's not get too friendly.' Tansy grabbed Beeman's cloak and flung it aside to reveal the white luckpiece. 'What's *that* then? Ain't you Wanion's man?'

'*No*. Absolutely not. I know how it looks.' Beeman sighed. 'I posed as her agent, I wear her token. It's useful. I've learned a great deal. Though it's been hard on my nerves.' Tansy still glared at him. 'Believe me. I would rather cut off my own hand than work for that woman. It was all pretence, a dangerous pretence.'

Perrin said to Tansy, 'He's telling the truth. Quick, go and check, make sure no one's followed us.'

Tansy slipped out.

Beeman said, 'I met with Bettenwey earlier. He let me think I'd be able to see Skir, but they stopped me.'

Tansy came back, shaking her head. 'All quiet.'

'I must see Skir,' said Beeman.

'He fretted about you all the way from Arvestel,' said Tansy.

'I must tell him I'm all right. Among other things. Are you sure you can't bring him here?'

Tansy shook her head. 'They got him locked up tight. Tighter than us. With guards outside his room and spies all around. We ain't allowed to leave the Temple. Skir ain't allowed to leave his room. We ain't seen him either.'

Beeman ground at his eyes with the heels of his hands. 'There are things I must tell him,' he repeated wearily. Penthesi whuffed softly at his ear, and Beeman gave an exhausted smile.

Tansy said uncertainly, 'Penthesi thinks you're all right.'

'Typical,' said Perrin to Beeman. 'She pays more attention to that horse than she does to me.'

'He's a handsome horse,' said Beeman.

'Hey. I'm a handsome man.'

'Penthesi ain't full of himself,' said Tansy tartly. 'That's why I listen to him. And he's smarter than you, too. You hungry, Beeman? I know where the stable boys keep their snacks.'

A few moments later she was back with a handful of apples

and a tin of biscuits. Beeman helped himself with a grateful nod. She'd also brought a lantern.

'Ain't no one around. I thought everyone in the Temple'd be out searching for you, but it's dead quiet.'

Beeman brushed crumbs from his moustache. 'They have more urgent business to attend to. Bettenwey has a plan. No doubt he's discussing it with the other priests.'

'Is that what your meeting was about?'

'Partly. Because of what I reported to Bettenwey, he will have to bring this scheme of his forward. He's not pleased about that.'

'What scheme?' demanded Tansy. 'What are you talking about?'

'Broken Fire,' said Beeman and, between mouthfuls of apple, he outlined the plan to Perrin and Tansy. 'Bettenwey plans to wipe out most of the leadership of both Baltimar and Rengan. He thinks that will win independence for Cragonlands. But it's much more likely that the Threelands would be plunged into chaos, anarchy and civil war. The initial explosion alone will kill dozens of people, but this foolish scheme could ultimately cost many more lives than that.' He picked up a biscuit, and put it back in the tin, as if he'd suddenly lost his appetite. His face looked old and haggard. 'Bettenwey plans to use Broken Fire, a notoriously unstable explosive. It might not just destroy the White Pavilion, though that would be bad enough. In untrained hands, it could wipe out the whole of the Old Quarter. And believe me, it will be in untrained hands. Bettenwey doesn't understand what he's playing with.'

Perrin said, 'I don't know Broken Fire. I don't think Rengan's Army has it.'

'No. It was sold to Baltimar by the weapon-makers in

Mithates.' Beeman's face was grim. 'They've been working on it for decades, and they don't have it right yet. I worked on Broken Fire myself, as a student. That's why Bettenwey asked for my advice; he wouldn't have told me about the plot otherwise.'

Perrin looked at him curiously. 'You're from the Westlands? Not Cragonlands?'

'Skir doesn't know. It's one of the things I wanted to tell him.'

Tansy said, 'Are you a chanter?'

Beeman barked a laugh. 'No! Anything but. When I was a student in Mithates, I helped develop the weapons that have torn this land apart. Now, I suppose, I want to do what I can to mend it.'

'But how can you stop Bettenwey?' said Perrin.

Beeman put two fingers in the corners of his eyes and rubbed them; his eyes seemed to hurt him. 'I know where the Broken Fire is stored. It's so dangerous they can't keep it in Gleve. It's in an abandoned temple up in the hills.'

'So go and chuck a torch on it,' said Tansy.

'If I did that, I'd be blown to smithereens. I may be flattering myself, but I'd like to believe I'm more useful alive than dead. But I do think I could disable it – carefully.'

Tansy and Perrin looked at him with the same question in their faces. Beeman gave his grim smile. 'I plan to. Tonight. Will you come with me?'

'What, now?'

'It must be tonight. Because of what I told Bettenwey.'

'Which is?'

'The leaders have decided to hold the talks early. Probably they suspect some trouble from the resistance. Wanion is already here in Gleve, and the others will arrive tomorrow.'

'Lady Wanion's here?' Tansy went white, and her hand flew to her throat in the automatic gesture. Her voice hardened. 'Reckon they should blow that evil witch sky-high.'

'If it were just a matter of killing Wanion, I agree,' said Beeman. 'A clean death is probably better than she deserves, after all she's done. But there are many other lives at stake. And if Bettenwey is determined to try his plan, it must be tomorrow. That means he will have to retrieve the Broken Fire tonight.'

'Unless we get there first,' said Perrin slowly.

'Yes,' said Beeman. 'The only way to neutralise the explosive is to cut it into small pieces. That will take time, and care. I might manage alone, but it would be easier with help. Will you come?'

'I'd rather not,' said Perrin frankly. 'But I can see that I'm going to.'

'You ain't leaving me behind,' said Tansy.

Beeman said, 'Will you stay with Skir? I don't like to leave him here alone. If something happened to Perrin and me . . .'

He let the end of the sentence hang in mid-air. Without looking at Perrin, Tansy said in a low voice, 'Reckon I'd rather come with you two.' She added defensively, 'I got very steady hands.'

Perrin let out a long breath. 'Pleased as I am to hear that you'd rather risk your neck with me than stay safely here with Skir, could I point out that this whole discussion is meaningless, since we can't get out of the Temple?'

'Yes we can.' Beeman produced a ring of strange, skinny metal objects from his pocket. 'Skeleton keys. They can open almost any lock, including the doors of the Temple.'

Perrin grinned. 'Oh. Tansy, what are you doing?'

'Saddling up Penthesi.'

The big horse tossed his head and pawed the ground, impatient to be out of the stables after being confined for so long. Beeman sorted through his keys. 'Let's go, before the priests finish their meeting. There will be a fierce argument, but Bettenwey will win. Pack the rest of that food in my rucksack; we may need it.'

Tansy was flushed, her eyes bright as she put the bridle on Penthesi. Perrin looked grim; he touched her sleeve. 'Tansy,' he said in a low voice. 'If we go now, we won't come back here. Beeman might, but we can't.'

'Good.' Tansy was busy with the bridle. 'I'll be gladder to get out of this place than I was to leave Arvestel – oh.' She swung round to face him, stricken. 'Skir. He'll think we ran out on him.'

'If Beeman tells him the whole story, I'm sure he'll understand,' said Perrin, feeling anything but sure.

'But not even to say goodbye . . .' Tansy bit her knuckle.

Beeman said quietly, 'I will see Skir again, whatever happens. I can give him a message.'

Tansy managed a smile. 'I suppose.' She turned away to fasten Penthesi's girths.

'You don't have any chalk, do you, Beeman?' said Perrin.

Beeman raised his eyebrows. From his pocket he produced string, coins, a folding knife, nutshells, a dirty handkerchief – and a blunt nub of chalk. 'Always useful, a piece of chalk.'

Perrin scratched some Signs on the wall of Penthesi's stall. 'Someone will let him know.'

Beeman looked quizzically at Perrin. 'You know the Tenth Power? You can read and write?'

'My mother taught me.' Perrin tossed back the chalk. 'I'm a chanter of the beasts, too.'

'Indeed? A man of many talents.' Beeman read what Perrin had written. 'See you on the other side?'

'It's what soldiers always say.'

Tansy put her hands on her hips. 'It ain't what *I'd* say.'

'And what would you say?'

'I don't know.' She thrust her chin up. 'Just give him my love.'

Perrin quickly scratched a few more Signs. 'Come on.' Beeman had found the key that fitted the padlock on the high double gates between the stable-yard and the laneway outside. 'Hurry.'

Tansy doused the lantern. Night had fallen; two almost-full moons were rising. Perrin swung up onto Penthesi, and hauled Tansy up in front of him. Beeman pulled his hood over his head and shoved the heavy gate open for the horse and his riders.

The gate swung shut with a muffled bang; there was no one to hear it.

Tansy guided Penthesi down the narrow streets. The city lights spread out below: yellow pinpoints that echoed the cold silver of the stars above. The streets were still busy; the spicy, greasy smell from the food-stalls made her mouth water. Men lingered, gossiping, on the corners; goat-carts clattered past from the market, laden with unsold goods. A tired child tugged its mother's hand and begged to be carried.

Beeman hurried on, and Tansy urged Penthesi forward. The streets grew more empty, and the horse's hoofs clopped loudly on the cobbles. His ears pricked left and right, and every so often Tansy had to rein him back from an eager trot.

'This way,' said Beeman. 'The east road out of Gleve.'

Soon they were on the flats, threading their way through narrow lanes. More and more doorways were barred for the night; the people who hurried by were alone, hooded, darting from shadow to shadow.

After a time the buildings spread out, lower and wider than in the city's cramped heart. The yellow glow of lamplight was replaced by the silver sheen of the moons. The cobbled street gave way to an unpaved track, and clouds of dust spurted beneath Penthesi's hoofs.

Ahead, a clot of shadow broke off and approached them.

Beeman murmured, 'Let me do the talking.'

'You there, halt!' A Baltimaran accent, with long, drawn-out vowels. A lantern swung from a soldier's hand.

Tansy halted Penthesi. The stallion whinnied and she quieted him with a pat. Beeman stood, his eyes watchful, Penthesi's bridle in his hand.

'You're out late.'

'We were visiting family in Gleve. Lost track of the time. We're heading home now.'

'Where's home?'

Beeman pointed with his chin. 'Velatran.'

'Fair way to go. Wouldn't your family put you up for the night?'

'Not three of us, and the horse.'

'Fine horse. Want to sell?'

'Not tonight. Come to Velatran tomorrow and ask me again.'

'Warm night for a cloak and hood. Not hiding anything, are you?'

Without a word, Beeman held his cloak aside. The soldier's voice, which had been bored, suddenly became hard and alert. 'A dagger? Don't you know the law? It's forbidden for natives to carry arms. Hand it over, quick smart.' The soldier clicked his fingers and Beeman unbuckled the sheath. The dagger glinted, and the white luckpiece winked in the lamplight. The soldier stepped back abruptly.

'Go on then,' he barked. 'Get out of my sight.'

Hardly daring to breathe, Tansy urged Penthesi forward out of the pool of lamplight. The soldier yelled at their backs, 'I'll be round tomorrow to collect that horse.'

Beeman murmured, 'The price for letting us go. Even Wanion's agents don't escape that easily. No, Tansy, don't make a sound. Just walk on. At the next crossroads, we take the left turn to Tarvan.'

CHAPTER 15

The White Pavilion

SKIR sat on the end of his bed, hurling a small rubber ball at the wall with such force it bruised his hand. He imagined the wall was Bettenwey's head, and he counted three hundred and seventy-two strikes before the ball rolled under the bed.

The light had faded. He'd have to light a lamp if he wanted to keep playing, but it seemed childish suddenly and he let his hands dangle, feeling anger surge inside him.

A prisoner again. He'd been a prisoner all his life, pushed around by other people. Before Bettenwey, it was Beeman, or the King of Baltimar. Even when he escaped from Arvestel it was Tansy who'd bossed him into it . . .

Tansy wouldn't sit here sulking. She'd find a way out. She'd do something to stop Bettenwey.

But Tansy was brave. She could ride and fight.

Well, he'd made it all the way from Arvestel, hadn't he? He could ride and fight, too. He was just as tough as Tansy and Perrin, and just as smart. If Tansy could do it, so could he.

The square of pale sky in his window was higher than his head, and covered with an ironwork grille. Skir stood on his bed and peered at it closely. He fetched a knife from his supper tray, and dug away at one of the metal pegs until he'd doubled the size of its hole. It was definitely coming loose.

As he worked, it grew darker outside. A deep blue seeped into the white sky. The first stars had appeared by the time he yanked out the first peg, and by the time he freed the second, the moons were up. As he wrenched out the third peg, he heard someone call 'Goodnight!' in the laneway below. He paused until their footsteps faded and the lane was silent. His fingertips hurt from jiggling the metal pegs. Then he tugged at the grille. With a loud clang, it came free; it was unexpectedly heavy, and he almost dropped it.

Skir listened, heart pounding, but the whole wing was quiet. That was odd. There were usually muted noises at this time as the priests retired for the night.

The window gaped naked in the wall. What would Tansy do now? A rope. Skir knotted together his sheets and tied them securely to the bed frame. Then he hauled off the mattress and tipped the bedstead against the wall. He was stronger than he used to be.

Balancing on the bedstead, he stuck his head out the window. The laneway was deserted. His room was on the second storey. Skir fed the sheets out the window and manoeuvred himself out backwards. There was a horrible moment when he thought he was stuck. Then he kicked himself free, slithered down the rope and fell, bruising his backside on the cobbles. The sheets hung white against the dark stone, pointing to his window. Skir scrambled to his feet, and ran.

Tansy glanced back and saw the patrol's lantern-light fade into the shadows below the silver gleam of the two moons. The lights of Gleve were hidden by a fold of the hills; the silent mountains reared black against the sky and blotted out the stars. Tansy shivered.

Perrin's arms tightened around her as they rode. 'Wanion can't see us, Tansy.'

'But she's so close . . . Maybe we oughta let her get blown up.'

'That's not the way to fight her,' said Beeman.

'What is, then?'

'She thinks she's a sorceress. Perhaps only true magic will defeat her.'

'You mean chantment?'

Beeman was silent for a moment, as if gauging how far to trust them. 'How much do you know of the revolution in the Westlands?'

'I know there's a Rising,' said Perrin. 'But not more than that.'

Beeman smiled ruefully in the moonlight. 'The Chanters' Rising began twenty years ago. It's not finished yet; it may not be over in our lifetime. There are many more chanters in the Westlands than here, which is why Wanion has got away with her false magic for so long. But even in the Westlands, chanters have been persecuted and forced to hide their gifts. They were taught to be ashamed. The Rising teaches them to be proud, to use their magic for the healing of all Tremaris.'

Perrin said, 'The Witch-Singer of the Westlands –'

Beeman turned his head sharply. 'The Singer of All Songs leads the Rising, yes, but she's no witch, not like Wanion. What have you heard?'

'Before my family left Nadalin, I remember –'

'What, Perrin?'

'My mother and father were afraid for me,' said Perrin

slowly. 'My mother said she'd give anything to make sure I didn't – I didn't fall into the Witch-Singer's hands.' He'd forgotten that, until he spoke of it. Beeman's words had drawn up the memory like a fish hooked from deep water.

Tansy shifted uneasily. 'The Westlands ain't nothing to do with us. We got enough fighting of our own to worry about.'

'The Rising affects the whole of Tremaris. Chantment does not belong only in the Westlands.'

'I don't know,' said Perrin. 'All the time I lived in Rengan, I never met another chanter. Even when I was a child in Nadalin, there was only one old woman who said she was a windworker – but she said she used to be beautiful, too!'

'The Singer believes there are chanters in every corner of Tremaris. She says the power of magic cannot be hidden. It must rise, as the sun rises, as the flame rises in the darkness.'

There was a pause; Penthesi's hoofs clopped on the track, and there was an indistinct thrum of crickets. Tansy whispered, 'Then how *does* Wanion do her magic, if it ain't real?'

Beeman kept his voice low. 'Those who believe in her magic give it power. Do you understand?'

'No.'

Perrin said, 'I think I do. If you'd stolen Skir's hair for her, she would have told him, threatened to make her magic with it. She'd try to frighten him into obeying her.'

Beeman nodded. 'Wanion's sorcery gains its power from fear. Take away that fear, and she would be powerless.'

'Mm,' said Tansy, unconvinced. 'She's still got the Pit and the shore fires. They're real enough.'

'But fear of the Pit is even more powerful than the Pit itself. There's no magical power in torture, or in leaving a body to rot as a warning to others. Wanion trades in fear and information.

235

Her spies are everywhere, and she knows everything – Perrin, what makes Rengan strong?'

'The Army.'

'Is it? Or is it unity? Rengan is organised around one purpose. Its people share everything they have, to stand behind their Army. That's what makes them strong. Not the Army itself, but the agreement that supports it.'

Perrin thought for a moment, then chuckled. 'All right. What makes Baltimar strong?'

'We're rich,' said Tansy.

'True,' said Beeman. 'Baltimar has fertile land, mines, dairy herds, treasuries, granaries stuffed with wheat. But –'

'It's the people.' Perrin was enjoying himself. 'It's the opposite of Rengan. Everyone in Baltimar is out for themselves.'

'They are encouraged to think of themselves,' said Beeman. 'That is their strength, but also their weakness. Just as Rengan's single purpose is its weakness as well as its strength.'

Perrin laughed. 'I should have been born in Baltimar, and Tansy should have been born in Rengan. Neither of us really fits the philosophy of our own land.'

Beeman said soberly, 'And it's those like you, the misfits, in both lands, who provide such a market for the rust-lords. You've had a lucky escape.'

Tansy didn't enjoy this kind of conversation. She said, 'So what's Cragonlands' strength, then?'

Beeman said, 'If you asked the rulers of Rengan and Baltimar, they'd agree that Cragonlands has no strength at all. It's been invaded, stripped bare, left with nothing. But it's a curious thing, you know. Poor and suffering and downtrodden as they are, hardly anyone in Cragonlands takes rust.'

'Maybe it's the Faith makes them strong,' suggested Tansy.

Perrin said, with a touch of bitterness, 'Strong enough to bend before every wind that blows.'

'To bend, yes. But not to break.'

There was a pause while Tansy and Perrin digested this. Tansy said, 'No wonder Skir's got a quick tongue, if you talked like this to him every day.'

Beeman laughed. 'Not every day.'

Perrin was silent. Everything he knew, he'd taught himself; he'd never had anyone to guide him or encourage him. Maybe if Tugger had lived, he'd have taught Perrin a thing or two. He'd tried, during the mission, but Perrin hadn't wanted to learn. He flushed with shame. He hadn't listened to anything the squad had to teach him. He hadn't even listened properly to the briefings about the raid . . .

Perrin went cold from head to foot. For the first time, he realised that if he had listened, if he had done what he was supposed to do – been in the right place, sung to the dogs sooner – the raid might not have been a disaster. Tugger and the others might have survived. Tugger's death was partly his fault. That was something he'd never admitted to himself before.

He wound his arms tightly round Tansy's waist and laid his cheek against her back. Perrin never cried, but there was a prickling behind his eyelids.

He heard Beeman's quiet voice. 'Take the left turn at the crossroads, Tansy. We're almost there.'

Skir's feet skidded on the cobbles as he ran downhill into the heart of Gleve. People stared, and he forced himself to slow to a walk. The streets were patched with light from open doors and windows. Skir walked briskly from shadow to shadow, not looking at anyone. His priest's robes were dark enough to pass for any plain clothing. Only the copper circlet on his brow might betray him, so he snatched it off and thrust it in his pocket.

Before long he reached the Old Quarter. The buildings here were crammed together, and the doorways were carved with elaborate, old-fashioned symbols, like the panels of the throne room: swirling clouds, twining rivers. Here and there were ugly holes where houses had been blasted away in the fighting, raw gaps like knocked-out teeth. Wild cats slunk through the ruins.

Two thoroughfares sliced through the Old Quarter: the Market Road, and the North Gate Road. Even at this hour, they were alive with food-stalls and music and spilled light. Skir headed for the noise of North Gate Road; he hunched himself inside his outer robe, and shielded his face with its folds. There might be people in the streets who would recognise him, as Diz and Lora had.

The North Gate Road wound uphill until it broadened into Sether Square, the winter square. In the bitterest winters, before the war, they'd sluice the paving stones with water so that children could slide on the ice. In summer, it was the home of flower-sellers. The White Pavilion formed the eastern side of the Square. Skir stood still while people jostled around him and soldiers barked orders. One gestured fiercely at Skir. 'Come on, son! What's wrong? Got no home to go to?'

Skir allowed himself a brief, wry grin; nothing had ever seemed more true. He walked, casually, to the gates of the White Pavilion. A smaller door was cut into the larger one, just high enough to duck through. Aware of the absurdity of his action, but somehow convinced it would work, Skir raised his fist and knocked.

Tarvan no longer existed. Tansy and Perrin rode Penthesi up the hill to the scattering of small houses, white and grey and silver in the moonlight. It looked like any other village, but the houses were as empty as broken eggshells, smashed and hollow, open to the sky. The black mountains stared impassively down.

'We're here.' Beeman nodded to the remains of a little temple at the end of the village. Its whitewashed walls were stained and crumbling, the roof was gone, and the whole interior was blackened and burned. Charred skeletons of courtyard trees thrust up above the broken walls.

Perrin and Tansy slipped from Penthesi's back. 'Where is it?'

'The cellar is intact,' said Beeman.

Wary, as if any footfall could set off an explosion, they picked their way to the ruined temple. It was cold in the hills, and Tansy shivered in her thin shirt.

At the temple steps, Perrin said, 'You stay here.'

Tansy shook her head; her teeth chattered. 'I got s-steady hands, remember?'

Beeman draped his cloak over Tansy's shoulders. 'Not too steady just now. Stay with Penthesi.'

'He'll wait here.' Tansy walked up the steps and into the blackened courtyard. Dead embers crunched beneath her feet. And – she looked quickly away – pieces of bone gleamed pale in the moons' light. 'Which way?'

Beeman nodded to the back of the courtyard. They passed under an archway and along a narrow passage, littered with debris. Stone steps led down to the cellar, disappearing into pitch darkness.

Perrin said, 'I don't suppose anyone brought a candle?'

'I always carry a candle stub.' Beeman patted his pockets, then plunged his hands into them and felt around. At last he cursed softly. 'Every day but today.'

Tansy let Beeman's cloak fall at the top of the steps. The blackness yawned in front of her, the breath of cold stone. She swallowed. 'Come on then. We'll have to feel our way.'

The little door swung open and a grizzled gatekeeper scowled out at Skir. 'Deliveries is round the back, in the lane.'

With relief, Skir heard the accent of Cragonlands in the gruff voice, not the drawl of Baltimar.

'It's not a delivery. I've come from the Temple.' He let the gatekeeper see his priestly robes. It was only then that he realised he had no weapon; but that was right, as it should be.

'Temple business? This time of night?'

'It is business connected with our visitors.' Skir stared at him hard, and the gatekeeper glanced over his shoulder and shuddered.

'She's a character, that Lady Wanion.' He licked his lips nervously.

Skir's heart jumped. *She* was here – here already. But he kept his voice even. 'Lady Wanion?'

The gatekeeper's scowl deepened; he knew he had said too much. 'I weren't told about any Temple business.' He tried to shut the door, but Skir wedged his foot in the crack. They stared at each other. 'Get out!' hissed the gatekeeper. 'Or I'll call the soldiers.'

Skir fixed him with a steely gaze. 'You have a priest of the Temple arrested here and there'll be trouble. These visitors are here under strictest secrecy. I don't know why you weren't told I was coming tonight. But if you call the soldiers, there'll be no secret left to keep, and the blame will fall on you.'

'I weren't told. I can't –' The gatekeeper wavered.

'*Let me in*,' said Skir. And, as if hypnotised, the gatekeeper stood aside.

Skir stepped into a large lobby, elaborately tiled and dimly lit. A pattern of golden stars and moons glittered high overhead. It was very quiet. Skir turned to the gatekeeper. 'Get back to your post. I'll find my own way.'

The man nodded uncertainly and melted away into the gloom. Without hesitation, Skir strode through the lobby and into a wide corridor with huge rooms opening off it. His soft leather boots were soundless on the tiles.

Skir ascended a massive marble staircase. Another long corridor stretched the length of the wing. This part of the Pavilion was in darkness, except where moonlight leaked through cracks in the shutters. Skir walked on, an urgent shadow. He felt invisible, untouchable.

Since the war, the White Pavilion had mouldered behind its gates, its ballrooms shuttered, its dining halls draped in dust sheets.

At the back of the Pavilion, a glow of lamplight filtered up the next staircase, and the sound of voices. Skir paused, listening. What next? He'd been so intent on getting here that he'd thought no further. Somehow he would stop Bettenwey's plot, that was all he knew ... And Wanion was here.

He guessed where he was; it was like Arvestel. He'd left the sprawling reception rooms behind; this part of the Pavilion contained the private apartments, the bedrooms and parlours of the noble guests. These rooms would have been opened up and aired for Wanion and the other visitors.

Skir slipped around the corner into the next wing. It was completely dark, with a strong smell of mould and mice. Skir bounded up a wooden staircase, swagged with cobwebs. The corridor here was dark, narrow and wood-panelled. Skir crept along, turned another corner and was back in the main wing, but a floor above the rooms that Wanion and her servants occupied. He felt as if he'd known these dark, neglected spaces in his dreams, as if he were following a map he'd drawn up himself long ago.

Ahead was a gallery, roofed with a dome of dirty glass. Skir moved silently to the edge and looked down onto a large, shabby drawing room.

Almost directly below him stood a square object, heaped with mounds of green silk and bone-coloured velvet. It took Skir a moment to realise that it was a huge litter of ivory, with long handles protruding from each corner, and the mounds of silk and velvet were the enormous reclining body of Lady Wanion herself. She was murmuring, too low for him to hear.

Skir's knuckles whitened on the railing. Crouched close to Wanion was a girl. Her chestnut hair glinted in the candlelight; she was massaging one of Wanion's withered, claw-like hands. Even before she turned her scarred face upward, Skir knew it was Elvie.

He must have made a sound, and Elvie's sharp ears caught it. She turned her blind eyes to where Skir stood in the gallery. He stepped back instantly into the darkness, but it was too late.

Wanion's head tipped back. 'Guards!' she roared.

Skir sprinted along the wood-panelled corridor. The stairway yawned, but the guards would come up that way. He flung open the nearest door and found himself in a bare room, streaked with moonlight: nowhere to hide. The next room held a single, sagging bed, swathed in cobwebs. He dived beneath it, trying not to sneeze or gasp as the boots of the guards thumped up the stairs and along the corridor. Doors crashed open, boots thudded and squeaked. The handle rattled, then the door smashed open. The boots made straight for the bed, and a spear was thrust swiftly underneath.

Skir wriggled backward, but a hand seized his leg and dragged him out. Two Baltimaran guards held him at arm's-length. Skir was convulsed with sneezes; his feet twitched grotesquely off the floor as if he were a puppet. A third guard marched back to the gallery and called down to Wanion.

'It's only some dirty little Craggish guttersnipe, mam. Shall we spit him on a spear, or throw him back in the street?'

There was a chance they might have let him go. But Skir had had enough of being disregarded. He was furious: with Elvie for betraying him, with the guards who'd captured him, with Bettenwey for trying to use him. He was angry with Wanion, with Tansy and Perrin, who'd left him to stew in his room alone. He was even angry with Beeman, who was not here when he needed him most. Most of all he was angry with himself for being caught. He struggled furiously. 'I am the Priest-King of Cragonlands!' he yelled. 'I am Eskirenwey, heir to the Circle of Attar!'

There was silence. Then Wanion's voice boomed from below. 'Bring him to me.'

With a violent wriggle, Skir threw off the guards and brushed down his robes. He extracted the copper circlet from his pocket and placed it on his brow. Then, with his head held high, he marched out of the room and down the stairs to Wanion.

CHAPTER 16

The Songs of Fire

'SLOWLY – very slowly,' warned Beeman. 'In its current state, the Broken Fire is extremely volatile. If it's shaken about, or squeezed, or, gods forbid, set alight, it will go up like a volcano.'

'Maybe it's lucky we don't have a candle.' Perrin's teeth flashed white in a nervous grin. 'What are we looking for?'

'A bundle about this big.' Beeman indicated an object about the size of a loaf of bread. 'Perhaps bigger. I'm not sure how much Bettenwey's got.'

'Don't seem like much,' said Tansy.

'Enough to destroy half of Gleve,' said Beeman grimly.

'Go, go, go,' muttered Perrin, but he gave Tansy a reassuring smile before they descended into the darkness.

Tansy put her hand to the wall as she felt with her foot for the next uneven step down. Beeman's big, warm hand was on her shoulder, and Perrin was beside her, humming softly. She smelled clean soap and sweat and a faint whiff of hair oil. How in the world had he found hair oil? Suddenly she felt giddy; the thought that something terrible might happen to Perrin was worse, much worse, than the thought of anything happening to herself.

'Perrin!' she whispered. 'Be careful!'

He squeezed her arm hard. 'You too.'

The darkness opened up ahead. There was a smell of cold stone, and a slow, erratic *drip . . . drip* echoed from a far corner of the cellar.

'This isn't right,' murmured Beeman. 'This space is too big. The Broken Fire should be tucked away somewhere smaller, more secure.'

'A hole in the wall?'

'Yes, maybe. You check that side, I'll check this side. Tansy, you check the floor.'

'Be careful,' said Tansy in a whisper. She felt the sudden vacancy on either side of her as Beeman and Perrin slipped away. She spread her arms wide, groping in the dark. A thought flashed through her mind: *this is how Elvie feels, every day*. How could she bear it, this crushing darkness?

And then she heard a faint hissing, rustling, like silk rubbed against silk. 'Beeman?' she called, her voice shrill. 'Is that it, the Broken Fire?'

'Ssh!' It was Perrin, on the other side of the cellar, his voice low. 'Snake. Quiet, don't move.' He began to sing.

Tansy froze, balanced on her right toe, left foot behind her, fingers stiffly spread. Perrin's chantment flowed past her, soothing and persuading, and Tansy heard the soft rasp of the snake's skin as it slid across the stone floor, drawn toward the steps, gliding up and outside into the night.

'It's gone,' came Perrin's voice in lazy triumph.

'Good,' said Beeman dryly. 'But be careful. There may be others.'

Shaking slightly, Tansy dropped to her hands and knees. The ground was cold and damp and rough. It *felt* like snakes.

She crept forward, sweeping the stones with her fingertips.

'Beeman?' It was Perrin. 'I think I've found something.'

'Found what?' Beeman's voice was sharp.

'A hollow place – like a little tunnel – there are stones missing from the wall.'

Tansy heard Beeman's cautious footfalls as he crossed the cellar. 'Yes,' he whispered. 'That's the place.'

Tansy edged her way toward their voices, holding out her hands until she brushed the cloth of Perrin's shirt. At once his warm arms wrapped around her, and he tucked his chin onto her shoulder. Beeman grunted as he groped inside the hollow.

'Can't – reach. It's too deep.' He swore. 'And I can't see if it's even in there.'

'It is,' said Perrin. 'It must be.'

'But I can't reach,' said Beeman.

'My arms aren't any longer than yours,' said Perrin. 'And Tansy's certainly aren't. We'll have to get a stick or something.'

'We are not going to *poke* at Broken Fire with a stick!' growled Beeman.

Tansy asked quietly, 'How – how big is the hole?'

'About as big as this,' said Perrin, making a circle around her with his arms. Then, 'Oh . . .'

'Maybe I could wriggle in.' Tansy tried to make her voice calm.

Beeman didn't notice the catch in her throat. 'Yes. Good girl. Come here.'

Perrin released her. Even Perrin didn't know how terrified she was of enclosed spaces; the thick black dark in her mouth, in her nose.

Beeman grabbed her wrist and guided her hands to the hole

in the wall. It was about waist-high; no more than two or three of the cellar stones had been removed, and the tunnel hollowed out behind them. It was just big enough for Tansy to squirm inside.

She reached all around the hole with her hands. It was just dirt, soft crumbling dirt. This was awful. She could taste the soil in her mouth: cold, claggy in her throat. She groped desperately with her fingertips, but there was only dirt under her hands. Her head scraped against the roof of the tunnel, and more soil crumbled down into her mouth. Tansy stifled a scream.

'Little bit further,' she managed to gasp, and Perrin and Beeman held her legs and pushed her deeper down the tunnel. Now just her feet were hanging out; she was almost buried. *Buried alive . . . No, no. Don't think like that. It* must *be here.* She groped forward, as far as she could reach. Nothing. Still the tunnel stretched deeper into the earth, narrower than ever. She shifted her hip bones to edge herself further, and then a little further. What if she got stuck in here? What if the walls collapsed? How would they ever dig her out?

Even as she formed the thought, her fingers touched something. A canvas-wrapped bundle. But she couldn't quite close her hand around it. She stretched forward, but all she achieved was to push the bundle a tantalising finger-span further away. 'No . . . no . . .' she moaned. A single hot tear of frustration squeezed beneath her eyelid.

'Tansy?'

The voice was so muffled, she couldn't tell if it was Beeman or Perrin. 'Tansy? Are you all right?'

Tansy took a deep, slow breath, inhaling particles of soil along with the air. She pushed her terror down, held her breath and dragged herself by the fingernails closer to the bundle – closer – she had it. She pinched a corner of the canvas between finger and thumb and pulled it toward her. Stars whirled behind her eyelids; her lungs were bursting. The hole was crumbling in on top of her. She tried to scream, *pull me out!* but the soft gluey dirt choked her mouth, her nose, suffocating her, and the terror rose, and pulled her under.

'Tansy!' Perrin's voice was frantic in the darkness. 'She's gone limp, she's in trouble!' He seized her legs and tugged hard.

'Gently, *gently*!' cried Beeman. 'The Broken Fire –'

'She's stuck – Tansy!' Perrin scrabbled around the edge of the hole with his fingernails. 'Help me!'

Beeman scraped carefully at the loose dirt. 'Slow down, Perrin!'

Perrin ignored him. He burrowed his arms into the hole. Tansy lay face-down, limp and motionless. Perrin grabbed her around the waist and dragged her out of the hole. He caught her as her body slid to the cellar floor, and carried her to the steps and up into the moonlight. He said, 'She's got it.'

Tansy's arms cradled a small canvas package to her chest. Beeman prised it free and carried it away to a flat stone where he set it gently down. Perrin lowered Tansy to the ground by the temple's ruined wall.

'She's not breathing!'

In two strides, Beeman was there; he tilted Tansy's head, and hooked the dirt out of her mouth with one finger. Tansy convulsed, and choked; then she was coughing violently in the circle of Perrin's arms, gasping in the fresh, cool breath of night.

'I thought – I thought I were going to die.' Tansy shuddered.

'I couldn't help you, I couldn't do anything! I wished I was an ironcrafter –'

'You did help, you pulled me out.'

'But I couldn't . . .' Perrin was shaking. It was the first time in his life that his two gifts, his quick tongue and his chantment, had been utterly useless. When Tansy's feet had gone limp under his hand, when he thought she'd suffocated, and there was nothing he could do to help her – it was the worst feeling he'd ever known. *So this was how it felt to care about someone more than yourself*, he thought dismally. He knotted his hands around her. 'You're all right? You sure you're all right?'

'Yes.' She leaned into him.

'Then come here.' Beeman's voice was harsh with tension as he turned back to the bundle, and peeled the wrapping from it with swift, delicate movements. 'You're here to help, not sit around cuddling. Fetch my cloak – over there, where you dropped it, Tansy, there, there! Spread it out. All right. Not too close.' The lump of Broken Fire sat naked on the canvas that had wrapped it; it looked like nothing so much as a formless lump of dough. 'Now,' said Beeman. 'I'm going to cut it into pieces.' He drew out his dagger; the blade glinted in the moons' light. 'If I get this right, it should send the energy of the explosion upward, not outward – it should minimise the area of impact.'

'Should?' squeaked Tansy.

'Of course, with luck, there won't be any explosion at all.' Beeman frowned; he lowered the dagger and made a slow, smooth incision in the lump, cutting away about a third of its mass. Beeman let out a wavering breath. 'All right. Now this piece into three. Tansy, are your hands steady again? Lift each piece *carefully* onto the cloak. Perrin, wrap a fold of cloak over each piece. They mustn't touch, understand? If we get this wrong... Whoomph. We won't be here to see it.' He brought the dagger down again, steady and slow, slicing the lump into smaller, uneven chunks.

Tansy lifted each small piece with both hands and lowered it onto the spread cloak. Perrin deftly wrapped the folds around it. Rushing cloud obscured one moon, and the first raindrops pattered on the backs of their necks: sparse, heavy, summer raindrops. Penthesi waited nearby, watching, with his head on one side.

'I wish to all the gods I'd never worked on this wretched stuff,' said Beeman grimly. 'Ah well. It was a long time ago. I was younger than you, Tansy, and so covered in freckles, everyone called me Trout...'

When the last piece was wrapped, Beeman took the unwieldy bundle and wedged it gently but firmly into his rucksack. Only then did he smile. 'Thank you, both of you. And well done, Tansy. I couldn't have done this without your help.'

'What now?' Tansy was shivering.

'We'll take it somewhere safe. I have a bolt-hole in Gleve, some rooms I've rented that Bettenwey doesn't know about. Once we're there, we can chop this damned thing so fine that it couldn't light a candle. And *then*, just to be sure, we'll drown it in the river... Come on. Let's go.'

Skir threw open the double doors and marched into the room. Wanion squatted before him on her immense litter, swathed in green silk and cream velvet. Emeralds dripped from her fleshy neck and glittered on her turban. Her eyes were narrow as a toad's before it strikes a fly; she watched his every movement.

Skir knew this, and he tried not to look at Elvie. But he couldn't help it. His eyes darted to where she perched on a stool at Wanion's side. Had she been Wanion's servant all the time? Had she betrayed them to the soldiers that night? But one swift glance convinced him otherwise. Elvie's face was a picture of misery and fear; her hands twisted in her lap in anguish.

Wanion sneered. She nodded to the guards, who retreated from the room, closing the doors.

Skir did not want to look at Wanion. He stared around. He was aware of a horrible smell, the stench of putrefaction, mingled with a sickly sweet stink of incense. The room was furnished with odd pieces from all over the Pavilion, perhaps from all over Gleve.

But there was one item that Wanion had obviously brought with her. It was a gigantic loom, darkened by a huge, half-finished tapestry. That was the source of the smell. Skir stepped closer. And then he saw what the tapestry was woven from.

Vomit rose in his throat, erupted through his nose. His throat burned, he stumbled back. The warp threads were not threads, but strands of strong wire. And the weft –

There were strips of leather that had once been human skin. There were desiccated fragments, some with splintered bones poking through, which had been human limbs. There was hair. There were blackened clots which Skir couldn't bear to look at. Some parts of the tapestry were still horribly moist. Skir pressed his arm against his mouth, fighting the urge to vomit.

'So, My Lord Eskirenwey,' said a soft, musical voice. 'You have come to me, after all. I see you have no weapon.' Wanion's voice became a slow caress. 'We are friends, yes? Welcome.'

Skir fought for self-control. His bold fury drained away; he felt sick and weak. Distant thunder grumbled over the mountains; the glass in the dome overhead rattled faintly. At last he choked out, 'Not friends.'

'Then why have you come to me, My Lord?'

Why indeed? What was he doing, creeping around the White Pavilion in the dark? He'd had a bright, vague vision of himself: he'd make a daring escape, surprise everybody, save the day and be a hero. But now he saw that he'd mostly wanted to defy Bettenwey. He'd wanted to appear clever, to show the High Priest that he couldn't be so easily controlled. And here he was, a prisoner again, and prisoner of the most cruel and ruthless person in all the Threelands. He *wouldn't* let her see he was afraid. He squared his shoulders and for the first time gazed directly at Wanion.

In the soft candlelight, she looked magnificent. Golden threads gleamed in her clothes; her shrivelled fingers were heavy with gems. She watched him through half-closed eyes; she looked almost asleep, but Skir sensed the sharp, glittering intelligence masked by her fleshy face.

'I wanted to see you,' he said.

A low rumble rolled around the room; Skir thought it was far-off thunder, but it was the sound of Wanion chuckling. Her head thrust forward. 'And I wanted to see you. I have wanted to see you for a long, long time. All the while you were in Arvestel, yes. How strange it is that we two, so close by in all those years, have never come together until now. And yet how fitting that we should meet here, in your own land.'

'You sent Tansy to steal from me.'

'Tansy? Ah, the laundry-maid, yes. You are an important

person, My Lord Eskirenwey. Do you wonder that I sought influence with you?'

Bitter laughter welled in Skir's throat. 'I am not important, Lady Wanion.'

'You are too modest, My Lord,' said Wanion softly. She watched his face carefully. 'Or is it possible that you do not know how important you are?'

She must have seen some change in his expression, because she rapped out a command to Elvie. 'Fetch a seat for the Priest-King.'

Silently, without hesitation, Elvie crossed the room, and carried a light chair back to Skir. As she set it down, Skir smelled her scent of herbs and wood-smoke. Her blind eyes gazed past him as she murmured, 'You burned her token. But she wouldn't – she wouldn't let me go.'

Skir did not sit down. He took hold of the back of the chair and gripped it hard. Elvie retreated to her stool; Wanion shifted her withered, jewel-laden hand to rest on Elvie's head, and Skir saw Elvie wince under its weight.

Wanion said, 'Please sit, My Lord. What an honour it is, to enjoy a private audience with the ruler of Cragonlands, the heir to the Circle of Attar.'

'You mock me. You must know I have no power. The Priest-King is a figurehead. The Colonial Administration rules Cragonlands, and the High Priest rules the Temple.'

The thunder growled nearby, rolling around three sides of the Pavilion.

'Yes,' said Wanion in her low, rich voice. 'And you are not even the true Priest-King, are you, no? You do not sing the songs to shake the mountains. You have not the gift of ironcraft.'

Skir jumped as if he'd been bitten. How could she know that? He said nothing, but he gripped the chair even harder.

'Your importance, My Lord, does not depend upon your position.' Wanion's eyes were fixed greedily on his.

Skir shook his head impatiently. 'What do you mean?'

Wanion let out a long breath, half-sigh and half-laugh. 'You do not know. You truly do not know who you are.' Her fingers tightened on Elvie's head, and Elvie whimpered as the rings cut into her scalp. Skir stared at Wanion, bewildered and angry.

'Let us make a bargain, yes?' Wanion's voice was deep and cunning. 'I will tell you who you are. Are you not hungry to know it? And in return, you will help me.'

The room tilted and spun around Skir; he clutched the chair so hard he felt splinters in his palms. 'How can I help you? I have no power.'

'Then there is no harm in the promise.'

'What do you want from me?'

Wanion flickered the tips of her fingers. 'Only to be my ears and eyes in certain places, at certain times. That is all, nothing more. You would hurt no one. I know you do not wish to hurt anyone.' Her voice lowered. 'I ask of each person only what they are willing to give. It is a question of finding the right price, that is all. You give to me, and I will give to you. You want to know what I know, yes?'

Skir closed his eyes. The sickly smell of incense and the stink of decay swirled around him; thunder rumbled overhead. It was true, he was desperate to know whatever Wanion could tell him. She said he was important, special; it was what he longed to hear. 'Yes,' he said recklessly. 'I agree to your terms.'

Wanion smiled. 'Good. Your name is not Eskirenwey.'

'I know *that*!' cried Skir in disappointment. The priests had given him that name. Was that all she had to tell him, the name his parents had chosen in that obscure village, sixteen years ago? He remembered what they'd called him. It was Tamm.

But Wanion said, 'Your name is Arraxan. You are the firstborn son of Calwyn, the Singer of All Songs, also called the Witch-Singer of the Westlands, leader of the Chanters' Rising.'

Skir stared at her. Whatever else he might have expected, it was not this.

Wanion smiled her wide, thin-lipped smile, relishing his surprise. 'No. I see you did not know. Even your priests do not know this secret.'

'But then h-how –' Skir stammered.

'You were sent to the Threelands as an infant, to keep you safe. You were to be hidden in the mountains of Cragonlands, fostered in a village.' Wanion gave her throaty chuckle. 'No one could imagine you would be chosen by the priests to be the next Priest-King. And yet so it was.'

Skir struggled to understand. 'But if I was supposed to be hidden . . . why didn't they fetch me back, when the priests chose me?'

'You were born there, but you know nothing of the Westlands, and nothing of the arrogance of chanters,' said Wanion harshly. 'To them, even the Palace of Arvestel is no more than the hut of a village chieftain. The Temple at Gleve is a roadside shrine. Your mother thought you would be as safe there, as hidden in shadows, as in your foster-parents' village. She was wrong. But by the time she knew, it was too late. All they could do was send a guardian to watch over you. And even he could not be trusted.' Wanion smiled in self-satisfaction.

'Beeman? What do you mean, he couldn't be trusted?'

'Your tutor was persuaded to work for me.'

'No!' cried Skir. 'Not Beeman!'

Wanion's eyebrow lifted. 'Why do you not believe it? Have you not consented to do the same yourself, just this moment ago?'

Skir felt a wash of shame. He was more certain of Beeman than he was of himself. *Beeman might have pretended to work for her*, he told himself fiercely, *but he would never have hurt me*. And suddenly he knew that Wanion must have known that too, or else why would she have ordered Tansy to steal from Skir? She could have ordered Beeman. But she hadn't. Skir hugged that knowledge to himself.

'So, Arraxan,' purred Wanion. 'Now you know who you are. But do you know *what* you are?'

'No more riddles!' cried Skir. He summoned up his earliest memories, trying to make them fit with what he'd just been told. The memories of the village were real enough, the smell of rust, the crowded cottage. His father, the man with dark curling hair on the backs of his hands — was that his foster-father, or the man who'd sired him? And his mother, that blurred figure, the one who'd sung to him in the thunderstorm — was that in Cragonlands, or before? Was that the woman who had fostered him, or his birth mother, the Witch-Singer?

Thunder cracked overhead, and Skir jumped and swayed. The taste of metal leaped into his mouth; only the chair-back held him upright. Wanion had begun to speak again. Skir wanted to scream at her to shut up, to let him think, but her voice filled his head like the thunder and drowned out everything else.

'You are no singer of ironcraft, Arraxan. You have always known this. Yet the priests who selected you made no mistake.'

Skir jumped again. 'What?'

'You are a chanter of fire, Arraxan. The first to be born in ten generations, excepting the Witch-Singer, who sings all songs.' Wanion's voice held a trace of scorn, as if it were somehow vulgar to be able to sing all the forms of chantment. *She's jealous*, thought Skir with a flash of insight. *She wishes she was a chanter herself. But she's not. That's why she had to invent her own magic —*

And then his mind got to work on what Wanion had just said. 'I'm not a chanter,' he said. 'I sing the chantments, but nothing happens.'

'But it will if you sing the songs of fire.'

This was absurd. 'But I don't know the songs of fire!'

'Oh, I think you do, My Lord.' Suddenly Wanion's musical voice was full of menace. Her fingers clamped Elvie's skull, tighter, tighter, until Elvie shrieked, and a trickle of blood ran down her face.

'Stop!' shouted Skir, but his voice was drowned by thunder. Suddenly he was drenched in sweat, his hands slippery on the chair. His terror of storms mingled with his fear of Wanion, and the huge, formless anger that swirled inside him. Elvie's face twisted with pain. Thunder cracked, so loud it seemed it would split the Pavilion in two.

Skir covered his eyes. Sobs of rage and grief and terror shook him. He was a little boy again, hardly more than a baby, and his mother was singing, and the storm whirled and flashed around them. He was in her arms, he was safe; he laughed and clapped his hands with delight and sang with her . . .

But as he sang, the lightning struck. White light cracked him like a whip from his mother's arms. He was hurled away, limp and helpless, smashed on the ground, and there were screams in his ears, and the metal taste of the lightning on his tongue.

That taste was in his mouth now. The thunder rolled and rumbled all around; the windows rattled, the tiles on the roof of the White Pavilion shook loose. Almost without knowing it, Skir began to sing his mother's song.

He sang louder as the chantment surged through him. It was a song with words that didn't make sense, nonsense words, a child's song. But the tune was strange and forceful; it belonged to the storm. The growl of thunder was in it, and the dazzle of lightning. He felt his mother's arms wrapped tightly around him, her warm voice close to his ear, the smell of her dark hair. He was no one then: not the Priest-King Eskirenwey, no one's pawn, no one's hostage, not a figurehead or a weapon or a great sorcerer, just a child too young to pronounce his own name. It didn't matter what anyone thought of him, or what they expected. He was simply his own self, safe and beloved in his mother's arms: the last moment that he'd ever felt truly safe. He called the lightning closer and closer, brighter and brighter, like fireworks.

A cold shiver ran over his skin, and his hair stood on end.

The lightning was in the room.

He knew it before he opened his eyes. Globes of cold blue fire danced across the threadbare carpet, lighting the room with a flickering glow. They dipped and weaved and spun slowly through the air.

Wanion's lizard-eyes followed them. Her mouth hung open, and there was a fleck of foam at the corner of her lips. Her breath came in heavy gasps, greedy and triumphant.

But Skir saw that she was afraid. She had created him, she had made a chanter of fire, and too late she realised she couldn't control him. Skir saw it. And he saw that even now her ringed hand pressed down on Elvie's head, and Elvie squirmed with pain, her mouth open in a scream of soundless agony, and Wanion did not let her go.

Anger surged through Skir, anger for Elvie's pain, not for himself. He was still singing. The chantment strengthened around him and through him until he was lost in the magic. Skir didn't exist any more: only the chantment of fire that streamed through him.

The windows shattered. Glass showered like exploding diamonds, and the room erupted into fireworks.

A dozen balls of lightning – yellow, orange, blue, white-hot – shot in through the windows and the smashed dome above. Lightning crackled from floor to ceiling; fiery spheres hurtled round the room, fizzing with sparks. Flames licked up the curtains.

Wanion cried out. Her wasted arms lifted uselessly, flapping against her litter. Elvie sprang up and raked the air with her fingertips, her scarred face contorted with panic.

Skir turned his face upward, and sang his mother's song. There was so much noise; the song reverberated in his mouth and throat, alive. So this was chantment, this was how it felt to sing up magic! His hair stood on end, his hands and feet tingled as if they'd burst. He raised his hands to summon the lightning, and the lightning came.

With a roar that echoed the cracking of thunder all around, the roof of the White Pavilion lifted off, clean as a cork from a bottle. For a heartbeat it hung in the air, then dissolved into a rain of fragmented tiles and rotten timbers. Skir stood with his arms outstretched, his red hair powdered with dust and plaster, and he sang. The lightning rose around him, enclosing him in a shaft of blue-white fire that crackled between the storm clouds and the Pavilion below.

'Ren? Ren – Skir! Oh, stop it, please, stop!'

Elvie screamed to him, but Skir could not hear.

Beeman, Tansy, Perrin and Penthesi walked, slowly and carefully, so as not to jog the Broken Fire, back down the road into the valley. Beeman gave his dagger to Perrin, in case they encountered Bettenwey's servants. There was a faint growl of thunder overhead.

'By the bones,' said Perrin. 'The storm's right on top of the city.'

They all looked down into the valley at the faint yellow lights of Gleve. The clouds were clotted, a thick, stormy mass above the city.

'Never seen clouds pile themselves up like that before,' said Tansy.

Penthesi whinnied and pawed the ground; the whites of his eyes showed. Suddenly he reared, black against the sky, and trampled his hoofs down like the clash of thunder. That instant, a silent blue-white explosion of light shot up from the heart of the city, flickering between the rooftops and the clouds.

'What in the name of all the gods –' cried Perrin.

'Sorcery!' Tansy's hand went to her throat.

Beeman swore. 'No! Skir! Oh gods. Let us be in time –' He began to run, heedless of the rucksack that bumped on his back.

Penthesi bolted. He snatched his bridle from Tansy's hand and careered down the track past Beeman, vanishing into the darkness.

Tansy grabbed Perrin's hand, and they sprinted toward Gleve, where the strange storm that was not wholly a storm raged in the space between earth and sky.

The column of lightning did not touch Skir. He thrust it away, called it near, sent it spinning up to the sky and back, wild with the power of it. Thunder shook the Old Quarter. Balls of lightning rocketed, fizzed, ricocheted about the White Pavilion; they punched holes in walls, scorched charcoal trails across marble floors, transformed clouds of dust into showers of golden sparks. And everything they brushed against burst into flame.

People rushed in and out of the roofless room where Skir sang; they tried to drag the bulk of Wanion clear of the fire-storm. Elvie crouched in a corner, arms over her head. Wanion's tapestry was a wall of flame; here and there a shard of bone showed dark against the glowing fire, then faded, crumbled into ash. The tapestry hissed and writhed as it burned, like a dying thing.

Wanion's litter toppled sideways into a pile of smouldering rubble. The carpet was on fire. Wanion roared as she struggled to free herself. The servants fled, leaping down stairs, smashing windows to escape. Elvie sobbed as the flames licked closer. She crawled away, and blundered into a burning sofa. The flames enfolded her, and she screamed.

CHAPTER 17

Arraxan's Choice

FINALLY, through the tumult, Skir heard Elvie's scream.

Abruptly he stopped singing. The blue-white column of lightning around him vanished. The room was ablaze, the roof was gone, and rain was falling onto his dazed face, but it was not enough to douse the flames. Elvie's dress was on fire. He tore off his outer robe. It seemed to take forever to reach her, to knock her down and smother the flames. She was small and light as a bird under his hands. There was a formless lump on the centre of the carpet. It did not move. Skir saw a gleam of gold, a fold of green silk, and knew that it was Wanion. The smell of scorched meat was so strong he retched.

Skir dragged Elvie to the doorway. It was ringed with flame, but the doors were gone, and there was space for them to run through. While Skir had been singing, there was no smoke, but now it billowed down the corridors, blotting out everything. Elvie wrapped Skir's robe over her face; she clung to his arm, pressing herself against him.

They stumbled along a wide hallway; Skir was certain there had been a staircase here, but he couldn't find it. A wall collapsed in a shower of sparks, and they ran, beating through the smoke. Suddenly they were in a larger space, open to the sky. Skir was lost. He opened an intact door, and found a narrow flight of stairs. He led Elvie down through choking smoke, but no flames, not yet. *How far was it to the ground? Could they jump from a window?*

Skir gripped Elvie's arm. In the smoke, he was as blind as she. Elvie coughed, shuddering for breath. They blundered down more stairs, then ran into a wall of flame and were forced to retreat up again. Skir slumped to his knees. They were trapped like rats, and it was all his fault. He'd been showing off, no better than Perrin –

Skir's head jerked around. 'Did you hear that?' he shouted.

'A horse!' Elvie's face lit up.

Somewhere through the smoke, a horse neighed, a high repeated call. Skir staggered up to follow the sound, through a warren of small rooms, then out into a wide reception hall, scattered with furniture. This part of the Pavilion was not yet burned, but the fire was chasing them; they felt its hot breath at their backs. Skir pulled Elvie out into the open air through a pair of glass-paned doors. The noise of the fire burst over them; above and behind, the White Pavilion blazed.

They stood on a ledge, too narrow to be a balcony. Below in the courtyard, a black horse reared, silhouetted against the flames. Penthesi called to Skir, just as Skir had called the lightning.

'This way!' Skir tugged Elvie to the carved stone railing. Trusting him, she began to clamber over. 'Wait!' They were high above the ground, the drop was as high as a house. Elvie clung, while Skir climbed the railing beside her. Penthesi neighed impatiently and pranced below. The fire shrieked above them, licking nearer and nearer. It roared into the room they'd just left; Skir saw smoke roll against the inside of the windows, and the red-gold glint of flame. He edged Elvie sideways; they shuffled along, clinging desperately, until they reached an outer set of steps and half-fell, half-slid down the wide railing to the ground.

Penthesi was there, almost trampling them in his eagerness. His eyes were white, and a long burn mark raked his flank. Skir hefted Elvie onto his back, then scrambled up behind her. Penthesi galloped through the gateway of the courtyard, a high, narrow arch outlined with flame, past stables and sheds and storerooms all ablaze.

Suddenly they were out in the street, and a wave of startled people fell back to let Penthesi through. He tore at a gallop down one narrow street, then another, and Skir couldn't control him. Penthesi veered left and right, and almost threw them off. Skir had just realised they'd circled the Pavilion and come out into Sether Square when someone grabbed Penthesi's bridle and managed to stop him.

'Beeman!' gasped Skir, and slithered off Penthesi's back into a bear-hug from his tutor.

Beeman released him almost at once, and helped Elvie slide down.

'What are you *doing* here? And Penthesi – is Tansy here? And what's that?' Skir stared at the rucksack that swung from Beeman's hand.

'Oh, gods,' whispered Beeman, gazing at it in horror. The rucksack was emitting a strange, high-pitched fizzing sound.

But then Penthesi bent his head and grabbed the straps in his teeth, shaking the rucksack from Beeman's grasp.

'No!' Beeman snatched for it, but Penthesi had already galloped away, tearing across the square, scattering people left and right.

Beeman screamed, '*No!*' The rain pelted down as Penthesi galloped toward the burning Pavilion; the whole frontage was a sheet of flame. Suddenly Tansy was there; she stood frozen, silent, her eyes fixed on Penthesi.

Hundreds of people were in Sether Square the night the White Pavilion burned. Those who hadn't seen it would never believe the tale they told: of a black horse who flew across the square, tail streaming like a banner; a horse that gathered itself, that seemed to float like a piece of the night itself against the roaring flame; a horse that leaped into the very heart of the fire, and was gone.

Perrin reached Tansy just as Penthesi made his mighty jump into the flames. He flung his arms around her to hold her back, but she was rigid as stone; she didn't even breathe.

The Broken Fire exploded. Beeman's work was more effective than he'd dared to hope, and it was a much smaller explosion than it could have been; but it was big enough. If not for Beeman, a wave of fire would have radiated out to engulf the Square, the crowd, and half the Old Quarter; instead, for the second time that night, a column of flame roared into the skies above Gleve.

Perrin shielded his eyes, Skir threw his arm over his head, and Beeman ducked for cover as debris showered down. But Tansy stared straight ahead as the yellow-golden fire, streaked with crimson and ruby, exploded up into the night, and fell back to earth in a rain of tiny glowing stars.

'Perhaps I should have told you sooner,' said Beeman. 'But you were so young, and always in such danger. Not just from Wanion. You're in danger still, you know.'

They had gone back to the large, bare rooms that Beeman had rented when he'd first arrived in Gleve, close to the Temple, near the top of the hill. From the window Tansy saw lights in the Temple, and shadows darting to and fro. She leaned her head on the window frame and thought of the message scrawled on Penthesi's stable wall: *See you on the other side.* Penthesi was dead. Wanion was dead, too. Suddenly she thought of Lorison; she was free of Wanion now, but she didn't know it yet.

Tansy's face was stiff and swollen with tears. Without speaking, she bent over the little cook-stove in the corner to make tea. The stove sputtered and did not want to stay alight.

Skir said, 'Shall I light it with chantment?'

'No!' said Perrin and Beeman together.

Beeman sighed. 'I should have realised that your ignorance of your gift was dangerous, too. Thank the gods there wasn't more harm done.'

'So it's true. I *am* a chanter.'

Beeman nodded. 'The first chanter of fire for many generations – apart from your mother, of course. But Calwyn is a special case.'

'I remember it so clearly now,' said Skir. 'How my mother was singing to me, when I was struck with lightning.'

'Yes. I was there that night. You wouldn't sleep. You were tiny, still a baby really. Calwyn couldn't soothe you, so she sang a chantment of fire to make lights in the sky, to stop you crying. And you copied her song; you sang with her.'

'Yes,' said Skir. 'I sang with her.' That song had stayed buried in his mind, etched in his memory, all these years.

'You called the lightning to you,' said Beeman. 'You called it *into* you. You were struck by the lightning of your own chantment.'

'But if – what about my mother? She was holding me. Did I hurt her?' Was that why she'd sent him away?

Beeman smiled. 'Calwyn wasn't harmed. She's the Singer of All Songs. You don't understand what that means yet, but she was strong enough to contain your magic. She blamed herself though, for singing the chantments of fire just to make her baby laugh. She thought she could have killed you. But then, they were elated, too, she and your father. Their child, the first chanter of firecall after so long, and showing the gift so young! They were so proud, so glad. We all were.' He nodded. 'Thank you, Tansy.'

Beeman wrapped his big hands around the steaming mug of tea she'd given him. Elvie sat in an upright chair, still clutching Skir's outer robe around her shoulders. Tansy leaned her head against Perrin's knees; they were quiet, sipping tea as Beeman talked.

'The early years of the Rising were dangerous times, Skir. Your parents were afraid for you. They had important work to do, and they were worried that they wouldn't be able to protect you from – from our enemies.' Beeman spoke hesitantly, watching Skir to assess his reaction. But Skir seemed to accept what he said.

'So they sent me away?'

'Yes. To the remotest place they could find: the heart of Cragonlands.'

'I remember the village. I remember the rust harvest.'

'Do you? You were only there a year before the priests found you.' He smiled. 'There was no mistake. Old Devenwey knew a chanter when he saw one. But he didn't know what kind of chanter you were; and Bettenwey has never believed that the Priest-Kings had any gift of chantment.'

'I wanted to show him,' muttered Skir. He stared fiercely into the depths of his tea.

Beeman put a hand on Skir's shoulder. 'And there lies the danger. A gift like yours is –'

'Worse than Broken Fire,' said Tansy.

'More powerful, because he can control it. Skir, you need to learn how to harness it. I couldn't teach you. It seemed wiser to leave it alone, let you believe you had no chantment. Perhaps that was the wrong decision.'

Perrin leaned forward. 'But why did you let the priests take him in the first place?'

'I wasn't there. Calwyn sent me when we heard what had happened.' He looked around the circle of young faces in the lamplight and smiled sadly. 'Calwyn and I are old friends. We first met when we were about your age. She still calls me Trout . . . She sent me to watch over you, Skir. But by the time I arrived, Cragonlands was at war, and it seemed the Temple would be the safest place for you. So I kept my distance, and survived as best I could. I was in contact with Devenwey, and, after he died, with Bettenwey. He knows the truth about your parentage, but he kept it secret. I have a feeling he intended to use that knowledge.'

Skir jolted. *We may have a use for the Singer of All Songs and her chanters in time.* 'He plans to use me to force the Singer – my mother – to help the resistance.'

'Yes, that would fit,' said Beeman slowly. 'Bettenwey has far too much power. The High Priest is supposed to speak for the Council, not the other way round . . . But he is such a capable politician, it would be better to find a way to work with him than to move him aside. I can foresee some difficult negotiations ahead.'

Skir put down his cup. 'I must be in the Hall of the Faith at dawn, to take the morning prayer today. Especially today. I have to explain what happened, before Bettenwey twists it around. Everyone will be there. I must let them see me as Priest-King. No more hiding away.'

'Bettenwey won't like it,' said Beeman. 'Which is another reason to do it.'

Skir thought, *I'm not scared of Bettenwey any more.*

Perrin tapped Beeman on the knee. 'You haven't finished the story. What did you do when the Baltimarans took Skir to Arvestel?'

Beeman frowned. 'I've always blamed myself for that. I should have realised the Baltimarans would do something of the sort; I should have prevented it. I've learned more about politics since then.'

'You followed me to Arvestel,' said Skir.

'Yes, I arranged it with Bettenwey. That took some doing. I've had to do a lot of things I wouldn't have chosen, to protect Skir.' Beeman glanced at Tansy. 'Like pretending to work for Wanion.' He rubbed at his eyes; suddenly he looked haggard. 'I'm not good at pretence, and these last years my whole life has been two, three, four layers of lies. It's exhausting.'

Skir was silent while he spun the copper circlet round his finger. He'd known that song, that chantment; it had been inside him all the time. But it hadn't come out until he'd needed it to save Elvie, until he'd broken out – however briefly – from his bubble of self-absorption. Was that what Beeman had been trying to teach him all these years? Was that what the Faith was about?

As if in echo of his thoughts, Elvie spoke for the first time. 'So what will Skir do now?' She turned her face toward him;

the scar across her eyes was livid from the heat of the fire. 'Will you go home to the Westlands?'

'He'll stay here, of course,' said Tansy. 'Where he belongs.'

'Where I belong?' Skir spun the copper circlet on his finger. 'All my life I've been sent here and sent there. I'm not Baltimaran, I'm not a Cragonlander, I've never belonged anywhere. If I went back to the Westlands, I wouldn't belong there either.'

'But his parents will want him back,' said Elvie. 'Won't they?'

'That's . . . complicated,' said Beeman.

Skir's eyes narrowed; he looked almost like Bettenwey. 'Complicated?'

'You're a chanter of fire, Skir. No one in the world knows the chantments of fire, except you and your mother. After tonight – well, I think it's imperative that you learn to control your gift. Only Calwyn can help you do that.'

'But?' said Skir.

'The night Perrin and the Renganis came for you, I wasn't there. I was meeting an agent from the Singer of All Songs. The message was that it's still not safe for you in the Westlands. Calwyn . . .' Beeman paused, and continued carefully. 'She would prefer it, I think, if you remained here.'

Perrin gave a low whistle. 'Sent him away when he was a baby, and she still doesn't want him back?'

'Enough, Perrin!' said Beeman. 'You know nothing. The Westlands are in turmoil. As the Singer's son, Skir would be at terrible risk. Here, as the Priest-King, he is at least partly protected. And besides . . .' Beeman hesitated. 'Calwyn never knew her own mother. I don't think mothering has come easily to her.'

'She made the decisions she had to make,' said Skir slowly.

'And she sent the best person she had to take care of me.'

'I have done my best,' said Beeman uncomfortably. 'But I've made mistakes. I'm sorry for all my shortcomings, Skir.'

There was a long silence. Everyone in the room watched Skir. He stopped twirling the circlet on his finger. He looked at it reflectively, then replaced it on his head. 'I'm the anointed Priest-King of Cragonlands. I'll be Priest-King until the day I die. No escape, no excuses. Just like Bettenwey said.'

'The meeting between the Baltimarans and the Renganis will go ahead, in spite of Wanion,' said Beeman. 'Do you want to attend?'

'Yes,' said Skir. 'If you come with me.'

'I was hoping for a rest,' said Beeman mildly.

'There's too much to do,' said Skir. 'Bettenwey said the Baltimarans *and* the Renganis want to stop fighting. We need to arrange it so both sides are appeased, but without harming the future of Cragonlands . . . Bettenwey can help – if we can trust him, and convince him to trust us.'

'Half the problem is rust,' said Beeman. 'If there was no rust trade, Baltimar and Rengan would lose interest in Cragonlands.'

'If there was no rust . . .' said Skir slowly. 'If all the chaka-weeds died . . .' His eyes widened. Could a chanter of fire sing a chantment to burn up every speck of rust in the Threelands? Destroy every chaka-weed, every berry, every leaf? Maybe he could travel, very slowly, through the whole of Cragonlands, singing as he went, burning the infection from his country. He didn't know enough about chantment. Perhaps his mother, the Singer of All Songs, would know. He could send a message and ask for help . . . The thought made him feel shy. But it would have to be done.

Beeman was off on another track. 'Cragonlands needs to

be rebuilt. Ideally, if we could combine the organisational skills of the Renganis with the wealth of Baltimar, *combine* the strengths . . .'

Skir looked at him. 'Any ideas on how to do that?'

'Not yet,' said Beeman.

'Me neither,' said Skir, but his face was alight with anticipation, as if he could hardly wait to work it out.

Beeman gazed at Skir with a strange expression, proud yet regretful. Perrin said to him suddenly, 'Did *you* want to go home?'

'Plenty of time for that,' said Beeman quietly. 'And there's no one waiting for me.' The shadow of an old sorrow crossed his face.

Perrin moved across to the window. The sky above the city had grown pale. He said, 'Well, I think *I'll* go to the Westlands.'

'You?' said Skir.

'There's not much for me here. A court martial in Rengan, or a life on the run in the mountains. I'd end up a rust-smuggler; men like me always do,' he added sagely. 'No, I'll join the Chanters' Rising. I'm tired of being a loner. My parents did what they thought was right, but I belong with other chanters.' He turned to smile at Tansy. But she did not smile back.

Quietly she crossed the room and put her arm through his. She drew him aside so the others couldn't hear. 'You know how much I care about you. But I ain't *part* of you. I won't go with you to the Westlands.'

He wanted to ask: *Is it because of what happened tonight? Because I didn't pull you out of the tunnel before you passed out? Don't you trust me, Tansy?* But he was afraid of what her answer might be. Then he had another thought. 'Is this about Penthesi?'

She held onto his arm. 'No, of course it ain't.' She hesitated. 'Oh, Perrin – you didn't sing to Penthesi, did you, tonight? Did you send him to rescue Skir? Did you tell him to jump in the fire?'

'No, of course not! Tansy, you can't believe that!'

Tansy shook her head.

A note of bitterness crept into Perrin's voice. 'So you're going to stay here with Skir. Can't you see he's got Elvie now? He doesn't need you any more.'

'Perrin, shut up. I ain't staying with Skir either.'

'What?' Perrin's face glowed with relief.

Tansy tightened her mouth. 'I could slap you. You don't care what I do, so long as I don't choose Skir over you!'

'That's not true. Tansy –'

But she was already speaking. 'I want to go up north. To Rengan. You said they need horse-tamers up there.'

'*Rengan?* Are you mad?'

'Reckon it might suit me. Better than it suited you, anyway.'

'But it's dangerous! And you're a Baltimaran girl, the enemy. Can you *imagine* what they might do?'

'I know it's dangerous. Reckon I can look after myself,' Tansy said. 'You know, I think I like danger.' Then she shuddered. 'Long as it ain't under the ground.'

'I won't let you go,' said Perrin. 'You can't.'

'Not forever. Just for a year or so. Perrin, I ain't never been free. I want to try it for a while.'

'And after a year?'

Tansy hesitated. 'If you still want me to, I'll come to the Westlands.'

Perrin took her face in his hands; her eyes were grey and steady, and she was not blushing. 'I'm not giving up,' he warned her. 'I can't let you go. I'll make you change your mind.'

'You can try,' said Tansy. 'But I don't reckon you will.'

Skir watched Perrin and Tansy at the window. He felt as if someone had punched him in the chest. He couldn't hear what they were saying, but the way they stood together told him everything. It was too late; he'd lost her. All the time he was locked up in the Temple, sulking, fighting with Bettenwey, he'd let Tansy slip away from him. And so Perrin had won. Skir thought, *I'll never forgive him for that. Not as long as I live.*

It was too painful to look at them; his gaze moved past them to the sky beyond. The storm clouds had all gone, and the sky was bleached white with the approach of sunrise.

'We'd better go soon,' he said. 'I have to be at the Temple by dawn.'

'It will be a long day.' Beeman scoured at his eye sockets with the heels of his hands. Elvie sensed the movement, and touched his sleeve.

'Do your eyes bother you?'

He blinked down at her. 'Yes, they do. I used to be very short-sighted, but Calwyn persuaded me to let her try her healing powers on them. It worked, more or less, but they always itch when I'm tired. Which is most of the time, lately.'

Elvie's face turned up hopefully. 'Your friend, the Singer. Could she heal my eyes, too?'

'I don't know, Elvie,' said Beeman. 'Perhaps. I'm sure she'd do her best.'

'It's a long way to the Westlands,' said Skir. 'And with no guarantee of a cure. It would be a hard journey even for someone who could see.'

'I'm blind, but I'm not helpless.' There was steel in Elvie's voice. 'I won't go back to growing rust for soldiers. My mother is dead, and Wanion is dead. There's nothing left for me in Rarr.'

'Of course. But you could stay here in Gleve. There are healers in the Temple. You could teach them about herbs.'

Beeman said, 'Perrin could take her, Skir . . . Perrin! Come. You'd watch out for Elvie, if she went with you to the Westlands, wouldn't you?'

'Certainly,' said Perrin promptly. 'Be my pleasure.'

On opposite sides of the room, Tansy and Skir both frowned.

Elvie was silent. Then she turned her face to Skir. 'I will stay here if you wish it. But you must tell me so. I won't give up the chance of sight for nothing. Give me reason to stay.'

Skir hesitated. He didn't look at Tansy. Then he reached for Elvie's hand. 'I do wish it. I want you here with me.'

'Very well,' said Elvie. She reached up to hold Skir's hand in both of hers.

Beeman said nothing, but the corners of his mouth turned down. He thought Skir would regret what he'd just done. Tansy saw it, and their eyes met for an instant; then she turned away.

'The sun's nearly up,' she said in a strained voice.

'We'd better leave,' said Skir again, but he freed himself from Elvie and joined the others by the window.

They looked out onto a scene like a charcoal drawing: grey and black and white. The dark carpet of the city flowed over the hills, sprinkled with pinpricks of lamplight. One high moon shone in the pale sky, a pearl nestled in grey silk. Perrin and Tansy stood together, with their arms around each other;

Perrin's hand was twisted into Tansy's sleeve, as if he were scared she'd run away if he didn't hold onto her. Smoke still rose in a thick column from the Old Quarter, and drifted black across the wide grey sky. Beeman sighed, and rubbed soot across his brow. Elvie stood quietly, a little behind the others, with her face turned to the window – no, Beeman realised, her face was turned to Skir.

Skir took an awkward step closer to Elvie, but couldn't bring himself to take her hand. He wondered if he had done the right thing. He was responsible for her now... He wondered suddenly if he had brothers or sisters. He must ask Beeman.

A line of flame blazed abruptly along the horizon, too bright to look at, and light spilled across the valley, slow and thick as honey. Then, with a stately leap, the sun bounded into the sky, and the whole messy, beautiful, broken world was stained with fire.

ACKNOWLEDGEMENTS

Thanks to Rosalind Price, Jodie Webster and Cheryl Klein
for improving my writing; the Constable and Taylor families
for endless support; Penni Russon for the title; and Michael,
Alice and Evie, the lights of my heart.

THE CHANTERS OF TREMARIS

The Singer of All Songs

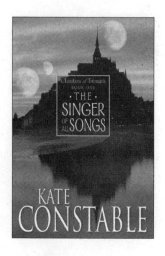

CALWYN IS A CHANTER OF ICE, BUT THERE ARE MANY KINDS OF CHANTMENT IN TREMARIS.

Calwyn lives quietly in Antaris tending the bees and learning the songs of ice-call. But then Darrow arrives, wounded, with terrible stories of hatred in the Outlands where chanters are persecuted and magic is a dying art.

Defying the Head Priestess, Calwyn and Darrow embark on a dangerous adventure, and soon they are pitted against the sorcerer Samis, who seeks the ultimate power of the Singer of All Songs.

'Kate Constable writes with such grace and clarity that she stands out from the pack. *The Singer of All Songs* is one of the most enjoyable fantasies I've read in a long time.' Sara Douglass

'A terrific book, beautifully written, with wonderfully rich imagery and fascinating magic.' Garth Nix

www.katecontstable.com